MW00436032

"Every once in a while a book comes along with the 'wow' factor. This book totally met all of my criteria for that. From the opening page, I was struck by the sheer beauty of the writing.... This is a definite book for anyone. I guarantee that there's a character you can identify with. Hopefully, it'll help you learn a little something about yourself as well. Join Vic on her journey towards self-discovery and allow yourself to be swept up."
— Minding Spot

"*No Story to Tell* tells a terrific story of a survivor finally taking a risk that will shake her world."
— Midwest Book Review

"This was a 'no holds barred' kind of read with a delicate touch that I definitely recommend!"
— Bookin' It Up

"*No Story to Tell* is about re-creating one's world—something to tell one's self more than other dreamers and idlers! Fascinating read, Ms. Steele!"
— Crystal Book Reviews

"This intriguing story of self-discovery should be on every readers' to-be-read list. It will have you questioning how you are living your life."
— Jersey Girl Book Reviews

"*No Story to Tell* by KJ Steele is intense and thought-provoking. In many ways it defies description. It has to be experienced and it is an experience not to be missed."
— Single Titles

THE BIRD BOX

KJ STEELE

The Story Plant
Studio Digital CT, LLC
P.O. Box 4331
Stamford, CT 06907

Copyright © 2014 by KJ Steele
Jacket design by Barbara Aronica Buck

Print ISBN-13 978-1-61188-186-8
E-book ISBN-13 978-1-61188-187-5

Visit our website at www.TheStoryPlant.com

First Story Plant Printing: February 2015

Printed in The United States of America
0 9 8 7 6 5 4 3 2 1

This novel is dedicated to the 1511 forgotten souls interred in the Lakeshore Psychiatric Hospital Cemetery. May you finally rest in peace.

Acknowledgments

As individual as each novel is, no work of literature forms itself into being without the influence of other people. This book is no exception.

I owe a debt of gratitude to Geoffrey Reaume who took the time to talk to me as I was formulating the early stages of this novel. His excellent book *Remembrance Of Patients Past* proved to be a tremendous source of inspiration and understanding for me.

I would also like to acknowledge the remarkable photography of Jon Crispin. His collection Willard Asylum Suitcases provided me with a great deal of insight into patients' lives. http://www.willardsuitcases.com

My heartfelt appreciation to Peter Murphy, who traveled the dark tunnels with me, deflecting the octopus so I could better glean the stories being whispered from the walls. Wendy Reimer, master sleuth, who unearthed much valuable information and sent it my way. And Sean Bacon, CD., who magically produced one of the key elements that appears in my novel and graciously allowed me to keep it on my desk for inspiration as I wrote.

Thank you is simply inadequate to express the gratitude and respect I have for my editor and publisher, Lou Aronica. Your ability to direct me back into the true heart of this story was visionary. You possess a rare gift.

I am blessed to be surrounded by a supportive family. Victor, Carrie, Chantelle, and Cara, your understanding and faith in me means more than you will ever know.

I'd also like to pay tribute to my friends at the Lakeshore Asylum. You touched me deeply and entrusted me with your stories. Laugh loudly my friends. Your voices are silenced no more.

Oh that I had wings I would fly like
a dove and be at rest I would fly out
of this asylum. . . . There is nothing
impossible with our Heavenly Father
all powerful He could give me wings
as easy as He

Ralph M.
1841-1911
Husband, father, farmer

His movements were cumbersome, with an awkwardness that didn't parallel with his strong athletic frame. His gaze washed over the ornate, carved stone bridge he had just traversed and slipped down the embankment to the waxen surface of Humber Creek. The night was hot and moist. A heavy calm weighted the air. Jakie flicked his head as if trying to awaken. He did not trust the calm—did not trust Dr. Davidson's pills.

Standing motionless, he struggled with the voices in his mind, sifting through them to seize on one that sounded familiar. To a casual observer, he might look like a contented man, idly caught up in a daydream. But Jakie Hewitt was far from a contented man. His internal being lived in constant distress. Distress at the mutiny of his mind. Distress at the loss of his soul. He began an argument within himself. Had he actually heard the noise? Or had it originated in his head? As time wore on, it got harder to tell.

Slowly he lowered himself into a crouch, his movements surprisingly fluid. Like a candle melting down over itself. Pulling up the bottom of his stiff jeans, his right hand worked the air to maintain his balance. Carefully, he lifted the flap of the pliable leather pouch strapped to his calf and extracted a glinting twelve-inch knife. Distracted by the beauty of his handiwork, he dropped onto his knees and admired the hand-forged blade with its carved bone handle. He murmured quietly, a long flat finger working its

way over the intricate symbols like he was reading Braille.
The knife was not allowed. Of this, there was no confusion.
Dr. Davidson ran his asylum with an iron fist. No weapons
or excessive force would be tolerated from either staff or
inmates. He had set out very clear procedures for everyone
to follow. Follow the procedures he believed and everyone
would stay safe. But then, Dr. Davidson was a very believing man. However, what Jakie Hewitt knew that the doctor did not was that the procedures failed on an almost
daily basis.

Sitting back onto his haunches, cocking his head like
a curious dog, he listened to the sounds of the night. The
unsteady bleep of a bullfrog. The occasional swoosh of a car
passing by on Lakeshore Road. The soft sudden shudder of
the trees as the night sighed. For a brief moment, he even
imagined he could hear the moon but then remembered
this was no longer possible since the moon had whispered
him those lies.

Below him, down by the big spruce, a movement alerted
his eye. Not much of a movement. Only a flicker really, but
he rose, electrified, his dark eyes scoped onto the site. To
the ordinary eye, to the eye dulled by a comfortable life, the
movement might have passed unnoticed. Or, if it had been
noticed, attributed to the brush of a branch as an animal
walked beneath.

But Jakie was an expert at interpreting the nocturnal
dance of the forest. And he knew that this had been a discordant step. A quick downward jerk of the branch. Like
the end of a fishing pole when a fish takes the lure. Or the
frantic tug of the rabbit finding itself suddenly immobilized by the snare around its neck.

Moving as swiftly as he dared, he made his way down
the embankment toward the tree. It was not a pretty sight
watching Jakie Hewitt walk. Years earlier, left unsuper-
vised to plow a field with another patient, Jakie had somehow gotten tangled up in the plow. Panicking, the other

man had fled, the horse dragging Jakie and the plow back to the stable. Dr. Davidson was able to get a specialist in Toronto to save the mutilated leg, but he'd always felt it was a patch up job at best and not really much of a success.

Ten feet from the bushes, Jakie stopped and listened to the darkness. Slowly, he melted into a crouch. It was an eternity's old game. Who could outwait whom? Who would be the first to break? The static position almost immediately caused burning pain in his damaged left leg, but he held his pose. The physical endurance was not what worried him. What worried him was his ability to harness his mind. He differed with the doc on that point. The doctor was unhappy about Jakie's tendency to spend so much time inside his own head. Encouraged him to socialize with the other patients. Tried to get him to speak of his thoughts so he could write them down. He knew the doctor considered him insane. He'd seen it written in his file. He didn't argue. But he didn't agree. He wasn't insane. Unless insane meant a good man lost and trying to find all the pieces once again.

From somewhere a soft mewling melody filled the air and then ceased. From where exactly, he couldn't tell. Deaf in one ear, he no longer perceived direction. He felt panic bubbling up his throat like bile as lurid images with ghastly smiles dove into his face.

"Not real...not real...not real," he chanted, the hard bone of the knife handle cracking in time against his prominent forehead. His lips, smooth and generous as slices of peeled peach, worked together silently, giving him the appearance of a man lost in an ecstasy of private prayer. The song rose again. An anguished, beautiful sound. Like God crying.

It was not impossible, he reasoned. God had visited him before. Visited him and Paul and Mary. Abraham and Joseph Smith and St. Francis of Assisi. There were even some in the asylum here who claimed visitations. But those he considered suspicious. Antichrists abounded. Dr. Davidson, who agreed he could accept the teachings of some, unequivocally dismissed Jakie's claims, a fact that bothered Jakie deeply and caused him to fear for the doctor's soul. God himself was silent on the matter. He imparted truth but seldom understanding.

Sheathing his knife, Jakie stood up and edged closer to the sound. He felt watched. Observed. And as he moved closer he could sense the thing in the forest recoiling in fear. Or disgust. He'd met the feeling before. Tittering girls attracted to his generous smile only to be repelled away by his dithering mind and crippled gait.

His eyes groped the dark shadows under the tree, finally coming to rest on a soft undulating shape rising from the ground like a miniature foothill. He held his breath and watched. A quiver. Shallow breathing. *A deer*, he thought, somewhat relieved. A small one. Perhaps even a fawn. Sick, he guessed. Or else run down by a passing car and come here to die. He knelt swiftly and pulled his knife clear. Coyote, his teacher in the wild, had frowned on his sensitive spirit. Admonished him to let nature be. Broken legs, abandoned pups. It didn't matter. Nature had its own way of taking care of things. But it wasn't that Jakie was squeamish about the death or the killing. He just preferred it fast, nature seeming a little heartless to him that way.

His body felt well oiled. This he knew. This he understood. To kill a sick animal fast was an easy thing. All it required was a certain fluidity of movement. He practiced the motion in his mind. The snapping back of the head. The clean, graceful sweep of the blade. Slowly positioning himself within arm's reach, he marveled that the animal did not even make a last frantic struggle to save itself.

Suddenly, before he had even realized that he had done it, his hand drove into the dark space, seized a handful of fur and exposed a slender white throat that glistened in anticipation of his arcing blade. A pandemonium of shrieks filled the night, but he was too terrified by the narrow miss of his knife hand to know if they belonged to the creature or to him. Stars exploded around him, blinding his mind. *The singing, the singing, the singing*, they accused and he knew that this should mean something. But for a long moment, it did not. *The animal was singing,* he repeated, trying to clarify his thoughts. And then the clouds disappeared from his mind and he saw the sun.

"Oh!" he garbled as he strained desperately through the darkness, trying to locate her.

She had scrambled as much as she could behind the trunk of the tree. And although the trunk was not large, the majority of her body was blanked from sight. Closer to him, he could see the outline of the blanket she had been lying under before he seized her.

"What's your name?" Jakie asked, trying for softness, because he could see the fear in her face. Hear it in the short ragged gulps of her breathing.

She said nothing. Gave no sign she'd even heard him speak.

"Didn't mean to scare ya. Thought ya was an injured deer, that's all."

Still, she was silent. Silent and watching through emotionless, wide eyes that glittered like polished river stones. She had on what seemed to be a tattered nightdress. Over the top of this she wore what looked to be an embroidered sweater. Riddled with snags, its sleeves ended far short of her twiglike wrists. The nightdress was an inadequate length, and Jakie was pleased but shy that he could see the bottom of her legs right up to her knees. Around one ankle, a thick chain shackled her to an overhanging branch. Around her shoulders he thought he could make out a frayed shawl, but when she moved her head, he realized it wasn't a shawl at all but rather the single mangled matt of her hair. Her angular face remained in the shadows, giving it the appearance of mottled bruising. However, a second later, when she lunged forward into the light and grabbed a bag from under the blanket, he was shocked to see the shadows remained. Scrambling backward, almost dropping his knife, he poised to defend himself. But, having pulled the bag into her lap, her demeanor changed abruptly. Her eyes were absorbed with something inside it, her hands busy rearranging its contents. It seemed as if in a split second she had forgotten Jakie was even there. And although he tried his best to focus, he could not be quite sure that it was a baby she was suckling at her breast.

CHAPTER 2

Extinguishing the reading lamp, the doctor slid the wire-rimmed glasses from his face and wished for sleep. Even without venturing a look at his watch, he knew it was already well past two o'clock in the morning. Strewn across the top of his worn oak desk lay almost a dozen books, articles, and papers. Malaria fever. Insulin coma. Metrazol convulsions. Lobotomy. Electroconvulsive shock therapy. And now this. Thorazine. It sounded promising. But then, in the beginning they all had.

Sinking deeper into the supple embrace of the leather chair, he relaxed his mind backward over the years. Treatments given. Outcomes recorded. Successes applauded and then relinquished as the twisted knots of insanity reformed inside his patients' heads. At times, he despaired that his life's work would amount to little more than a blind, impotent pseudo-surgery of the mind.

Dr. Gerald Isaac Davidson was older than his years. A life spent in the pursuit of other people's health with little regard to his own having extracted a heavy price. Much to his chagrin, as time slipped by the mirror began to reflect a picture of himself he was not pleased to see. As a young boy, he had faithfully believed he would grow up to look like his mother. It was not to be. By his thirteenth birthday, it had been grudgingly accepted that he had inherited the squirrelish face, receding chin and yellow, corn kernel teeth of his father. It had been small consolation at the time that he had been fortunate enough to have at least gained the quick intellect of his mother. A formidably brilliant woman who was beautiful right to her dying day. It had remained a mystery to everyone why she had ever married his father in the first place. The fact that she had severely regretted her decision had not. Laced to the marriage by deeply embedded religious views, she had sought relief by honing her intellect into a dangerous tool. Over the years, she had all but emasculated the man who called her *wife*.

The old house creaked and groaned around the doctor as it settled in for the night. He wondered idly if it made such sounds in the daytime as well. He, himself, had no idea so little was he there. He preferred to take his meals in his office in the administration building. It was a convenience of time. And he thoroughly enjoyed the view afforded him by his fifth-floor window. He found the orderly symmetrical layout of the hospital buildings restorative. After particularly difficult or harrowing treatment sessions, he would stand beside his untouched food, systematically tracing and retracing the square, four-storied structures that flanked the central administration building at right angles. He was proud of his hospital. Proud of its forward-thinking Cottage System: four solid brick buildings housing the male patients to the north reflected back by four nearly identical female wards to the south. Expansive, tree-dotted lawns, meticulously kept flowerbeds and a small apple orchard combined together to paint an almost pastoral scene. And each time he stood musing out his window, he was again struck by the juxtaposition between the austere, regal façades of the hospital buildings and the bedlam and commotion residing within.

Personally, he would have preferred to take a small suite next to his office. It was foolishness, him living alone in a place as massive as Cumberland House. But, the hospital had its protocol and reasons for housing their superintendents there. There was an unspoken agreement that detached aloofness was required of the doctors to maintain a sense of structure and control among the staff and patients. Indeed, the architecture of the institution itself had been designed to act as a form of psychological restraint. In this, Kivas Tully, the provincial architect of the day, had hit the bull's-eye dead-on when designing Cumberland House. Three opulent stories of red brick offset by soaring rooflines, a central turret and a white-columned veranda. The house had an almost pretentiously hostile air. Only a row of gracefully arched windows adorning the second floor redeemed it from being altogether too severe. In anybody's opinion, it was a magnificent structure. Beautiful. But certainly not welcoming.

Taking a burl pipe from the pocket of his beige cashmere sweater that wrapped itself limply across the back of his chair, he loaded it with sweet-smelling tobacco, tamped it, reloaded it and tamped it some more. He did not light it. Could not abide the smoke. But, he savored the routine. Enjoyed the *clack-clack-clacking* of the tip against his lower teeth as he lost himself in thought. He was not a man given to vices. Indeed, he was a strong advocate of the principles the Lakeshore Insane Asylum had originally been founded on. Fresh air. Exercise. The restorative effects of hard work. The discipline of a kind hand. For years, he and the others had believed that these procedures in and of themselves would be able to restore the ailing mind. They had been proven wrong. Over and over again. As the years passed he had watched and participated in almost all of the new treatment options that had been presented. Varying degrees of success had been observed in the mostly indigent patients who had received the experimental treatments. Varying degrees of success and some truly horrifying failures. The latter he tried not to dwell upon. At the core of his being he passionately believed that the mentally ill could be healed. That no one had to be damned to a life of such unproductive, hopeless misery. Encouraged by the almost desperately optimistic reports of his colleagues, he would struggle to contain his disappointment and forge ahead. Doubts. Insecurities. Fears. The agitators of the soul he pressed into submission.

He was encouraged with what he read about the new antipsychotic drugs. Yes, the results definitely looked promising. Perhaps not just as another treatment but possibly even a cure. *The* cure. And, Dr. Davidson knew, with so many of the brightest minds committed to the race, spurred on by the luminescent light such a finding would cast over their careers to say nothing of the credibility it would bestow on the field as a whole, the eventual discovery of a cure was all but inevitable. But how many years and how many patients that eventuality would encompass was anyone's guess.

Standing, a chronic stiffness seized his lower back and stifled his movements. He hesitated for a moment before he straightened up and moved slowly around the desk to lean against the thick pine frame of the arched turret window. Sliding a finger across the sill, he squinted his eyes through the gloom. He would have to speak to Margaret about the dust. Below him, in a seam of moonlight bordering the yard, he saw a figure standing beside the lilac bushes. Sighing heavily, he took the pipe from his mouth. He could tell by the sad slouched countenance that it was his gardener and cemetery custodian, Jakie Hewitt. He shook his head in amazement. And, he had to admit, a certain amount of admiration.

"Damn Houdini," he mused, rubbing tired eyes with the back of his hand.

There had been a few of them over the forty years of his practice. Patients who could defy a full lockdown and the carefully adhered to procedures of the wards to gain their freedom, seemingly at will. Although he had never committed the thought to paper, he had to admit that they exhibited a level of cleverness that challenged him to acknowledge a little genius might coexist along with their insanity.

A long-term patient, Jakie had been hauled into the asylum by the police and promptly committed. An incoherent, rambling mess of a man, he'd arrived along with a large, muddy, steamer trunk and some tattered papers filled with vague symbols. Besides his many phobias and suspicions, he seemed to present with a rather acute case of amnesia. Considered delusional but harmless, he had full grounds privileges during the day and was, in fact, one of the best gardeners the institution had ever had. Nights he was supposed to remain in the locked ward, but over time he had developed a penchant for slipping away and sleeping in the cemetery caretaker's shack instead. An irritating indiscretion, but one which Dr. Davidson chose to overlook.

Unhooking his tie from the arm of his chair, Dr. Davidson refastened the noose around his neck and made his way downstairs. Tired and irritated by this patient's imposition, he also knew the poor fool was deathly afraid of grass and would stand hovering at the edge of the lawn to his dying moment if someone didn't intervene. Originally, he had tried for weeks to coerce Jakie into clipping the lawns surrounding Cumberland House. Convinced the extensive grass areas were really the Red Sea and would someday swallow him up, he had steadfastly refused. Threats, restrictions, and finally punitive discipline were of no avail. Eventually, Dr. Davidson relented. But it still prickled his academic pride to see his gardener skirting around the grassy areas as if his very life depended on it.

Crossing the yard under the shadow of night, the plump grass swallowing the sound of his footsteps, Dr. Davidson called out softly so as not to startle the half-deaf man.

"You are in direct violation of procedures, Jakie," the doctor said, as usual cutting straight to the point.

"Happens, sir."

"No. That is erroneous. You do not retire in your bed at night only to find yourself an hour later, awake and strolling about the grounds. It does not just happen. Does it?"

"Suppose not."

The unconvinced note in the other man's voice greatly annoyed the doctor. He felt a hot rush of blood run to his head followed by a hesitation of uncertainty. Perhaps it was the truth. Perhaps that was precisely how it happened. A simple case of somnambulism. He quenched the suggestion, standing straighter, aware of any slights his posture or voice could deal against his authority.

"We'll have to rescind your grounds privileges."

"No!"

"It's not my call. You know the procedures."

"But sir, I have found her."

"Found whom?"

"The Madonna. And child."

Taking a deep breath, exhaling as he grabbed Jakie's arm firmly, the doctor started directing him toward the administration building. In his forty years he had heard them all, the current one being no exception.

"But it's true, sir. I did. Down by the bridge."

"Well, perhaps they'll see fit to make you a saint then, Jakie."

"Do you think they might?"

The doctor looked away from the exuberant puppy-like face. "Perhaps."

Jakie stopped walking and looked at the doctor earnestly. "I should like it very much if they did, sir."

"Of course. Of course. Now, let's get back to the ward. It's late and I'm tired."

"But I can't just leave her down by the crick."

The doctor did not like the resistance he heard growing in Jakie's voice. He was even less happy about the resistance he felt growing in his arm. The man might be crippled, but he was strong. And with no backup to call, the doctor knew he was in danger of losing control of the entire situation. Increasing his grip on Jakie's forearm, he established direct eye contact with a condescending, fierce glare.

"You will come now, Jakie, or you will force me to apply disciplinary action."

"But she is the Madonna, sir."

"She is a delusion."

"Forgive him, Father."

"Do you want to end up in solitary, man?"

"I'm called of a higher—"

"Don't begin—"

"There are mysteries—"

"There are ice baths—"

"One does not choose his cross—"

"Metrazol—"

This touched a nerve. "Forgive them, Father. They know not—"

"For God's sake, man!" the doctor exploded, exasperated and exhausted beyond caring. "Grab hold of your faculties for a moment and be reasonable."

At this Jakie broke, loping down the hill toward the creek with such a terrible loss of equilibrium that the doctor was already envisioning the fall and subsequent stitches. Following the younger man down toward the trees, the doctor started at an unfamiliar sound, straining through the darkness to see.

"Jakie," he whispered. "Where are you? I can't see a damn thing."

"Here, sir."

The doctor followed the voice to the dark shadows surrounding the base of the trees and saw Jakie's hunched-over form, looking beneath. A simple grin lit up his face as he looked back at the doctor and pointed into the darkness.

"You see, sir. She's right there."

CHAPTER 3

Dear Dr. Davidson,
May 14, 19--

I hope Sir that this letter finds you well. I
am writin you once agin to ask you to please
be a good soul an post the letter I include
to my dear Husband an Children. I implore
you Sir an beg of you to make sure it gets
done cause I have no news of my loved ones
for so long now I think it is possibly 2 or 3
years. You can not even begin to unnerstand my pain sir at having to wonder for
so long what has befell them. As you know
I was broght in here to this asylum after
the birth of my 9th child. I would admit Sir
that my brain was tired an not working rite
for a while there but I can assure you doctor that I am not insane as some in here
are. I am not an educated women this I am
sure you can tell as my father was not of
the opion that it was nessarsary to educate
girls as we mostly ending up marrying an
settling down. Which seems to be the truth
of it Sir as that is surely what I did myself
although as a child I had thoughts to
become a doctor of medicine like your self
an I would spend any spare moments which
were not many sitting on the porch of my
grannies house trying to read my grandfa-
thers books which filled two large book

cases although no one else thought them of much interest. I could not read much of the words Sir but I could get by looking at the pictures an some times I would lose sense of the time an I took more than a few beatings for not getting the hogs fed on time which was one of my jobs then. But I did not mind the beatings so much Sir as when I was reading I felt in a different place an it was worth the beatings to get to go there if only for a short while in my head. I did not get to know my grand father Sir an I am sorrowed by this as they say he was a lerned man an had studied at a university for some years before his own father was killed an he had to quit an go work in the mines to take care of the large family left behind. An they say he was killed by the Pleurisy Sir but I am inclined to doubt it as I have seen how my mother looked away when it was spoke of an I know too Sir something of the symptoms of that dread disease an when I asked of his health my mother would only say he was fine one day an dead the next. Which makes no sense Sir as you know in the case of Pleurisy but I suppose I was not to know any different an I am sure in this case the truth is best left unsaid. My mother was only a young girl of fifteen when my grandfather passed but she was expected to make her own way Which she did Sir an became a housemaid for some folks called newmans an shortly after she married my father who was a farm hand about the place an 20 years her senior. Wether she chose to or had to I would never of dared ask an I suppose it is best left that way. As I have told you before Sir my father was a very hard working man with little time for nonsense an we children were needed to help on the farm so not any of us got much education. But we always did have food in our stomaches an a roof over our heads an we were not beaten often but only when we needed it an even then not terrible hard as some did who got broken bones to show for it. Sir I wonder after my children every day an my Husband as well. An I think it must be going on 3 years now at least an I find it an intolerable thing to be locked away like this when I know my babies are growing up without me an surely you agree Sir that this is not rite that a child should grow up without its mothers love cause she is unfairly locked away an can not return home evin if she would like to do so. It is not rite Sir to keep me locked away like this. This place is like a prison an I have done nothing wrong. You do not know what it is like in here and I know that is not your fault as so many patients need your care but I can assure you this is an awful place not fit evin for a dog. I could tell you things that go on in here that would make you very mad sir if you saw them for yourself. The nurse here are very meen sometimes not all of them but some of them for sure, Nurse Jenny is kind an genteel with everyone evin Myrtle who is crazy as a bat an thinks nothing of going #2 on peoples beds Oh Sir can you evin begin to unnerstand my despair of being in this place??? I work hard from erly morning an am always the last to bed cause the night brings me nuthin but the most painful kinds of despair. I dream I am home with my family an happy to be so sir an then I wake an I am still in this writched place and I cry great sobbing tears I cry Sir I am not ashamed to tell you cause what kind of

mother would I be if I did not??? You do not
know sir what it is like to pass the day in
here. If it was not for my duties in the
kitchen preparing the meals I think I
should have already gone completely mad I
do not know Sir if you have hear from my
dear Husband but I would beg of you to tell
me any news that comes your way I do not
unnerstand why I have no answer to my
many letters sent surely my childs will of
missed me by now??? An you can not imagine the sadness filling my heart to know my
baby has grown without me all these years
an would cry if I took her in to my arms to
hold cause she would be fritened and not
know who I am. An can that be rite Sir???
Surely you agree that is not a rite thing
Sir??? I want sir that you would come to see
me an see for your self that I am good now
to return home. I was a good wife to my
Husband Sir an a good mother to my children I worked from dawn till late at nite
each an every day sir an it were no burden
My Husband had said I was quarlsome sir
an I do not defend my self in this regard I
some times was so an I relies the errors of
my ways now I was young an foolish once
sir but I will assure you I am no longer that
way But sir it is now 2 or 3 years past an I
am much improved from my time here you
should come test me for your self an see
how good my brains is. You can ask of me
any simple question an I can give a good
answer please doctor I ask you to do so I
beg it of you please it would not take very
long to do so an then you could see for your
self I am good enough to go back home to
my family. If I am not allowed to go home
soon sir I fear for the worst I am not a crasy
women but I fear I will become one if you

do not tell my Husband to come an take me from this place, I just want to have the little comforts of life agin the things that make one there own self I want to sleep in my own bed agin an when theres a chill I want to wear my warm swetter with the flowers on it that used to belong to my great aunt Helen I want to brush my hair with my soft brissle brush that were my own mothers. You shoulda seen my hair doctor. I aways had the most lovly hair. It were the color of mollases taffy an it grew down to <u>there</u>. An I pulled it to one side with my pearl comb that looked like a buterflie it were the most beatiful comb sir but someone gone stole it from me I think it was Dolores. In this place my hair has got so corse an ugly my dear Husband will be ashamed. I long evry day to have a cup of tea in the dainty tea cup my grannie gave to me on my wedding day It was a real tea cup Sir A real Bone China tea cup made in England with pink flowers I think they were carnations an it was expinsive sir course it would have been rude to say so but you could tell it by the feel light as a newborn chick it was an like all things of money sir it could make evin the cheapest of tea taste ready for the Queens table. I would like to have my tea when I like to sir an not when the nurse tells me to do so am I a child I should listen to her??? I think not sir I am a mother myself an I think my mind is up to knowing when I would like a cup of tea or not. I like to go outside when I like sir as well an not be locked in here like a beast only taken out when the nurse sees fit to take a walking tour An I want to hear the laughter an noise of my own children sir an not aways the sound of this place the

constant screeming an moaning it is like
purgatory but worse cause we do not know
what sin we committed to get our selfs into
this place or what we can do to redeem ourselfs an we can only be silent or start screeming ourselfs an try to not hear for awhile
Myrtle who never shuts up about her poi-
sin stomache an who shits every where
with no more shame than a mongeral dog
in a alley who at least trys to cover it up
before it goes away. This asylum is a tomb
for the living doctor an I know they do not
call it a asylum any more but when I came
in here that is what it was called an sir you
can change the name of a place all yous
want but it do not change what a place is.
An surely yous yourself has seen that
writched creture up under the eves of Cottage 5 doctor. Grinning down at us as if we
weres somethin to laugh at. An I s'pose to
somes we are. But still...its not welcome to
look up an see that horible thing. Some in
here talk of ghosts an such nonsense an are
scared of the groans an screams we hear at
night but I tells them it is folloshness to
think so an why would any ghosts want to
live here??? This place has enough torment
alredy without them adding to it but some
of the ladies here seem to think the ghost
of Mrs. Molly Miller haunts the tunnels
down below but I can tell you straight sir
that Molly Miller was terrified of those tunnels an the things that went on down there
an the nurses would sometimes put her in
to the shackles down there when she got
carried away an I know for certain sir that
since she fell from the window an died that
is the last place Molly would be. Some of
the nurses like to tell the ladies differently
though sir an I can see it is only to scare

the weak of mind into doing what the
nurses want an some times they make us
do there work for them, Some of them are
lasy as cats in the afternoon sun sir an it
works very well for them to say they will
put the ladies in to the tunnels if they do
not do as they are told. I do not believe such
nonsense sir as I am not crasy or feeble of
mind but I go a long with it cause I have
seen what can happen when one makes
troubles here There are things I know to be
true Sir as I myself have been wrapped in
cold blankets an strapped to my bed until I
was exhausted from fighting an then had
nurse B...I will not tell you her name but let
it be knowd sir that she is a wretched creature an enjoyed poking at me an threatened to cut my tongue out evin once I was
too tired to care. An that is not the worst of
what happens to us here sir an I speak from
experience and should you like to know
more I would be happy to tell you the truth
of what goes on here in cottage 4 once you
go out an the sound of your foot steps leave
us. You should know sir that none in here
blames you for things as the nurses remind
us almost daily that you are busy an not to
be bothered with trifles cause you have so
many patients under your care. An I can
see sir that this is the case an I do not hold
aginst you that you are not aware that certain of the nurses are downright sneaks.
Not all of them for sure but nurse B...is one
we all thinks should be locked away herself. She is mean of spirit sir an were she a
cow or horse you would sneak her off to
auction in a distant town an rid yourself of
her to someone who is fool enough not to
know to look beneath a pretty eye. It is
nothing for her to give us a slap or jab us

with her keys when she goes by an if we are
fool enough to do any thing back as the
new ones always is before they learn the
rules of this game then she calls for help an
we are strapped down while she tells lies
and stares down at us smiling as sweet as
mother mary an not an ounce of shame
either I tell you. Not an ounce. Sir I would
wager all I have that if one were to cut out
that womans heart it would be as black as
the ace of spades.

But sir, I should not speak ill of others just
tell the truth which seems to be the course
of my troubles sometimes An I shoulnt like
you to think I am ungrateful for the care I
have got here sir cause mostly it has bin
good an to be sure at first I was most happy
to come here when my husband said I
should do so an he made it sound so delitful
saying the patients got to stay in cottages
by the lake which made such a lovely picture in my head which turned out a great
disapoinment sir when I first chanced to
see the big brick buildings which were no
more cottages than a cow is a kitten. An
although I was frightened to stay here
alone without my Dear Husband I still
thought it a beautiful place sir with its
green fields an the milk cows standing so
lazy sunny them selves an I suppose sir
that comforted me as I felt it a bit like going
home to my fathers farm an I remember
some of the men patients were out gathering potatoes in the North field an it all
looked so paecful an not unlike my fathers
farm at all in that respect an I suppose I
felt a bit like I was goin to a place where I
could rest as I was so tired an it seemed a
wunnerful thing to be able to come here an

be looked after till I felt myself agin. I do
not mean to complain sir but I was so terrible tired after the baby cause I had a bleed
an evin tho she slept alot there was somethin not quite rite with that child I never
knew what but I could feel it in my bones
an 2 of the other little ones was got up with
some sickness to an I had them to care for
an my stupid head would not stay straight
with all the kids sick an crying an wantin
food an fresh diapers an having to haul up
the water from the creek to wash the
clothes an get the meals on time an of corse
help my dear Husband out in the fields
from time to time as well an my son Ezra
who was only just beginning to learn to do
the milking an so I still had to help him
some an Lou-Bell was not always the easi-
est of cows to milk just like her mother an
there were times I hit my son with the
switch sir when I should have hit the cow
but I knew he would feel it more an I felt
my mind was coming apart an I am not
proud sir to say it but I put more than a few
welts across his face. An I live with that
sorrow sir an if I had only one wish I would
wish him to remember them as kisses
rather than blows as is befitting a mother.
An sir I have no good to say for my self and
I do not know why I did not hold up better
as others have done the same an more an
with a smile upon there face as my Good
Husband was to remind me an I know such
to be true. But I could not sir hard as I tried
an I did try so very hard sir an would cry
from the effort of it but each day had too
many chores an not enough hours an then
I fell behind an the spring was gone an the
garden lay waiting an as you know sir
planting waits for none of us an my

husband grew furious with me when he found I had not got it done in time. An that is when the neighbor girl began to come around but I am no ones fool sir an I saw straight away what she was about An it was not long after my Husband wanted to hire her to help out about the place but I am not a sheep with the wool pulled over my face sir an I can smell a rat when a rat is trying to make a nest in my house. An I tole my Husband pleasantly enough that I had no wish of that girl helping about my place but said I had a cousin who still lived with her parents just outside of Carrot Creek who would be sure to come an help An that is when the unpleasantness started Sir an I do not wish to speak ill against my Husband sir an shall not do so but there were things that happened that should not of an I protested an that is when things got worse an then the kittins got drowned an I set to screeming an sir I did not know it were just a joke an when my husband tole me so it were to late I just could not settle my self back down agin. An I do admit sir I have a foul temper when crossed sir an always have an have oft been told to learn to hold my tongue but I was foolish sir in the way of youth an did not. It is hard sir to feel your self in an injustice an not speak your thoughts but I am pleased to say sir I have lerned to do so since being in this place an I should like you to tell my Husband that I have lerned to do so an am no longer quarlsome an he would find me most agreeable should he come an get me from this place. An could you ask him sir to do so as soon as he can find the time as I would like very much now to go home as I felt I was only coming for a short rest an I fear 2

or 3 years have gone by since he last came.
An could I bother you to ask him to bring
my brown dress as I have grown skinny in
here an I fear neither of the others would
stay on me any more but please sir also
could you tell him if it is any trouble to not
worry hisself but to just please come an get
me an I will wear the garb of this place evin
though I am loathe to wear it one more day
than I must. I am so weary of only the same
dress each day an no color or hair orda-
ment to speak of as Angel Queen Supreme
has had that sneak Dolores steal them all
away an it is tiresome sir to each day put on
clothes that do not differ from one day to
the next or one person to the next unless
one has money enough to buy new things
as some are lucky enough to do but I am
not sir an I feel it would not matter at all if
I dressed or stayed in my nightgown all
day. Not that nurse B...woud allow such a
thing any ways sir She is most strict about
that sort of thing an if we tarry to long to
gase out a window at a bird or the clouds or
the sunset she is right there to prod us
along just as if we are cows going home to
be milked. An she is most anoying to be
sure sir an maybe evin black in heart An I
know a thing that happened here sir that I
am sure you do not cause I feel sure sir a
just man likes your self would not let such
a thing pass but when Ethel was sent over
here from Brockville she was not happy
about it an not well behaved at all sir an
carried on something awfull an fought like
a polecat with anyone who come near her.
She has no family to speak of sir or none
who is willin to make them selfs known at
any rate an no friends neither cept for the
one she had in Brockville an she was angry

sir at being taken from her one friend an
that place where she had bin since a young
girl her self an after so many years sir a
place must become like ones home evin if it
is not the place one would have choosed to
live out most there life here on this earth.
So one can unnerstand well enough sir her
displeasure of been takin from that place
an then nurse B making a point each day of
saying Ethel you will never get back to that
place so you might as well quit feeling sorry
for yerself an content yerself that you will
only see your friend if yous both gets to
gods kingdom which she doubted cause
Ethel was fond of foul words an was not shy
to use them. An nurse would makes jokes
of Ethel an pretend to find worms in her
hair an say it was cause Ethels brain was
eatin full of worm holes an then Ethel
would get scared sir an one can not ritely
blame her can they an she would begin to
her screeming agin an one day after theys
got her tied down sir I heards nurse B...say
she would be happy to cut Ethels voice
cords right out if she did not quit screeming like a stuck pig an her eyes was rolling
back sir an it scared the rest of us to see it
happen an she was yelling for some one to
help her but we minded our own as we all
knews what were to come next sir an in no
part eager to get caught up in it an sir I do
not wish to say unkindly against another
but nurse B...does seem to have a mean
streek in her an if I were to say the truth sir
I have more than once seen her poke or
pester one of us till we can stand it no further an then she calls the other nurse an
tells some filthy lie or another an has us
strapped down or put in the pit sir where
the darkness is thick as death an things

are done to us that the devil hisself would
not allow. She has a wire sir you would
never know where she hides it as she is
crafty as a fox an even tho I have at times
pretended sleep to see where she puts it I
still do not know but it is a stiff wire sir an
thin an in this you can take my own word.
An I have seen her take it from her skirts
an whip it over the high flesh of the patients
legs when they are tied like brute beasts an
she is clever in an evil way an knows to hit
us there where the skirts cover our legs an
none are to see that place but there are
some here that do see an I know I have said
so before in my letters sir an I hope you will
forgive me my crass way sir but there is
some in here sir who do things to us that is
not rite. An I can tell you more sir if you
would like to know what goes on behind
you once the sound of your foot steps leaves
our ward an I should like to tell the names
of those sinners but I would fear to do so sir
as long as I must stay here as I fear I would
be stuck with pins an maybe even burned
like I was before sir even tho I know they
told you it happened a diffrent way. But I
am no fool sir believe me that an I know
what they were about an they were angry
with me cause I had told how Molly got her
black eyes an they meant to teach me not
to say the truth of what goes on in this
place. An I was paying no one mind sir just
doing my chores in the kitchen as I do
every day an am thankful of that but they
come up behind me sir an I can not tell for
sure who it was as I did not see their faces
but one gets to know the smell of others an
I smelt there vinager smell an heard that
huffing like a winded nag an I knew whos it
was. An sir my head was held over the

boiling pot for so long sir I could not see an it were many days fore the scalds left me an my eyes are still poor on account of it an I know doctor that you think it did not happen that way an they tole you I had tried to harm my self an was stopped by them. But I can assure you sir that is not true an I will swear on gods name it did not happen that way. There is an evilness that lives among us sir as surely you your self know an it does not aways hide behind an evil face an you would be surprized sir of some of the things I could tell you that goes on in here when the lights are out for the night an the creatures begin there evil crawlings. Things that should not happen an are of the darkness an I would be ashamed to speak even the words of it but would if you would be inclined to know for your self an should ask it of me an I would tell you in secret when my husband comes to take me away as I fear for my life here an some are set to kill me an I have heard it spoke of in the cover of night when they think me asleep sir but I have a gift of hearing sir an could hear a gnat chewing its tail six rooms away. An I know sir it may be hard for you to beleave that such things happen here but you do not live inside this place an I think sir it would be wise of you to ask me of it so you can know the truth of it for your self. An I should be happy to tell you any thing you should like to know sir once my dear Husband has come to take me away.

Sir, I very respectfuly submit you this letter an agin I can only beg of you your favor to pass the other letter on to my dear Husband an Children an request sir you advice him as well that my mind an dispisition is

much improved an he should be happy now
to have me home as I will prove to be of no
further trouble to him.

Sincerely, Mrs. John Mason (Anna)

Ξ Ξ Ξ

Leaving the letters lying on his desk, Dr. Davidson rose,
walked into the stream of late afternoon sunlight spilling
through the window of his office and looked out at the
white-blossomed cloud of the apple orchard. Off to his left,
closer to the lake, he could see the hospital's cricket team
practicing on the oval. His eyes picked out the tall figure
who was batting, stroking the balls away with elegant
drives and glances. Obviously having a better day today,
the doctor noted. Dr. Davidson knew and loved the game
and was proud to have Norman Headly on his team. Made
up primarily of staff, it had been given an enormous boost
with the recent addition of Headly. Prior to his breakdown,
he had been one of the best batsmen in the country and
a great favorite among cricket followers, a fact his family had used to demand his immediate transfer out of the
archaic Provincial institution, 999 Queen Street West.
Which hospital he would be transferred into had been a
vigorous source of debate among several of the local superintendents. Dr. Davidson had personally shown Headly's
family around the Lakeshore grounds, pointing out all
the advantages of a hospital designed in the Cottage-style
system. He had proudly explained to them that the Cottage concept of institutional care incorporated some of the
most advanced theories of the time: restorative landscapes,
industrial, occupational and recreational therapies. He had
explained that the very layout of the buildings themselves
had been designed to simulate a village-like atmosphere in
order to provide the patients with a sense of security and

community. He supposed he had to concede to Mrs. Anna Mason, however, that perhaps it was a bit of a misnomer to call the buildings that housed the patients *cottages,* as they were in fact four-storied brick units each capable of housing almost seventy patients. And although it was a small slight, it still bothered him immensely that she insisted on pointing out at every opportunity the grotesque stone gargoyle that had somehow been added without detection to Cottage Five during construction. But then there were so many things about Mrs. Anna Mason that bothered him. That she felt the hospital had been misrepresented to her in the first place. That she had made so little progress and indeed had begun to slip more and more deeply into her suspicious paranoias. That she had felt she was coming to the hospital for a short rest, which had turned into twenty-three long years, a fact her disturbed mind either would not or could not accept. That her husband had quietly divorced her, married the neighbor girl and requested Anna's letters no longer be passed along to him. That her children, whom she held so dear, had grown up calling another woman *mother*, believing their own long dead.

Sighing, he walked back to the desk, added the two new letters into a tattered file thick with yellowed papers and placed it back onto the bottom shelf.

CHAPTER 4

A wind burst of mildewed air rushed out to confront him as he wrested open the massive wooden door. He detested this part of the hospital. This subterranean intestine that so conveniently connected the buildings above. A design marvel in their conception, the tunnels had proven a colossal failure in their final application. A utilitarian series of narrow corridors with arched brick ceilings, a chaos of motley colored wires, strings, and pipes ran along the walls at varying intervals. At several junctures some of the wires had broken and been hastily repaired, a fact that accounted for much of the fluctuating power and blackouts, which beleaguered the hospital on a regular basis. Central to all the tunnels was the Services building. Initially, all the meals and laundry for the institution had been delivered to and from the various buildings through the tunnels. This enabled the groups of patient-workers to travel between their Cottages and the Services building without ever having to go outside. It was a design detail that should have made the job of the nurses who oversaw the transfer of the patients immensely simplified. But the tunnels were too dark, too claustrophobic. And in the susceptible minds of the patients and far too many of the staff, too easily compared to medieval dungeons. Inevitably stories arose, were believed, and thrived as abundantly as did the ever present rats. Dr. Davidson had little time for such nonsense. Of course, he too had experienced the vague and sometimes not so vague noises that arose seemingly from just around the next corner. But he was not a superstitious man. If there was a noise, there was a reason why there was a noise. It was as simple as that. And while he could forgive his patients for their naïvety, he had to admit some of the most foolish minds belonged to his own staff.

He did not like the dank, cheerless tunnels or their adjoining treatment rooms, but that did not stop him from feeling slightly put upon when some *higher up* in the government made the decision to take a section of it out of his control and offered it to the eminent American psychiatrist Dr. Harold Uldrich. Uldrich was the sort of man whose reputation preceded him. And, in Dr. Davidson's opinion, greatly exceeded him as well. The sort of man who had his detractors but few who were willing to voice their dissent publicly. In the psychiatric community his legendary status was well established. The fact that this status had been gained by conducting some extremely risky and sometimes dubious new treatments did not seem to be a topic of concern for those who paved his way with government grants and additional funding.

Dr. Davidson headed toward Cottage Four, the building that housed the severely insane female patients. The hopelessly insane, as some referred to them. Dr. Davidson felt otherwise. He passed by the heavily barricaded door that led to Uldrich's rooms. *Authorized Personnel Only*. In spite of himself, he was curious as to what was going on in there. Prior to Uldrich setting up in the hospital, Dr. Davidson had been asked about volunteering some of his patients for the research. His hesitations and concerns about the project had been politely but pointedly dismissed.

His footsteps reverberating around him, he walked toward what was now the isolation chamber. It was inappropriate, housing nonviolent patients in cells intended for the safe incarceration of those who threatened harm to themselves or others, but with the incessant overcrowding such things could not always be avoided.

Slowing his pace, he approached the door and then continued on by. Despite attempts to calm himself, his breathing had grown into shallow rapid gulps, his heart a wild horse thundering in his chest. Silvery beads of perspiration prickled his back. He would need a moment alone. Maybe more. Clenching his jaw, he cursed his failure to bring something along in case he had to self-administer. The fear he understood. Its obvious root could easily be traced back to a single childhood incident. As a young boy he had often been left in the care of his grandparents while his parents went off on extended overseas travels. Unaccustomed to the stifling inactivity of the older couples' congested flat and perhaps feeling more than just a bit rebellious at being left behind yet again, he one day had snuck away to go exploring in the hills. Coming upon an abandoned mine shaft, he did what any inquisitive boy would have done. Ignoring the faded warning signs, he found a length of old rope in a nearby shed and lowered himself down. It was not much of a discovery. The floor of the shaft was turgid with stagnant water, a distinct putrid smell violating his nostrils.

Grabbing hold of the rope to climb back up, he had watched as his knot frayed free, the remainder of the rope curling down on top of him. The urgency of his situation did not touch him at once. With the falling of dusk, however, that was to change. As the darkness began to blind him his sense of smell sharpened to compensate. The foul odor pulsed and grew as if it were feeding on his fear. Suddenly it had occurred to him that he did not know where the smell originated. Whatever the thing was that emitted it, he knew one thing without a doubt. The thing was dead. At first he'd imagined small, furry woodland animals. By the time a search party stumbled across him thirty-four hours later, however, the decaying, mutilated thing had become himself.

Pushing the memory away, he recited a litany of reassurances which gradually enabled him to focus forward on the task at hand. The hospital's newest admission, the young girl Jakie had found tethered to the tree, needed to be assessed, diagnosed and, hopefully, identified. He wondered if the nurses had been able to garner any further information. Names, dates, marital status, religious persuasion, personal and familial histories. All the seemingly mundane details that the nurses were so chronically careless about gathering but that often provided him with the interlocking key as to why the patient had ended up in his hospital in the first place.

So far, this new girl was proving something of an enigma. She could sing but refused to speak. Her repertoire seemed limited to just three songs, traditional Protestant hymns, suggesting a Christian upbringing. Beyond that, no other clues were forthcoming. Save for those provided by her physical self. Caucasian female. Late adolescence to early twenties. Blue eyes. Blonde hair. Unkempt, malnourished, extremely emaciated, her frail frame a riddle of lesions and contusions.

Positioning himself in front of the door, he drew a purposeful breath, released it and then rapped resolutely on the gray metal. He was profoundly dismayed to be met by the soft pudding face of Nurse Mildred, a woman he found so contumacious he told himself he allowed her to retain her job only on account of the dire shortage of others willing to take it.

Orphaned as a child, Mildred had been raised on the Saskatchewan prairies by a simple, hard-of-luck couple whose abundant superstitious beliefs almost formed a religion in themselves. Far from simple herself, however, Mildred knew her mind and spoke it freely. And her verbal veracity was fully supported by an incredibly fluent body

language, which was in no way muffled under her generous layering of fat. He would have much preferred to be
attended by one of the younger, less obstinate nurses who
did as they were told and would never have dreamt to question his authority. He tried to keep the thought from his
face. The woman was uncanny in her ability to see beyond
what people chose to say. And he already had the unhappy
suspicion that she had warned the other, prettier nurses
away from him, claiming his affections for herself.

Shuffling aside she let him enter, almost smiled. Perpet-
ually winded, her mouth gaped as her moist pink tongue
plunked away absently inside her cheek. Averting his eyes
he tried not to focus on the heavy scraping behind him as
she relocked the door. Quickly, he surveyed the room. It
did little to alleviate his misgivings. Yellowing walls peeled
their paint. A single light bulb hung from the ceiling,
ensnared by a protective covering of industrial-strength
wire mesh. Cryptic poems and messages deluged every
available space, scratched into eternity by the inspiration-
ally insane who had dwelt here before. Shoved into the
left corner of the back wall was a spare metal cot, the thin
mattress still tightly encased by the sheet and worn wool
blanket. A melancholy fear crept through him. He tried not
to imagine the grip of total darkness that would seize the
room should that one dim light bulb choose to flicker out.

"Nurse! Where's the patient?" he said, his voice too
loud, too harsh.

"*Phht*," erupted Nurse Mildred, as if she were farting
from her face. She rolled her eyes toward the far wall. He
followed the motion. Took in the empty room, the empty
bed, and then stared back down at her with empty eyes.
She stared back.

Unease began to crawl up his spine. Like there was an
obvious answer to a riddle that only he could not guess. It
was a game his mother had enjoyed. Querying him beyond
his capabilities then happily solacing his frustrated tears.

A shadow of pity briefly caressed Mildred's face, and Dr. Davidson instantly blocked the emotion from his own. The woman's intellect confounded him. One moment dangerously sharp, the next dulled beneath a burden of superstitious stupidity.

Hands placed firmly on her knees, she bent over slightly, peered beneath the bed, and then smiled back up at him. "So I'm s'posing you weren't never much good at hide and seek then neither, hey?"

He stiffened, offended.

"Nurse Mildred, it may seem all fine and well to you that the patient is hiding underneath the bed. I, however, rather expect to find them on top of it when I come in, waiting to be examined. Whatever is she doing under there anyhow?"

"Playing billiards for all I know. Can't rightly say I've been under there as yet to find out."

He could see by the protracted stiffening of her body that he had cut her, and he instantly regretted this. He had no wish to quarrel with this woman who had it within her power to either simplify or greatly complicate the next half hour of his life.

A deep breath, a measured exhale. His eyes sought refuge against the far wall.

"Well, perhaps you could get her out from under there so we can proceed."

"Hoof! No thank you. Last nurse tried that got bit on the cheek."

He hesitated, struggling to suppress his rising frustration.

"Well...what do you suggest then, nurse? We most certainly cannot carry out the examination with her stuffed away like that."

"Be easier. I'm telling you, this one is nuttier than a whole nest of squirrels."

"Nurse. Please." He frowned.

"What? Just calling the kettle black, that's all. Even ol' Angel Queen's going to have trouble with this one. And filthy as sin when they brought her in too. Ain't no telling what she's got."

"Ears, Nurse Mildred."

"Huh?"

"Ears. She has ears. And seeing how she can sing, I am assuming she can use them."

"Well-well-well. Ain't we just a whole slop bucket full of sunshine today?"

He pressed a hand up against the tight drumming at his temple. It was like the woman drew him into these arguments by sheer osmosis.

He cleared his throat. "Look. It's been a hectic morning, and I still have a daunting number of tasks to attend to before lunch. Could we please just carry on?"

"Shore. Suit yourself. But I ain't going under there alone to drag her out."

A tendril of panic wound in his gut.

"Well. Are there no attendants available then?"

"Not a one. You know how short we are."

He did know. Staff shortages were a perennial problem. A problem he had once hoped would be remedied by the building of the on-site Nurse's College. Each year it produced an eager crop of fresh-faced girls primly smiling in their flawlessly starched uniforms. A few stayed on. For the vast majority, however, the rigors of institutional work soon proved overwhelming. They dissolved into tears, into marriage, into less demanding careers or, on more than one occasion, into insanity itself.

The drumming in his head had intensified, joined now by the whole marching band. He squeezed his eyes shut. Removed his sweater although he knew the room was not hot—the thick stone foundation kept the basement permanently cool. He searched in vain for somewhere to hang the sweater and finally cast it onto the bed. A mental list scrolled through his head. Cottage rounds to complete. A death certificate to prepare for Mr. Hampton, who had not fared well after yesterday's electric shock treatment. Finish the report on budgeting requests. And then at two o'clock, the game against Brockville. It was going to be the first time Norman Headly would play for the Lakeshore team, and Dr. Davidson was hoping not to miss a minute of it.

It was obvious to the doctor that this examination would not proceed unless he was willing to go under the bed and drag the girl out himself. The thought was unfathomable. The walls compressed, deflated him like a balloon. Feeling lightheaded, he reached out to grip Nurse Mildred's elbow.

She looked at his hand. "Everything all right, sir?"

"Yes. Yes, of course. Just short of air down here, that's all. Is she violent?" He removed his hand and inclined his head toward the bed.

"Like I tole you. Bites like a beaver. But she seems not so bad if you keep the quilt wrapped up around her head. Cides, she's just a wee whip of a thing really. And she ain't had so much as a bone to eat yet. I'd shore think the two of us could handle her okay."

"What do you mean, 'She's had nothing to eat?'"

"I mean she's had nothing to eat."

"At all? But it's been hours since Jakie found her down by the creek, and who knows how many more hours she'd been tied up there before that."

An exaggerated shrug. "Sir. We are not magicians here. Surely you have heard that you can lead a horse to water, but you cannot make it drink."

"Rubbish. What about Molly?"

Molly. Years earlier, Molly Miller had been the sole survivor of a tragic house fire that had consumed her entire family. Once her condition had been stabilized, she had been transferred out to the Lakeshore Asylum, broken-spirited and in constant pain. Facially disfigured, most of her once beautiful hair burned to baldness, she felt herself grotesque. On her thirty-sixth birthday, she had decided she would no longer eat. She had only one birthday wish she said and that was to die. Dr. Davidson had personally taken on her case. Molly's miraculous survival from the fire had struck a deep chord. Newspapermen followed her story relentlessly and often inaccurately. Politicians, anxious to encourage a country oppressed by war, were quick to march her name out and wave it as a flag of victory and courage.

It had not been beyond Dr. Davidson to foresee the effect news of Molly's demise would have on the public at large. Nor had it been beyond him to foresee the effect her full recovery would have on the reputation of his hospital. Indeed, on the reputation of psychology as a whole. A chance to finally redeem its name in the minds of the ignorant masses who still believed the institutions were little more than torture chambers housing the demonically possessed and dangerously insane.

"Without intervention, she would have died within the week," he mumbled quietly.

"True," Nurse Mildred allowed.

He thought back to the devastated, bird-skeleton frame and his treatment plan. Twenty-eight days strapped into bed, an intravenous tube inserted through her nose forcing nourishment into her stomach. By the end of the eighteenth day, Molly had begged to be allowed to eat on her own again. Her strength had returned rapidly. By the end of the month she had been strong enough to walk unaided and shortly thereafter gave her nurse the slip, made her way to the top floor of the administration building, broke a window and threw herself to the ground.

"Wasn't our fault. What happened," he said to the floor. "We did our best."

"Perhaps, doctor. Perhaps."

Working against the resistance in his joints and mind, Dr. Davidson stirred himself back to the present and stiffly lowered himself to one knee to look under the bed. A tattered patchwork quilt lay scrunched into the corner. Had he been a betting man he would have bet with confidence that no one lay beneath it. Even the thought of such dark confinement unnerved him.

"Is she under there often?"

"Every time I've come into the room."

"But why?" he whispered hoarsely.

"Because she's a nutter, sir," the nurse whispered back, mirroring his incredulous look.

"No. Well, yes, of course. But what do you think would drive someone to do that?"

"S'pose she feels safe that way."

Dr. Davidson considered this, striving for objectivity.

"Want to know what I think?" Nurse Mildred offered and then carried on without waiting for an answer. "I think she's one of the *Unspeakables*."

"A what?"

"An Unspeakable. Child of Darkness. You know. One of them kids born not quite right in the head, and the parents get to thinking there must be some kind of devil or bad spirit in them. I once heard about a family who had one they kept locked in the woodshed, and one night he got loose and chopped them all up to bits to make himself some stew. Ain't no one knew a thing till the hired hand went in to get the fire started next morning."

"Nurse Mildred," Dr. Davidson replied sharply, "such stories are nothing more than poppycock bantered about between the undiscerning of mind."

"Well," she huffed. "When Mr. Brewster was doing the burying, he told me about that there law and you got to admit it sure does seem to support the possibility of such things."

Dr. Davidson knew at once which law she referred to. It was an outmoded relic of the *Medieval Anatomy Act,* which forbade using the unclaimed corpses of mental patients for medical research as their evil spirits might jump out and possess the body of the researcher. For years, the doctor and several colleagues had been pressuring the government to have it abolished.

"Surely you do not believe such nonsense?"

A noncommittal shrug.

"Well. I myself firmly hold to the opinion that such ideas will cease to exist as the study of the mind continues to enlighten our understanding and beliefs regarding the mentally ill."

"Ah. And I, sir, firmly hold to the opinion that one belief can blind you just as well as another."

"What is that supposed to mean?"

"Only that ignorance is timeless, sir. That's all."

An uncomfortable impasse grew between them before Dr. Davidson brusquely suggested that they carry on with the examination.

"Perhaps if I talk to her I can coax her to come out of her own accord."

"Perhaps you can. But ain't no one had any luck with it yet."

He swallowed. Unsuccessfully attempted to square his rounded shoulders. A simple matter really, he assured himself. A quick reaching under the bed and hauling the girl out.

"All right then," he said thickly. "Let's get to it."

"Shore," Nurse Mildred agreed cheerily. "I'll get her legs. You can have the teeth."

He winced. "And how does one tell one end from the other?"

"Easy. Her head'll be crammed into the farthest spot."

Taking a deep breath, he tried not to think. "All right. Count of three then."

In unison, they attacked. The bony blanket erupted beneath their grasps, and they found themselves engaged by a surprisingly strong opposition. The girl's hands locked tightly around the leg of the bed, which was in turn bolted to the wall. The jostling partially disrobed her from her quilt, and Dr. Davidson instinctively shrank his face out of striking distance as flame-blue eyes seared into him. The closeness of the space suffocated him, and he felt a desperate temptation to release his grip and scramble out from under the bed. But, like the man burdened with holding the head of the snake, he didn't dare let go.

"Hang on then," came a raspy pant from somewhere behind him. "Hang on. I'll give her a jab."

Before he even began to comprehend, Mildred had unsheathed a hypodermic needle from her pocket and stabbed the sole of the girl's right foot.

Buckled by the startling pain, the girl's hands released just enough to sway the advantage. Displaying a surprising agility, Nurse Mildred snared the kicking legs, heaved back onto her ample backside, yanking the girl clear of the bed as if pulling a stuck calf. Exploding into a thrashing, boiling cauldron, the girl howled and spit as she tried to twist loose. Deftly spinning her away from him, Dr. Davidson hooked her elbows through his own and immobilized her. Her body was hot and sweaty against him, shaking with rage and fear and exhaustion. Looking down at the bleached driftwood arms intertwined with his own, he saw yellowish-green and violet bruises interspersed with a scattering of scabs and open sores. Prominent cheekbones jutted out so sharply they looked in danger of piercing the paper-white skin covering them. Someone had changed her out of the sweater and too-small nightdress Jakie had found her in and placed her into a pale green hospital gown that was far too large. Were it not for the intense wildness in her eyes she could have been mistaken for a small child playing dress-up.

Regaining her breath, she resumed her struggle, flinching, at the pain this caused her twisted arms, but did not cease. The doctor held her easily now, the earlier burst having depleted her. Through the awkwardly gaping neck of her gown, he was peripherally aware of the rapid, injured-bird beating of her small breasts. He felt like a beast. Ashamed of the brute strength with which he so easily incapacitated her. Afraid the spindly twig-arms would snap and she would crumple to the floor at his feet. He looked to his nurse for help, and she again produced the needle from her pocket. She stepped closer, her eyes roving for a suitable muscle. Instantly the girl stiffened, an unnatural groan escaping her. Suddenly slumping against the doctor, her arms and legs began a spasmodic, rhythmic jerking; her head lolled back to reveal a foam of bloodied spittle on blue-tinged lips.

Taking a step back, Nurse Mildred quickly crossed herself.

"Good Lord, Mildred. It's a seizure, not a possession," the doctor said with intense irritation. "Now, help me get her on the bed before she swallows her tongue."

Eyeing the girl dubiously, she swept the doctor's sweater onto the floor and carefully helped lay the girl down. Already the violent movements were ceasing, and Dr. Davidson observed a great swell of pity cross over Nurse Mildred's face as she looked down at the fragile form.

"Ah, look, sir. Her baby got dropped in all the ruckus. Poor thing."

Dr. Davidson gave a tangible start as he followed her gaze to the small pink arm poking out from under the bed.

"For God's sake, Mildred," he hissed. "It's just a doll."

"Not to her it ain't, sir. Not to her."

CHAPTER 5

D r. Davidson could see that Norman Headly had no wish to play. It was a wish the young doctor, who also doubled as the cricket team's trainer, seemed intent on not understanding. Headly's six-foot-five frame was slumped into that of a smaller man. His shorn head hung to deflect a barrage of insults. The scorched, infuriated face of the doctor shoved in close with each new round, arms flailing like a broken windmill. Headly's maple-leaf hands rose up to cover prominent ears. His body swayed sideways, like a circus elephant remembering its lumbering gait.

Dr. Davidson tapped his pipe hard against amber teeth. He'd been so encouraged by the improvements he'd seen lately in Headly's condition. Now, watching the man shuffling about like a baffled buffoon, he had to wonder if those improvements hadn't been little more than his own wishful thinking.

A collection of Brockville supporters stood off to the left of him, impatiently waiting for the game to proceed. With the score tied at twelve points apiece, everyone knew the outcome would be decided by the next swing of Norman Headly's bat. If, in fact, Norman Headly could even be coerced to swing the damn thing.

A few piquant looks were driven Dr. Davidson's way from the Brockville group. He responded with a leisurely search out across Lake Ontario, as if he were profoundly interested in a minute speck on the horizon. He felt the smug humor simmering around him. More than just a few toes had been crushed in his quest to secure Headly for his Lakeshore Hospital team. Now, it was beginning to look like he may have paid a hefty price for a horse unwilling to even leave the gate.

Quickly he reassessed the situation. *Talk-talk-talk.* He disdained the younger doctor's new-fangled training. Reasoning with a madman. Where was the sense in that? Not that he wasn't an advocate of a compassionate approach. He was. In fact, he applauded himself on such advanced thinking. But still, there were times when just the mere mention of one or another of the treatments could vastly hurry patients along.

A rustling of laughter erupted behind him, and he turned to see Dr. Uldrich and his entourage of glowing nurses crossing the field. The man did not simply walk. He strode. With long, elegant, self-important steps that had a couple of his shorter-legged nurses scurrying along in his wake. An erect, athletic man, Uldrich expressed his sharply cut suit well. A slash of navy blue tie was set off by an impeccably white shirt. On his head sat a jaunty bowler, conjuring up impressions of mobsters or movie stars but certainly not a doctor. Dr. Davidson's mouth puckered.

Since arriving in Toronto two months earlier, Uldrich's staff had kept primarily to themselves. With few exceptions, all invitations to attend various hospital functions had been turned down. It was a practice that had not fostered good relations. Suspicions, hostilities, and rumors had flourished like spring weeds. Nurse Mildred had demanded Dr. Davidson personally investigate what was really going on in Uldrich's *Sleep Therapy* rooms.

"*Sleep Therapy,*" she'd hissed. "*More like Zombie Therapy from what I hear.*"

Patiently, Dr. Davidson had tried to explain what little he knew and was rather irritated to find himself defending a man he would have much preferred to condemn. Dr.

Uldrich was, he had tried to explain, apparently research-ing a new procedure whereby it was hoped a patient's mal-functioning brain chemistry might be repaired through a combination of electroshock treatments and the restor-ative effects of prolonged sleep.

"*Restorative effects of prolonged sleep?*" Nurse Mildred had guffawed loudly. "*Why, if us nurses didn't keep prodding some of those old codgers awake, they'd sleep themselves right to death.*"

"Wonderful afternoon for a game, wouldn't you say, doctor?" Uldrich boomed, interrupting Dr. Davidson's thoughts as he strode to a stop, pulled out a gold lighter, and leaned across to light Dr. Davidson's pipe.

"Uh, no. Thank you, I don't smoke."

Skeptical eyes nudged the pipe.

"I'm allergic," Dr. Davidson replied as he plucked the pipe awkwardly from his mouth and slipped it into his sweater pocket.

Feeling his space radically impinged, he eased aside slightly and fixed his gaze on the far wicket. His gut churned in a slow roiling boil. Could the man not ascertain that some stood alone not because they had to but rather because they chose to?

"How are we doing?"

"Poorly," Dr. Davidson replied vaguely, annoyed at the other man's presumptuous inclusion.

"Hmm. How's our boy doing?"

"Mr. Headly is not at his best today."

"Too bad. He was one of the best you had up here in Canada, wasn't he? I had hoped to see him play."

"Well, good god. The man is not dead yet."

Dr. Uldrich looked down unswervingly. "Your point?"

"You speak of the man in the past tense. As if he were dead rather than just temporarily incapacitated."

"No. You are mistaken, sir. It was not Headly of which I spoke."

"But—"

"It was, rather, his legendary ability as a batsman to which I referred."

"Oh. I see," Dr. Davidson conceded stiffly. "So, you see no hope for the man's recovery then?"

Mercurial gray eyes slid over the field to where Norman Headly was now scribing jagged circles around an old woman who sat statue-still on a stone bench, the young doctor still pestering along behind like an agitated terrier.

"Not much hope. No."

"Well, with all due respect, it does seem somewhat pessimistic to declare a patient hopeless when one hasn't even had the opportunity of examining them."

"I don't make it my business to declare any patient hopeless, Dr. Davidson. I shouldn't think I'd make much of a researcher if I did. And, as to examining Headly, I already have."

"Under whose authority?" Dr. Davidson burst, puffing up in spite of himself.

"I examined him while he was still up at Queen Street. I've worked with a few of his type. And to a one, doctor, if it had not been for my intervention, they would still be shuffling about some ward shitting their pants and bawling for their mammas."

Dr. Davidson passed a quick, apologetic glance over the nurses. His eyes fretted toward Headly, his thoughts lingering over the farcical ghost of a once proud man.

"This intervention you speak of," he said dryly, squinting up into the sun as he attempted to catch Uldrich's eye. "Is that the nature of the research you're doing here?"

"It's part of it, yes."

Dr. Davidson's peanut-knuckled fingers fidgeted his pipe.

"And Headly? You think he'd make a good candidate?"

"I think he'd make an excellent candidate."

"How so?"

"Well, as you know, Headly suffered a major emotional trauma. But still, it was only a singular trauma. Up until he ran over the child—"

"It was his son."

"Yes. I'm aware of that. But the important thing is, up until that, the man had led a fairly normal life. You see, one day he is a normal, functioning, even gifted member of society, and the next he is a bumbling lunatic unable to even tie his own shoes—"

"The boy died in his arms, for God's sake. He didn't see—"

"Yes-yes-yes! I know all that. And of course it is an unspeakable tragedy for a father to bear," Uldrich said impatiently as he lit a cigarette. "One would expect some sort of transition period to be sure. But the problem is, Headly has failed to transition. It's like his brain keeps short-circuiting around the memory of that moment."

"Well, surely one cannot blame the man—"

"The point is not to blame, doctor. The point is to cure, is it not?"

"Yes, of course," Dr. Davidson huffed. "Which is why I had him transferred here. Queen Street was little more than a warehouse. Here, he's exposed to some of the most advanced care available."

"And how is that working?" Uldrich asked pointedly, as Headly's wavering tenor scraped the air with a shaky rendition of "Amazing Grace."

"*Amazing Grace, how sweet the sound. That saved a wretch like me. I once was lost, but now am found. Was blind, but now I see—*"

Dr. Davidson sighed deeply. "You think you can help him?"

"Yes."

"How?"

"How? My Sleep Therapy."

"Yes. But what exactly does that mean? What is it that you actually do down there?"

"Ahhh. Well, it's surprisingly simple really. We induce prolonged stages of sleep—"

"How prolonged?"

"Hard to say exactly. Depends entirely on the patient and the individual progress. It could be days, weeks, sometimes even months."

"Months! Good god, how is that even possible?" Dr. Davidson blurted.

"Drugs, doctor. Drugs. We've an excellent combination of them."

"But what about food, water—"

"Well, of course we wake them for feedings. And treatments."

"Treatments? The ECT then?"

"Yes. We like to work with multiple treatments in the beginning in order to remove any unnecessary debris."

"Debris?"

"Troublesome memories," Dr. Uldrich returned unctuously. "After that we can begin to reprogram them using a constant looping of self-affirming messages. As you can see, it's a relatively simple process. Basically, we endeavor to de-pattern an unhealthy brain and then reprogram it."

"Hmm. And for Headly then? What sort of messages would he receive?"

"Well, of course it would take some thought. But for Headly, I would probably de-pattern him back before the accident. Blot out that nasty bit of business entirely, while still attempting to retain his athletic brilliance, which was learned at a much earlier stage of his life."

"And can you do that? Select what will or won't remain?"

"I'm pleased with the progress we've seen so far. But we're still in the experimental stages, doctor. Nothing can be guaranteed."

"Fascinating," Dr. Davidson murmured, his mind firing with possibilities. "But surely, even if you can successfully negate the memory, it would only be a matter of time before Headly sees an old newspaper account of the accident—"

"Perhaps. But it would not retain any ownership over him. He may be momentarily disturbed, as would any of us over such a senseless tragedy. But then he would be called off to supper or some such thing and it would evaporate from his mind. The accident would be, as it were, as if it happened to somebody else."

"Brilliant," Dr. Davidson concurred, his mind already searching among his patients, braiding unfortunate pasts to eventual committals.

"Of course, long-term effectiveness is being redefined almost daily. You should come down one day. I'd be more than happy to show you around."

"Yes, perhaps I will," Dr. Davidson responded, warmed by the unexpected invitation and temporarily forgetting his extreme claustrophobia.

"Good. Wonderful. And perhaps you could arrange to have the young epileptic girl brought in at the same time. I've never had occasion to work with one of those before."

Dr. Davidson bristled. "An epileptic?"

"No. An Unmentionable. Indeed, until this girl was brought in, I thought they were little more than a silly, superstitious myth."

"Well, let me remind you, sir, that we still know precious little about this girl's circumstances—"

"True. But, it is possible, is it not, that her sunless complexion, fear of the light and relative comfort in the dark recesses of the isolation room do suggest she may have spent an inordinate amount of time hidden away. Perhaps even in a dark cellar, as Nurse Mildred has suggested?"

"Well, of course anything is possible. One certainly learns that well enough in this line of work. But still, it's all just speculation and conjecture. Neither of which seem very helpful to the girl's condition. Nor do I see, sir, how your Sleep Therapy would be an effective treatment for her epilepsy."

"No. Not for the epilepsy. But for the other. Think of it, doctor. If we could de-pattern the horrific psychological abuse she's evidently suffered, we would stand the chance of reprogramming her so she could live a normal life with no more than the epilepsy to ail her."

"I can't see that working," Dr. Davidson replied tightly.

"And why not?"

"Her parents, for one. It would be impossible to secure their consent."

"Her parents! It is my understanding that the girl was found abandoned. Chained beneath a tree. Surely, that in and of itself suggests an acquiescence of parental rights?"

"To the contrary. Considering that these are obviously simple-minded folks, burdened beneath an overwhelming superstitious fear, the fact that they risked bringing her here at all suggests a certain amount of concern for her well-being."

"Ha!" Dr. Uldrich cried derisively. "And were it not for the total lack of basic care the girl has evidently received, I might be inclined to see it your way."

"See it whichever way you choose, doctor."

"In my line of work, sir, we endeavor to see things how they *are* rather than how we would choose them to be."

A bridled impasse grew between them until a noisy shower of color down by the lake diverted their attention.

"What about one like that?" Dr. Davidson asked, his eyes on a spiritless group shuffling up from the ladies' pavilion, a heavy figure wearing a glittering yellow dress and purple sweater gaily skipping out ahead.

"Good god! What on earth is she wearing?"

"Miss Lawson is quite fond of sparkles."

"*Quite* fond? I should say so. She rather looks like she's wearing the entire Milky Way!" Dr. Uldrich enjoyed a rather mirthless laugh. "What's her history?"

"Real—or imagined?"

"Well, generally I like to stay on this side of delusion."

"Indeed. Myself as well," Dr. Davidson agreed, pleased to feel the tension recede. "She's a Lawson. Have you heard of them? No? An enormously successful bunch around Ottawa. Extremely well connected. You know the type. Anyhow, the father had her committed a couple of years ago. Apparently, she was always completely insufferable as a child. As she got older, things went from bad to worse."

Dr. Uldrich arched his brows.

"According to the father, her behavior became completely unbearable upon adolescence. Small injustices became catastrophic events, melancholy prevailed, tantrums and tears the order of each day. And as if that were not enough, she began to develop a rather robust interest in the opposite sex."

"Not so unusual for a girl of that age," Dr. Uldrich mused. "Most of them seem to go through their silly hysterics and begin to exhibit a certain fondness for young gentlemen."

"Indeed," Dr. Davidson agreed, his face flaring. "Unfortunately, the gentlemen Miss Lawson was exhibiting a certain fondness for were far from young."

"Ahhh. Indeed. Indeed. So, what do you think, doctor? Is she mad? Or simply immoral?"

"I try to assume neither. Before she was brought here, the father had her examined by a psychiatrist in London who diagnosed her as manic-depressive."

"And you concur?"

"No. Not fully. I suspect the father would have kept paying people to examine her until someone told him what he wanted to hear."

"I suppose it happens. So, what *is* your opinion of her mental health then?"

"Honestly Dr. Uldrich, there are times she seems to me little more than a profoundly overindulged child. Of course, the father refutes that vehemently. He's a self-made man. Extremely effective not only in his business dealings but in his political wrangling as well. Some say he has aspirations to run. So, you can see that the girl had become—how should I say it? She had become somewhat of a liability to the family's fortunes."

Dr. Uldrich studied the gaudy spectacle skipping oafishly toward them with a renewed interest.

"Do you suppose, doctor, that the father would be receptive to our using her in the Sleep Therapy program?"

"I can assure you that he would be. But, I can also assure you that once the girl gets wind of it she'll kick up such a fuss he'll be hard-pressed not to give into her."

"But surely, if he does entertain thoughts of running for office, he must be aware that a scandal like this could scuttle his chances?"

Dr. Davidson sighed heavily. "Yes, I am sure he is well aware of that. But for now, he seems content to have her here, sending a seemingly endless stream of gifts and money to keep her happy."

"And *is* she happy?"

"Oh, yes. Indeed. Deliriously so. She seems to think this is her private estate, the nurses her personal staff. She's even convinced a couple of the patients to be her ladies-in-waiting."

"And you?" Dr. Uldrich laughed. "I suppose you're one of her stable boys?"

"No," Dr. Davidson flushed hotly.

"Name?" A thick, phlegmy voice demanded, so close to Dr. Uldrich's ear that he gave a visible start.

"Good god, man! I didn't even hear you come up."

"Name?" the man repeated impatiently, undeterred by the doctor's stormy scowl. He wore a well-cut velvet jacket and sharp-creased trousers. "Come now, I haven't all day. I'm a busy man I'll have you know. A busy, busy man."

"This is Dr. Uldrich, Mr. Seymour. He's carrying out some research down in the tunnel rooms."

"Family name first, followed by full given."

"Uh...Uldrich. Harold Bruce," the other doctor replied, scanning Dr. Davidson's face.

Unhitching a tattered ledger book from under his arm, Mr. Seymour painstakingly scratched down a rather imprecise spelling of the name, busily returned his stub of a pencil into its little wooden case, and carried on importantly across the field, striding toward the statue-still lady sitting alone on the stone bench.

"And who in God's name was that?" Uldrich asked.

"Mr. Seymour," Dr. Davidson repeated.

"Yes, but what is it that he does? Some sort of record keeping?"

"Of a sort, yes. He enters names into the Book of Life. Apparently yours was missing."

"Ahhh! A patient then. With half of them running around in civilian clothes, it gets hard to tell."

"I'd have thought his big Bible might have tipped you," Dr. Davidson chided quietly. Surprised, Uldrich looked again at the departing man. Indeed, alongside his ledger book he carried a massive old Bible, its crepey pages sticking out in an explosion of various angles.

"He occasionally rips out pages that contradict his beliefs. Then—when he's had a change of heart—he gathers them up and adds them back in," Dr. Davidson said by way of explanation.

"I see," Dr. Uldrich murmured, shaking his head. "What's with the old woman there?" he asked, watching curiously as Mr. Seymour spoke sternly into the ancient, embroidered face that gave no indication he was even there.

"Not much. He's been trying to get her name for the last twenty-five years."

"Why won't she give it to him?"

"Doesn't speak."

"Doesn't—or can't?"

"Doesn't. Apparently his eyebrows are too furry for her liking."

Dr. Uldrich furrowed his own black brows together.

"She says it means he's not to be trusted," Dr. Davidson explained, chewing down a little grin.

Dr. Uldrich raised an eyebrow at the obvious swipe. "She talks to you then?"

"No. She talks to one of the other patients sometimes. Jakie Hewitt. As far as I know, she's never said a word to anyone else—including me.

"She was here when I came. According to her file, as a young girl she set fire to her family home, killing both her parents in their sleep. The neighbors found her outside on a swing, singing sweet as a canary while she watched them burn. Apparently, doctor, she confessed quite cheerfully about the whole thing and then clammed up and hasn't said a word about it since."

"Hmm. Maybe you should bring her down as well. It'd be interesting to see what we could do with her."

"*Interesting?*" Dr. Davidson said peevishly, and both men bristled. "Well, I can't see much point in it, sir. She has to be close to eighty. Seems best to just let her live out her days in the peace and quiet of her own head if that's what she chooses—and quite clearly she does."

"And you assume there is peace and quiet in her head, doctor?"

"Yes. I guess I do. She's never any trouble. Rarely even moves from wherever the nurses choose to sit her. Indeed, this whole hospital would be a much quieter place if I had more like her," Dr. Davidson murmured, judiciously

deciding he would refrain from mentioning the several suicide attempts the old woman had made over the years.

"Well, perhaps I can assist you with that. I need more
patients to work on. If you could give me access to maybe
three or four new ones a month, I can almost guarantee
you that in a year from now this hospital would be one of
the best run in the state."

"We call them provinces...sir. And I can assure you my
hospital already is one of the best run. We're very proud
of what we do here, doctor. Our patients are treated with
dignity and care and for the most part, respond well to the
calm control that prevails."

"Gerald! Oh, Gerald!" a shrieking voice cawed out, cutting short Dr. Uldrich's reply.

The two men turned to see the young Lawson girl break
from the walking group and start galloping toward them
in her awkward, Percheron gait. On top of her head, both
hands fumbled to secure a crown made of bent spoons, her
sorrel ponytail whirling around, wild as wind. Behind her,
a nurse erupted into a storm of blistering, unheeded warn-
ings, her frenzied loss of control startling the rest of the
patients, who bolted like a spray of starlings. Myrtle, buckled over with both arms wrapped around her ample girth,
ran back toward the lake, screaming at the top of her lungs
that her guts were falling out. The rest of the group clustered together, racing after Mary Lawson like an audible
nightmare, their individual screams, the screams of those
running beside them and the screams of the nurse who
roared behind in furious pursuit, all combining to breed
their most horrific delusions.

Roused by the commotion, a drowsy attendant shook
himself awake and scrambled across the field to intercept
Mary Lawson's beeline course to Dr. Davidson. Seeing
him approach, Mary laughed and veered off to the right.
Anticipating her, the attendant shimmied right as well.
Mary diverted left. The attendant, a scrawny scrap of a

man, quickly shuffled sideways. Barely ten feet separated them. Hunkering down like a linebacker, he braced, ready to absorb her blow. Squealing with delight, Mary rammed both arms out in front of her and flattened him beneath her like a dry reed.

Gasping and giggling, she raced up to Dr. Davidson, reached around and pinched his behind, hard.

"You're it, pookie-poo!" she yelled breathlessly and then turned to Dr. Uldrich, fluttering her eyelashes into his rather astounded face. "Well, hullo there. I don't believe we've met. I'm Angel Queen Supreme...Dr. Davidson's wife."

Before he could react she was off again, joined by a carnival of shrieking patients, nurses and attendants in an anarchistic game of chase. One of the attendants seized the back of her sweater, which she shimmied out of, leaving him holding it in his hands like a shimmering purple lizard tail. Cursing, he threw it to the ground and jumped on it soundly. Pulling an equine-size hypodermic needle from his coat pocket, he shook it menacingly at Angel Queen who had stopped to catch her breath. Giggling, she hiked her dress up and slapped her bountiful pinkish rump as if to give him a place to aim.

The pandemonium was too much for Norman Headly. Splintering away from the nippy doctor he ran large, loopy circles, swatting his cricket bat at nurses, doctors, attendants, trees, flowers, a cloud of invisible bees. His song had fragmented, his raspy voice rocketing off, convulsing him with hysterical laughter. *"Was blind, but now I see...was blind but now I see—"*

The old woman sat alone on the stone bench. She did not move at all.

CHAPTER 6

A silver-plate moon hung in a silent sky. The brilliance of its light shimmered across the lake, illuminating the ladies' pavilion built over by the rock cliff. Jakie eyed the moon, fearful it would again begin its vile whisperings. Turning its face from him, it pretended he was not there. Slowly, he began to relax into the embrace of the ancient oak tree, absorbing the peacefulness of the night. A lullaby breeze rocked him. It was late. The deep curve of the night when he felt most alone. Alone and at home in his aloneness. He knew that soon he would have to rouse himself and steal his way back across the asylum grounds undetected. He lingered against the thought. He preferred it here. Muted from sight by a canopy of leaves, the calm heart of the forest pulsing around him.

Here, his mind could sometimes almost grow quiet. Only here, cradled in the soothing, whispered hush of the forest. Away from the constant attack of noise and commotion that plagued the rest of the institution. Birds in a box. That is what they were. He'd tried to tell the staff that birds could not thrive in a box. It was a violation of nature. That they would become dependent and needy. In time, they would forget their desire to fly free. Invariably, the doctors and nurses had found this amusing, shushing him impatiently away with too-busy hands.

For Jakie, the asylum had become a strange place of refuge. An island of woodland surrounded by the impenetrable city. He had escaped—once. Slipped away easily under the veil of night. But before long, he had again sought the security of the asylum's brick walls. He did not understand the city. It frightened him in a way the wild beasts and dangers of the forest did not. Unable to find its heart, his spirit growing parched among its asphalt rivers and industrial breath, he had lost his way.

Sometimes he glimpsed back to the life he'd known before the city—before the asylum. When he could sit quietly for hours, focused on a single thought, or non-thought, in the way that Coyote had taught him. It had been a battle hard-won, a way to harness the demons that roamed through his mind and tormented his childhood dreams. Using this singular focus, he had developed into an excellent huntsman, able to level any animal from a seemingly impossible range. Once, Coyote had asked him how he achieved this, but words had failed him when he tried to explain. It was more something he felt than something he did. His eyes simply settled on the animal, waiting for their hearts to begin beating in unison. And then the shot would ring out—as if of its own accord—and the animal would fall. This too he would feel, he had tried to explain. This releasing of the body as the spirit took flight. Coyote had looked at him for a long while, saying nothing. Then he had stood up, wrapped his blanket around him, and walked off into the woods alone. Jakie had not followed, could not read the current of his mood. But as he had sat alone by the fire, he'd savored the memory of what he had taken for a flicker of pride in Coyote's deep eyes.

An owl hooted. Loudly. The sudden outburst failed to startle him. He was intimate with the wakefulness of the sleeping forest. He had grown into a man within its shadows. Owl had been his brother, River-falls his best friend. Elusive Wolverine had been the ever-present watchfulness dogging his young tracks. That much he remembered. But still, he remained troubled by one thing. Were the memories real or simply imagined?

He stretched long, his head rolling to one side, his stubbly cheek pressing against the cool comfort of the tree. The screen of his mind imploded and then instantly flashed forward with an image of raven hair and hypnotically soft eyes. He struggled against the eyes. Their docile, whimpering need. He thrashed out at them wildly, almost losing his balance in his attempt to wave them away. It was not her. That is what the doctor had said. Only the sickness of his mind trying to make him believe it so. He squeezed his eyes closed. But here she lingered also. Two beautiful eyes, gazing into him with a pleading mother-love.

It couldn't have happened the way Coyote said. The old squabble started up again in his mind. A mother did not abandon her pup. Not unless she was sick. Unless she was sick—or the pup was.

They had spoken of it only once.

"Why did she leave me?"

It had taken a long time for Coyote to look up from the log he was wrestling into the fire. Jakie, barely breathing, had braced himself in anticipation of the answer, but Coyote had merely taken out his pocketknife and started flicking the dirt out from under his long fingernails.

Jakie's heart had run rampant as rabbits had those shameful times when the snare had been misplaced, capturing but not killing as it was set to do. He'd looked up at Coyote angrily, knowing he was being silently warned away, but now caught up in a current of emotion so forceful it was beyond him to control it. He *had* to know. It was his right to.

"Why?" he'd spewed, too desperately, too brashly in the quiet of the forest night.

Coyote had looked up sharply, Jakie's harsh tone a violation of their usual earthen speech.

"She didn't want you," he'd said simply.

Jakie staggered under the weight of what he'd always known.

"But why not?" he'd challenged.

Coyote shrugged heavily.

"Why?" Jakie pressed, hysteria beginning to weave itself through his veins, causing a vibration of trembling to erupt in his long sinewy limbs.

"You were sick."

"But...but, I got better," Jakie had protested impotently.

"Yes." Coyote sighed. "You got better."

Jakie had cast about frantically for something solid, a place to root himself as the words of his rejection swirled menacingly around them.

"Did *you* make me better?"

Coyote shook his head. "The forest made you better. I only helped."

Jakie looked through the flames at the arms like gnarly roots and the bronzed, open chest. Tears quivered in his thick, dark lashes. He'd wrestled desperately to release the words buried deep within him.

"Are you..." he stumbled into silence and then pressed on as Coyote glared up at him fiercely.

"My father...are you my father?"

He'd snapped his eyes to the live coals spitting out toward him from the fire, attempting to evade the intensity of the moment by dodging the hot embers. He'd busied himself kicking dirt over the coals, snuffing them out one at a time as silence again descended over them, the dense hush of the forest draining away the imprint of his words. Finally, he'd snuck a quick glance up at Coyote.

Coyote, although not altering his gaze from where he had fixed it on the distant mountains, had seemed to know at once when the boy's eyes had looked to him again. Softening his shoulders, he exhaled thoughtfully.

"You *want* to know who your father is?"

Jakie had nodded furtively.

Coyote lowered his head solemnly. "Okay. I think maybe he is...Sasquatch."

Jakie erupted into a storm of protest, hurling himself, a whirlwind of limbs into Coyote.

"It's not funny!" he'd squealed, his voice cracking with emotion.

"No," Coyote agreed, easily catching him up and folding him into a blubbering blur of fists and tears. "No, it is not funny."

He'd held Jakie this way until sleep threatened to pull both of them away.

"So...you remember nothing of it then?" his voice lulled thickly into Jakie's ear.

Jakie shook his head weakly, not wanting to stir the night awake with their words. Even though he was still very young, he could not remember ever having been held in such a close embrace. He knew that only in partial sleep would he be allowed to remain there.

"No," he'd whispered against the warm leather of Coyote's vest. "I don't remember none of it."

Coyote's dark head bobbed in the shadows.

"Good. Good. It will be best that way."

☰ ☰ ☰

Jakie started from his deep reverie. Rebalancing himself in the arms of the tree, he flung a suspicious glance at the moon. It glowed white and serene. A porcelain lie. He struggled to discern whether Coyote had actually visited him—if they had spoken aloud—or if he had simply traveled into the past inside the sanctum of his own mind. He strained to hear the echo of his own words, but only the rushing roar of silence returned to him. He stretched his body awake. A cold river of unease dislodged itself from his spine, spiraled down the trunk of the wise oak that held him, and disappeared into the damp ground. It was like a silent snake—the unease—slithering up behind him, weaving itself through each vertebra, and then slowly engulfing him in raw fear, suffocating the very life from within him.

Hands loosely cupping the strong arms of the tree, he swam down through the branches and then dropped lightly to the ground in an alert crouch—a cat's shadow. For a moment, he hovered motionless, senses scanning the breath of the forest for any sign that he was not alone among the flora and fauna. Finally satisfied, he reached inside a crevice at the base of the tree, withdrawing a glass Mason jar. Twisting off the metal lid, he drew back the sleeve of his shirt, deft fingers extricating a long line of white pills from an inside seam. With the utmost care, he placed each one of these into the half-full jar. He did not like the way Dr. Davidson's pills made him feel, clamping down over him like a depression of bad weather. There was something untrustworthy about those pills—so small and yet so able to alter one's basic nature. As Dr. Davidson's fondness for the pills had grown, Jakie had watched in silent horror as some of his friends in the asylum had slowly morphed into people he no longer knew. Dropping the pills one by one into the jar, he was extra vigilant to make sure that none of them found their way into the soft earth-body of the mother. Tightly securing the lid again, he quickly vanished the jar from sight.

Jumping up suddenly, he broke into a lanky lope, his limber limbs ropes of freedom propelling him forward through the dense underbrush with great agility. A wide smile festooned his face as he ran. It felt so good to release his body into the wind it was meant to be. At times the burden—the sacrifice—of having to live as a cripple was almost too much to bear. But, queerly, his decision to live that way—to live within such self-induced physical restrictions—had actually funneled a great deal of extra freedom into his life.

Before the head attendant, a surly bastard with a preacher's smile, had run him over with the horse and plow, Jakie's natural physical strength and abilities seemed to fly above his head like a flag of war. Doctors, nurses, attendants—all those assigned to his care—felt an innate challenge just being in his presence. And, although Jakie knew the doctor had been told a different story about how he'd been run over, Jakie chose against trying to correct it. He unsettled his caretakers and, in response, they attempted to limit him with invisible, as well as visible, restraints.

The abject mutilation of his leg had shifted all of this. Jakie, a sponge of perception, had noted the subtle signs of the staff's newly acquired comfort in his midst. Accordingly, as their fear of him relaxed, so did their restraints. They became less wary. Less aware. Like he was an old tiger with no teeth and a crippled paw. It was a ruse that suited him well. So, as the leg eventually healed, he pretended that it had not. No one ever thought to question this claim. They much preferred him this way—an odd fellow with a comical, crippled gait. Harmless, as it were.

Tonight the rush of green-scented air streamed his dark hair back from his face. He felt like a boy again. Young, free—hopeful. The beautiful girl he'd found down by the creek—the young Madonna—was carved eternally into the marble of his mind. Just the thought of her exploded his heart into a wild animal. An animal unknown—far beyond a name. A violent swell of emotion staggered him to a stop, and he fell onto his knees. Clasping mudded hands before him, he sobbed for forgiveness. For what sin, he knew not.

Reaching up he buried his hands deeply into his untamed hair, pulling himself forward, and pressing his face fiercely into the loose belly of the pungent earth. Filling both fists with thick mud, he painted his face black. He dared not think he'd been blessed with such a beauty. He was far too defiled for that. By what, he did not know, could not remember, but he sensed the root of it, alive and well, living deep within him. At times, if he were prone to forgetting his unworthiness, a tiny tentacle of torment would reach forward and pierce him with some small remembrance, this always providing him with far more than he wanted to know.

He stretched himself prostrate across the forest floor, and his heart broke him into great sobs. He could not ask for forgiveness but perhaps only for the chance to redeem even some small part of himself. His gatherings from the cornucopia of healing gifts offered so freely by the forest had already enabled him to help many of the patients and, in secret, a couple of the nurses. And he felt sure that if he could find a way to get them to her, several of the herbs and tinctures he'd already prepared would be certain to aid the young girl—the Madonna.

A vengeful, caustic voice boiled up around him as he thought of her. It swirled menacingly, everywhere at once, hurtling accusations, threatening to pull him into its gnashing rapids of darkness. Useless. Murderer. Liar. The voice was not unfamiliar to him. Crushing both hands over his ears, he tried to keep the words from entering him, futile he knew, as they just continued on, driving up from the inside.

Driving *him* up from the inside, they drove him onto his feet. Black shades shadowed through the trees. He could feel their whisperings. Fear gripped him and rode him hard toward panic. How had they found him? Here. Among his camouflage of trees. It seemed years—a lifetime of years— since they had last stolen into his world. He suspected at once the willows, seeing clearly now their long antenna-like arms, pointing directly at him in the low breeze. How could he not have seen them before? Blinded by love. A fool blinded by love. A fool to even think for a moment that such love and loveliness could ever allow his entry. A vile, foul thing. That is what he was. Belonged here, alone in this mad-marsh of hatred, these muddy voices accusing him of things he knew to be true.

He broke from them suddenly, trying to outrun himself, the forest a traitor now, tripping him with newly placed roots and rocks, shouting his darting whereabouts back to them as they pursued like yapping dogs. The creek emerged before him—black-red. The water a depthless bloodlust, an evil destructive force. The way was clear. It was written in the sand. He must drown himself to save himself—a baptism of redemption. He struggled against the thought, but there was clearly no other way. The cold metal truth rained like shrapnel on his naked heart. The creek curled itself into a molten stream of lava, drew him forward, its slit cobra mouth spewing hot poison at his eyes, trying to blind him. He would not allow it. He would blind himself. Gouge his stumbling eyes with a helpful stick. His penance. A just penance. Never would he behold her beauty again. Not enough...not enough. He had already made a graven image of her upon his heart. Such blasphemy. They would have to cut her from him. She could not dwell there. It was a polluted place, and she was too pure. Surely, they would both die if she were allowed to stay.

The trees blinked their eyes. The traitors. The bastard traitors. They'd all swung over to the other side. No wonder they'd found him so easily. A fish in a waterless lake. Didn't matter. Even if the trees hadn't helped them, they would have found him anyway. They could read his thoughts from a million miles away. Read his heart. The happiness the Madonna had awoken within him would have set off a cosmic storm of protest. It was not his to feel that way. He had known from the beginning that they would put it to a stop. He only wondered what had taken them so long. Quickly, he slashed around behind him, his fast knife sweeping through them, bloodless bodies spurting bile, unsilence-able heads taunting as they rolled. He longed to kill every last one of them, but he knew it was useless; they were hell incarnate—already dead.

Desperately, he whispered for Coyote. Too late...too late...he was being swept downstream in a torrent of his own despair. Suddenly the lucid, earthy voice emerged, centering him once more in the vast ocean of his storming thoughts, and he crumpled face down to the ground beneath him.

She. Is. Not. The. Madonna. The Madonna belongs to the sickness of your mind. There is only the girl. The girl and the beauty of the girl. Remember this. Fight to remember this.

And then he was gone. And with him, the horror and the terror that only a moment before had threatened to tear Jakie from himself. He rolled over onto his back and closed his eyes, exhausted. The unexpected emotion, the unbridled attraction he had felt upon encountering the girl—and every day since—had disrupted him from himself. Like he had been placed in a small boat, pushed upon an uncharted and turbulent sea, denied even the small comfort of a paddle in which to attempt some form of control. He was adrift in a bewildering universe of frank desire. He knew not how he'd arrived there nor how he was going to find his way home. And in all of it, the steady stream of unknown currents, circling him like cunning sharks, ready to upend him completely and drag him away.

Pulling himself onto his knees, he gazed full at the circular moon and then shook his head hard. Looking around him at the soft forest, he felt as if he'd just awoken from somebody else's dream.

CHAPTER 7

J akie rose early. Long before he had to make the ten minute walk across the cemetery and over to the dining hall for breakfast. Just before the bleary-eyed sun began to blink herself awake. His foraging the night before had gone extremely well. Bark from the sassafras, leaves from the mulberry, and a prickly handful of stinging nettles filled the wooden bucket that sat just inside the cabin door, next to his dry-mudded boots. A bright mound of red-lacquered reishi and brilliant cinnabar-red chanterelle mushrooms garnished the top of the greenery. The distinct pungent smell of wild cranberry spiced the crisp morning air. Jakie inhaled deeply. He loved the way the cabin smelled when he brought the forest home with him. Reaching down into the driver's seat of the little car, which positioned itself more or less directly in the center of the living room, Jakie carefully extracted a double handful of the dried ginseng roots he'd collected over the summer. The car, a makeshift but viable roadster, had been systematically built over the years by the cabin's previous inhabitant, Mr. Brewster.

Jakie had enjoyed long afternoons digging graves alongside the older man—A personable, talkative fellow— listening to the fascinating tales he told about life-back-when. An ingenious but forgetful sort, Mr. Brewster had been openly perplexed, finding upon the completion of the vehicle, that he was entirely devoid of an exit plan. The cabin's door was too small, its few windows rudimentary. The car was trapped within its own birth canal.

After recovering from the initial shock of this rude discovery, Mr. Brewster had found it to be a terrific joke on himself. He'd laughed merrily about it for days, then weeks, and on into the years. When he finally died of weariness and old age, the institution had interred him in their own cemetery, in a grave Mr. Brewster himself had dug not all that many days before.

Jakie had been the logical choice to inherit the cabin—and the gravedigger's job—after the old man's passing. He had hesitatingly accepted both. He still chose to spend a good many of his nights in the ward, however. Too much unrestricted time alone had a way of pressing forward the dark thoughts lurking about inside of him.

Attempting to free the cabin of some of Mr. Brewster's clutter, Jakie had stumbled across a set of meticulously drawn maps, an intricate web of roads and highways and backwoods trails leading out of the asylum, down through the United States, and on into Mexico. All those years. All that patient devising for the day when he had planned to finally make his great escape. Jakie had refolded the maps with great care, entombed them in a large Mason jar, snuck out under a moonless sky, temporarily unearthed peaceful Mr. Brewster, and placed the insurgent maps under his eternally stilled hands.

Stepping around the car, Jakie shuffled over to the wooden bucket and carefully extracted a loose handful of the pinky chanterelles. He played them gently across the faded kitchen counter, a miniature collage of upside-down umbrellas in full bloom. One eye glanced at the clock as he filled a small cast iron pot with water, lit the stove, and set it down to heat. Scooping some dark walnuts from the windowsill, he shimmied free a stuck drawer, withdrew a hammer, and shattered them open. Deftly sorting out the fleshy meat, he popped some into his mouth, took the pot from the stove, swept the remaining battered carnage into the bubbly water, and set it back on the flame. The pine-plank floor protested loudly as he crossed over to the rustic oxblood table that sat beneath the perspiring kitchen window. Picking up a small blue jar, Jakie held it up to the light, rolling it gently as he inspected its contents. An herbal tincture he had made for Myrtle. He was hoping it would be effective enough to settle down her agonizing stomach cramps. His own stomach growled, and he scanned the open-plank cupboard to see what he had to eat. A coffee can full of smoked trout sat high up on the top shelf. Reaching up on tiptoe, he stretched forcibly in order to bring it down. Cats, weasels, other patients; his cabin knew no real privacy. Taking a large piece of the flat jerky from the can, he was set to tear it in half with his teeth when a light scratching outside the cabin alerted his ear.

Slowly withdrawing the fish from his still-open mouth, he hushed his breath, listening intently into the mute air. No sound traveled forward and yet his deeper sense, the one not impaired, confirmed he was no longer alone. Gently cursing the complaining floor he attempted, unsuccessfully, to move stealthily back over toward the window so he could have a peek outside. Edging the gingham curtains aside, his gaze swept over the cemetery. It lay quiet and serene, as cemeteries are wont to do. A few light branches bobbed lazily in the breeze. Nothing else moved. And yet, the feeling was inescapable. He was not alone. He stepped across to the rough door, unhitched the metal clasp, and eased it open. The cemetery held its silent slumber. Still, he knew something—or someone—was eyeing his every move.

Finally, he saw her. Slit green eyes studying. A sly, closed grin on her clever face. Sitting still in the camouflage-shadow of the large spruce tree across the road, the red fox waited, alert to his every move. Jakie regained his breath, laughing heartily at himself. She'd managed to sneak up on him yet again. A furry phantom beggar, they'd spied on each other's movements for so long she'd finally decided he might be a useful friend. Standing up, she licked her chops, stretched and almost wagged her full bushy tail. Stepping back into the aroma and warmth of the cabin, Jakie pulled a few more sticks of fish from the can and then stepped back outside onto the bright-filled porch.

"Come on then," he coaxed, as he extended the silver sliver of fish toward the curious fox. She watched, unmoved.

"Come on now, young miss. Ya be wanting some breakfast, ya got to come get it."

The pretty fur head remained motionless, the eyes intelligent, ears pricked to attention. She sniffed the air eagerly but held her ground. Jakie laughed out loud. First at the antics of the fox and then at himself, as he crossed the dirt road in his bare feet, quietly remonstrating the young animal.

"See here now. Look how spoiled you're getting. Begging my food and expecting me to bring it right to ya as well."

Eyeing him cautiously, she allowed his slow approach to within six feet of her and then abruptly she swung around and padded off, creating a few extra feet of safety between them.

"Oh!" Jakie said lowly. "Playing hard to get, are ya, princess? Come on now. I've a bunch of things to get done today and feeding you isn't even on my list."

Listening intently, the little fox relaxed onto her haunches. Jakie shadowed her. They sat this way, locked in a mutual stare as the morning continued to drift away. Jakie felt the standoff a bit unfair, his pot left on the stove, the water slowly boiling dry. The fox seemed content to just sit and stare. No duality pressed her from the inside. Jakie envied the animals this, their free singularity of purpose.

Finally, relenting to the complications of his humanness, he broke the moment and extended his hand slowly toward her. The fox's nose quivered, tasting the offering of fish from afar. Still, she sat disciplined, watching.

"Holy—moly—foxy," Jakie muttered, admiring her sound discipline but feeling slightly aggravated now by the steadily seeping passage of time. With a smoothness of hand, he flipped the fishy morsel toward her and she responded eagerly, gulping it down. Then she sat back again and waited expectantly.

Smiling at her cunning, undisturbed patience, Jakie realized suddenly how well the little fox had trained him to play her game. Grinning, he quickly threw a couple more offerings her way, each one a little closer to his feet. Warily, she took the bait. Knowing that this was the way their little game was played. Her approaching and waiting. He relenting and feeding.

He threw her the last of the fish and rose back up to his feet, as the fox receded back into the forest, disappearing into the underbrush that fringed the trees. Jakie always felt a little lighter after one of her visits. Her instinct of trust in him helped him to trust himself. Suggested to him that whatever lurked unknown inside his hidden memories might not be innately evil after all.

He slipped back into the cabin. The little remaining water in the iron pot was tinted a stiff black. He hoped the color would not prove too dark. The whole cabin felt hot and dewy, filled with the perspiration from the boiling pot.

Taking Mr. Brewster's silver flask from the plywood dashboard of the car, Jakie carefully siphoned off the dark liquid. Wrapping the flask tightly in a red, strawberry-embossed tea towel, he stuffed the whole concoction into his jacket pocket. His stomach grumbled again and again. He glanced out the misty window at the rising sun. He'd have to hurry if he wasn't to forgo breakfast before he made his rounds.

Grabbing a basketful of herb-posies, he carefully added the blue bottle tincture on top, stepped into his rubber boots, and set out across the cemetery grounds toward the tall brick clusters that formed the hospital.

He walked respectfully and as slowly as time would allow between the long rows of faceless graves. The disinherited were buried here. Those whose dying had raised no cries of alarm. No remorse nor any attempt by the living to at least ensure that in death they would be treated with a dignity denied them in life. Society's castoffs. Fearful and feared. Disposable and despised. Some had just been forgotten. Others had merely, wearily, outlived all those they had known. Each one of them was laid here in the asylum's cemetery for eternity. An eternity spent in a place each one of them had only envisioned visiting for a short time. A brief resting place in the chase of life where they could catch their mental breath. They were boxed and folded neatly away underneath the cover of ground, their meager belongings gathered together, stored in whatever suitcase they had arrived with, labeled, and promptly forgotten among the rafters and rats in the various buildings' attics.

Harangued voices arose from the buildings in front of him and for a moment, Jakie thought to turn around. To turn back—turn his back—on the oppressive anger that so often contorted the beautiful asylum grounds. Briefly, he vacillated. And as he did, he felt for a moment the struggle that he knew must occur each day within all of the staff as they walked through that vaporous barrier. Left behind their families and friends, lives constructed on the shifting, but accepted, scaffolding of love and hope. Crossing over each day some invisible border that diminished them all. Entering into this world of broken beauty. All of them— patients and staff alike—reaching blindly for a stability and answer that eluded them all.

Jakie approached a seldom-used door, juggling his basketful of herbs with one hand, while he slipped a rough-hewn key into the lock, admitting himself in through the back entrance of Cottage Five. A functional room, the dining hall's low ceiling hung like an oppressive cloud above long rectangular walls. All were smudged the same dull gray. Running down the length of the room, several elongated tables stretched out like wooden feed troughs.

The efficient clank and clatter of the morning's breakfast being cleaned up permeated the close air. A few scattered patients still lingered over their crumbs, procrastinating the beginning of yet another day. Two bored attendants leaned heavily against the back wall, chewing over the results of the previous day's game, sipping cold coffee from cracked mugs.

"Morning," Jakie offered as he walked by.

"Morning," they returned, heads bobbing in unison. A large, shaggy hand reached out and caught Jakie by the elbow, reversing his forward momentum.

"Hey! What's that?"

Jakie looked over at the scarred, jowly face. It was florid. Pimply. In dire need of a good shave. The attendant was new, transferred over from the Brockville asylum. Ethel claimed he'd had quite a reputation among the patients there. One to steer clear of. Having observed the man since his recent arrival, Jakie was inclined to believe her. There was a certain terseness about his perfunctory movements that suggested a latent roughness. A simmering capacity for violence. Slowly, Jakie eased his arm free of the man's restraining hand.

"Just some leaves and berries. That's all."

"Leaves and berries?" the attendant repeated, grunting as he pushed off from the wall, his buffalo-body energized with suspicion. "What you bringing that junk in here for?"

"To heal the sick, sir," Jakie replied quietly.

"Ha!" the man snorted explosively. "What you think you are? Some gaw-damn loony-bin medicine man?"

Jakie held his tongue, casting a quick searching glance at the other attendant. Frowning back a mute apology, he also shuffled free of the wall now and attempted to defuse the situation.

"Ah, come on, Oswald. Leave him alone. Jakie don't never hurt no one. Maybe some of that stuff even does some good. Who knows?"

Oswald grimaced as if he'd been pierced with a hot stick. Tipping his head stiffly to one side, he glared down at the short, balding, pumpkin-faced attendant.

"Holy Mother—Teresa! What kind of place you fellas running around here? No gaw-damned way we ever let them run around playing doctor like that up at Brockville."

"Jakie just likes helping people, that's all. He don't mean no harm—"

"Helping people? Christ, even the doc's got a hard enough time figuring out who's real sick and whose just sick in the head around here. Bunch of hocus-pocus. Can't help no one feeding them a bunch of rabbit food," Oswald said, giving Jakie's basket a heavy nudge with his leg.

The basket tipped sharply, almost falling free from Jakie's hand.

"Hey!" Oswald accused sharply. "What's that? Sure ain't no leaves."

Jakie and the other attendant looked down to see the spectacular, shell-face of a mushroom shining through the leaves.

"It's a reishi."

Oswald sneered. "Don't talk mumble-jumble to me, mister. What is it?"

"A mushroom."

"Hah! A mushroom," he repeated, looking over at the other attendant for support. "Well, that just tops the story, don't it? Just what were you supposing to do with that thing?"

"It's medicinal," Jakie murmured.

"Oh no. Absolutely not. You are not going to be feeding that thing to no one. End up poisoning half the ward. Go chuck it in the garbage."

"Well, just a minute there," the short attendant began nervously. "Jakie here knows quite a bit about these things."

"*Knows about these things?*" Oswald spat, raising himself up straight, shaking his head vigorously.

"Have yourself a look around, will you, Don? You know where you are, right? The loony bin, that's where you are. And this guy here?" He jabbed a thumb toward Jakie. "This guy—he's locked up in this here loony bin because he's crazy. And there ain't no way I'm letting this crazy guy go 'round and poison all the rest of the crazy guys. You follow?"

Don hunched his shoulders up around his ears as he absorbed the onslaught, glancing around self-consciously to see if his tongue-lashing was being observed. No heads turned their way, the routine of the dining hall carrying on as usual.

He nodded his head. "Yeah, I suppose you're right."

"Damn-diddling, I'm right," Oswald triumphed. "Now, dump that shit into the garbage there."

Jakie sighed as he stepped across to the garbage, lightly shaking his head as he watched a good part of his summer's foraging join the toast crusts, oatmeal globs, and bits of once-chewed bacon fat in the bottom of the bin.

"Gotta keep these buggers tapped down a bit or they'll end up running the whole gaw-damned place, ya know?"

Jakie stood a few feet apart from them, head bowed, feeling forgotten as they continued to speak as if he were no longer there. The burly attendant's pointed words and misuse of the holy name, stung relentlessly at a tremulous place deep within Jakie's heart. He longed to leave. To cover his ears. Anything to keep the hateful words out. Knowing, however, that any unauthorized movement would now be perceived by the new attendant as a challenge, he struggled to maintain his ground.

"*What?*" Oswald spat suddenly. "What's that you just said?"

Jakie visibly started as he looked up into the furious face, only now hearing his own voice, chanting rhythmically.

"Father forgive them. They know not—"

"Forgive who, you crazy bastard?" Oswald shot out, brusquely grabbing Jakie by the back of the neck. "Maybe you need some reminding which one of us is locked up in this hellhole, huh?"

Jakie's stature livened as he straightened, rising up to his full height as their eyes collided.

Oswald smirked. His greasy nails clawed deeper into Jakie's neck.

"Whoa—whoa—whoa," rushed the smaller attendant, placing a hand on Jakie's sweaty back and pushing him forward. "Come on now. Let's get you some breakfast before it all gets thrown away. I'll see you over in Four in a few minutes, Oswald. Okay?"

Jakie walked obediently ahead of the attendant, relieved not to be provoked any further. Things happened sometimes. Things he didn't remember. Except for a few jagged splinters that remained trapped in his mind.

"You okay?" the attendant, Don, whispered.

Jakie nodded his head as he rubbed the pain out of his neck.

"Sorry about your stuff."

"That's okay," Jakie whispered, without looking back. "I can bring you some more herbs for your knee tomorrow."

Accompanying Jakie right up to the serving counter, the attendant gave Jakie's shoulder a light pat and then continued on his way. Taking a porcelain bowl from the stack, Jakie picked a piece of dried remains from its rim and pushed it across to the pencil-thin man who stood on the other side of the counter. The man did not take the proffered bowl. He stood, eyes shuttered, head and arms hanging as limp as a disused marionette. He looked as if he were asleep. Or dead, while somehow still standing. Assuming the former over the latter, Jakie loudly cleared his throat.

"Go away. I'm not here," a pearly voice claimed.

"Looks like you're here to me."

"Well, I'm not. That's why you can't see me."

"I can see ya, Phillip."

"Philly, please."

"I can see you, Philly."

"You have magic powers?"

"'Course not."

"Well then—how can you see me?"

"Because you're standing right in front of me, Phil... Philly."

"Don't be ridiculous. I am not."

Jakie took a long breath and sighed. So far his morning was not adhering well to his busy plans. Such an occurrence was not totally uncommon in the asylum he had found.

"Okay," he relented. "If you're not here, where are ya then?"

"Somewhere," Phillip teased. An impish grin trickled across his still-shuttered face.

"And...where is somewhere?"

"Somewhere, is somewhere else."

"And where is somewhere else?"

"Not *here*—" Phillip replied emphatically.

"Fair enough," Jakie agreed, standing up on tiptoe to try and see if the big silver pot still held any leftovers from the morning's fare. "So, what is it that you're doing *somewhere else?*"

"Dancing," Phillip cooed seductively.

"Hmm. With who?"

"None of your business!" he exploded, head and arms bursting up and then down abruptly, as if he'd been electrocuted. Still, the red-rimmed eyes remained closed.

Startled by the abrupt, disconnected behavior, Jakie took a closer study of the pale fine face. There was an unhealthy puffiness about the eyes—not enough water, or too many tears—he couldn't tell for sure. The skin was an unnatural white. Black brows retained a constant startled state, a partially swept away corner revealing they had been meticulously charcoaled in.

"Well...when you're done dancing, could you please come back and scoop me up some porridge?"

A shrug of dainty shoulders.

Rubbing his face into his hands, Jakie searched around, located a stool, and plunked himself down to wait. Becoming aware of an agitation of energy circulating behind him, he turned ever so slightly and watched without looking. Oswald was at it again. This time with Mr. Seymour, who had somehow managed to remain in the dining hall long after the others had been swept back up Cottage Five's stairs.

Jakie winced as Oswald picked a dirty fork up from beside the big Bible laying open on the table and ground it into Mr. Seymour's velvet-coated back. Swatting with impotent, flailing arms, Mr. Seymour attempted to wave him away. Grinning, Oswald ground the fork in harder. Suddenly—as if he were a pierced balloon—the older man collapsed heftily onto the table. Jakie's body tensed, watching acutely for any sign of continued breathing. Slowly, Mr. Seymour's square head began to roll back and forth across his folded arms, as he emitted a loud, low moan.

"No more. No more. Wifey said there is no more..."

Casting a furtive glance behind him, Oswald stuffed his big paw into the leather-trimmed pocket of Mr. Oswald's purple paisley smoking jacket, pulling out a handful of something Jakie could not see. Another moan escaped the

flaccid, saggy heap of a man as Oswald's hand withdrew.
The sound of the moan rankled the nerves down Jakie's
back. It was not a moan of pain that escaped the old man; it
was the haunted moan of deep despair.

Jakie worked to drop his guard as Oswald turned and
started to walk his way. He wanted nothing to do with that
man. He had met his kind before in the asylum. Attendants
like him readily came and went. And from what Jakie could
remember, nothing good had ever come out of any of their
meetings.

"You're late," a thin voice accused.

Jakie jumped his attention back toward the kitchen.

Phillip snapped his bulbous blue eyes awake just as he
did so.

"You're always late when it's my day to serve," he complained, flinging his head dramatically around to one side
and again shuttering his eyes with long, feathery lashes.

"Late? Me?" Jakie said innocently as he pushed up the
sleeve of his coat and checked a wristwatch that wasn't
there. "Well, maybe just a little."

"Maybe just a *lot*," Phillip pouted playfully. "Say...what's
that?"

"What's what?"

"That," Phillip pointed to Jakie's arm. "That little picture you have painted on there."

"Just a tattoo."

"*Well*! I can see that plenty good enough," Phillip
exhaled, with an exaggerated roll of his eyes. "But what is
it? What does it mean?"

Uncomfortable, Jakie tugged his sleeve down as he
shrugged.

"Don't be so coy with me, Jakie Hewitt. I've seen one
like it before." He leaned over the counter toward Jakie
and whispered quietly. "Black Devil. Right?"

"I've no idea what you're talking about," Jakie said
with uncharacteristic brusqueness. The arrowhead tattoo,

the shards of memory. They all pointed him uncomfortably toward a life he had had—and evidently—lost. "You look a little pale today, Philly. You feeling all right?"

"Oh! That!" Phillip sparked, gently patting his cheek-bones. "Potato flour. Mar-ve-lous stuff."

Jakie frowned lightly as his stomach issued a very pub-lic complaint.

"Think you could scoop me out some of that?" he asked, gesturing to the silver pot.

"Well. No promises. It's pretty stuck-on today. Myrtle burnt it again," Phillip said, digging out a ladleful and sus-pending it high above the counter. "I don't like that one," he whispered.

Jakie said nothing. Just continued watching the non-movement of the porridge.

"*You* know," Phillip persisted. "That monster-beast that made you throw your flowers away."

"Thought you weren't here for that." Jakie chuckled.

Phillip's direct blue eyes searched into him queerly. "Of *course* I was here, Jakie. I've been right here, standing behind this stupid counter all morning."

Jakie's mouth opened to reply just as the reluctant oat-meal released its grip and belly-flopped onto the counter—just beside his waiting bowl.

"Glass of champagne with that then?"

"Uh...no thank you, Philly."

Scooping most of the moosh-pile up with his hand, he wiped it into his dish, turned, and made his way to a lone dark corner at the back of the dining hall.

After a few attempts at swallowing some breakfast, Jakie helped Mr. Seymour back up to his ward, depositing the still-distraught man into the able hands of a concerned nurse. Descending the vocal front steps of Cottage Five, he peered long into the high sun. Maneuvering over the grid of sidewalks that connected the Cottages, he made his way closer toward the lake. The ladies' pavilion reposed in quiet silhouette against the seemingly tranquil view. Less austere than the rest of the asylum's buildings, it was still a large step short of lavish. Prim and pretty, it sported a sloping octagonal roof, supported by an equal number of turned wooden posts, decorated at the top with matching fans of latticework. These joined together to form eight delicate archways. A flat wooden bench ran around the circumference of its inside, and it was here that most of the walking group sat, modestly trying to shield their faces from the devilishly hot sun. They sat resigned rather than ready. As if they'd all boarded a carnival carousel only to find it had long since ceased to function.

Beyond them, a half-dozen trumpeter swans glazed across the sparkling mirror lake. The tinkle and murmur of the ladies' light voices carried toward him, occasionally accompanied by heartfelt laughter. It was easy to get lost in this place, Jakie observed. In these moments that flirted with an absurd sense of tranquility. And yet they happened. More often than one would think. Slowly, he pulled the ribbons of his thoughts back around him. It never paid to get too interwoven with the deceit of the world. Where any moment a great rift could appear in the crackled canvas of this Victorian sketch.

He stepped off the sidewalk and started across the immaculate cricket oval, heading toward the lake. His roving eye caught on clumps of weeds and sprigs of trees around its edges, each one determined to reclaim its rightful heritage. The discrepancy between the outer world Jakie viewed and the inner world he walked in—the one that stumbled him with half-memories and cryptic tattoos that for him no longer held any meaning—had no common place to settle. He was engaged in an endless exhaustive battle to maintain it all. There were days, or more often—nights—when he simply did not know how much longer he could hold it all together.

The voices started—as he knew they would. He'd been fearing their outbursts since his run-in with Oswald. He lowered his head as he walked, his disjointed gait hampering him even more now, slowing him down. The great halls opened and the abuse began. Raining down old pronouncements and profanities. Nothing new but crippling just the same. He was a fool—a loser—a moron. Such a simple matter—bringing a bucketful of herbs and leaves from his cabin to the Cottages. A child could do it. But not a sick child. No, even as a child he would have gotten it wrong. The voices continued to beat him down like November rain. Dark and dirty. Unrelenting in their morbid drizzle. He fought against the temptation to turn around. Scuttle back to the cemetery. Dig his own grave. Everything in him wanted to avoid seeing the displeasure on Nurse Mildred's face when he told her that he didn't have the promised herbal remedies. The stark disappointment. He would understand her dismay. Her desire to help the others, although shadowed to most, was clear to him. As with many things, it was Coyote who had whispered him this.

The thought of Coyote brought his remembrance starkly forward into Jakie's mind. Ceasing to walk, he closed his eyes, watching as Coyote's weathered hand flashed a knife next to him, its sharp blade dissecting away the accusing voices with an uncomfortable closeness. Finally, the scraping ceased and Jakie continued on his way.

A few heads turned, idly gawking as he walked toward them. Others could not be bothered. Or perhaps, were already too bothered to be much interested in his lumbered approach. Most of the other patients treated Jakie as if he had always been there. Comfortable, innocuous, at times even charming. Drifting among them like the soft shadows playing beneath the tall oaks. Crossing off the distance between him and the ladies' pavilion, he noticed several hands dancing up to offer him a welcoming wave.

These, Nurse Mildred efficiently redirected back to the task at hand. A mountain of socks—waiting to be darned—while the ladies absorbed the freshness of a beautiful day.

"You're late," Nurse Mildred said by way of greeting, as she waddled down the pavilion's narrow plank steps and repositioned herself on the pebbly sand.

"Am I?" Jakie exclaimed in mock disbelief. "Again?"

Following a thin silver chain from her starchy lapel to an overstuffed front pocket, Mildred pulled free her watch. She tapped a finger into its round little face.

"Certainly are. By a good half hour." She adopted an imposing, wide-legged stance, hands on hips, raised eyebrows demanding an answer.

"Sorry, ma'am," Jakie mumbled. "Ran into some trouble."

She silenced Jakie with a frown, obviously aware the current of voices behind her had suddenly fallen off into an eavesdropping eddy. Largely disenfranchised from the outside world, the asylum women keenly felt their deprivation. When some new news finally made its way past their doors, they were bloodhounds on blood, all senses keenly tuned in order to devour the fresh morsel.

"We'll talk over here," Mildred said, half-directing, half-pushing Jakie along in her path as she made her way up the shore toward a lone gray bench. She searched out impatiently over the hospital grounds.

"Miss Lawson, I'm leaving you in charge here until Nurse Bea gets back," she shouted over her shoulder to the women mingling in the pavilion. "Those socks aren't all finished up by lunchtime, there'll be no card games this afternoon for anyone, you hear?"

"You'll not be bossing me around, nurse!" Mary Lawson replied haughtily. Still, she enthusiastically sparkled herself into the center of the ladies' group and began widely gesticulating with her hands as she gave orders.

Huffing heavily as they approached the bench, Nurse Mildred turned her back on the scorching sun, positioning herself under the canopy of a hemlock tree. She gestured Jakie onto the bench, full in the sweltering heat, and cued him to retell his story. There was much humming and harumphing as she candidly let her views on the matter be known as he mumbled along. Not quite waiting for him to finish, she plowed in over top and began telling him yet again about her cumulative health woes. She, along with several of the patients, had been heartily anticipating a handful or two of Jakie's healing remedies.

Jakie's attention wandered, his eyes subtly making their way back to the ladies' pavilion as he listened to Nurse Mildred talk. He was disappointed that the girl had not been included in their walking group. The sunshine and fresh air would have done her well. And besides, he'd truly been hoping to refresh his vision of her. Not that the original had faded. It hadn't. Not at all. But rather, he knew that she would have outgrown it by now. Become someone slightly new. Already shaped by the asylum around her. He resisted the thought. He had borne witness too many times to the slow scars that deformed those who tarried too long in this place. Anger steeled about his heart. Dr. Davidson had no right to keep her locked away here. She was not dangerous. Or even sick from what he could tell. She was simply misplaced. An angel fallen from heaven into this pit of hell.

He took his kerchief and wiped his brow. Oblivious to the suffering heat, Mildred rambled on and on. Like a lame freight train dragging itself across the prairies. Curious, he watched as Mary Lawson exited the pavilion, followed by a small complement of women. Tottering precariously on the loose ground, they made their way across the shore, down to the edge of the lake. Each one had their sock basket in hand, these being plunked unceremoniously down on the ground. Then, following the silhouette of Mary's lead, they each bent over, took up a holey sock, and scooped its dangly belly full of sand.

Straining his eyes in order to see better, Jakie resorted to tipping his head slightly to the left in an effort to catch the dictatorial orders Mary Lawson was spewing. Suddenly, all of the women straightened up as one being, drew back an arm, and catapulted the dark socks high into the air. Quickly stifled shrieks of laughter burst out as the pregnant socks hit the water and then sank.

"What on earth—" Nurse Mildred said, interrupting herself as she half-turned around.

"Swans," Jakie reported innocently, as the offended flock took flight.

"Gadabouts, those women. The whole lot of them. Well, they won't be so frivolous come noon, and their baskets are still full of undarned socks," she huffed.

Jakie straightened on the bench, his focus diverted by a large, stooped woman shuffling oddly toward them. A prominent Roman nose seemed to have perched itself incongruously in the center of her otherwise nondescript face, a dowager's hump having claimed her back. She wore a dark green, sateen scarf that suppressed her hair tightly back from her face, promenading the obtrusive nose even more.

Jakie nodded to her as she approached, trying not to stare at her nose, which appeared to be everywhere at once. Placing a hand over her mouth, the woman ducked her head into her chest and mumbled a sort of greeting. She continued past him toward Nurse Mildred in her short, mincing gait. Slowing to a hovering halt, she continued shifting from foot to foot as she talked, her conspicuous hand still covering the lower half of her face.

"Bad today, is it Myrtle?"

"Aye. Poisoned me again, the brutes. In me sleep, I s'pose."

"Nonsense," gawed Nurse Mildred. "Like I tole you before, it's just the medication."

"Feels me skin wants to come off, you know."

"That's normal—"

"But, I can't hardly sit still no more—"

"Don't be such a fuss, Myrtle. You'll get used to it."

"Did he bring the stuff? For me stomach?" She nodded toward Jakie.

"He did. But they made him throw it away."

Myrtle's face lifted and then fell. "Why'd they do that?"

Nurse Mildred shrugged.

"But, me stomach, the poison. It's getting worse you know. Can he bring me some more?"

Nurse Mildred threw her hands in the air. "I got nothing to do with it all. Ask yourself. He's sitting right here."

"Can't."

"And just why on earth not?"

Myrtle dropped her head even lower, covering her mouth with both hands now as she whispered into Nurse Mildred's ear.

"Gawd! Don't be so silly. Jakie here's seen plenty of you gals without your teeth. Haven't you, Jakie?" she said, forcibly turning Myrtle on her thick heels and maneuvering her heavily onto the bench beside him.

"What happened to your teeth, Myrtle?" Jakie asked.

"Threw them away."

"Why'd you do that?"

"Didn't fit."

"Well, I'm sure they'll make you a new set if you ask."

"Had a new set. Twice now. Hurt. I just want me own back."

Jakie glanced up at Nurse Mildred, who'd failed to suppress a snicker.

"Don't think they can do that for you," he replied gently. "Once they's all pulled out, I don't think they ever do come back."

"Not *those* ones," Myrtle said sharply. "The ones I had when they put me in here. They didn't never hurt me so much."

"You throw them away too—"

"'Course not. They got left in me suitcase an stuffed up in the attic."

"Well," Jakie offered, "maybe Nurse Mildred could bring them down for—"

Nurse Mildred scowled him quiet.

"I tole you before, Myrtle. Them suitcases is emptied of anything you might need before they're put away. You must have forgot to pack them."

"Didn't forget—" Myrtle replied tightly.

Jakie hesitated, rolling his thoughts through his mind carefully before he rolled them off his tongue.

"Do *I* have a suitcase up there, Nurse Mildred?"

"Did you have one when they brought you in?"

Jakie looked at his hands, folded neatly in his lap.

"Don't remember? Me neither. But if you did, it'll be up there till you leave—"

A sense of discomfort grew around the oft-unspoken words. The question that haunted all of the patients' minds. Their eventual leaving. Or not.

"Ah, now what are those gals getting themselves up to? Here now—" Nurse Mildred turned back toward the lake, hollering as a dozen arms drew back, ready to release another volley of undarned socks. "Stop it now, ladies! Stop that right this instant! There'll be ice baths for the lot of you if—" she fumed, as a sudden cloud of socks cannonballed through the air.

Jakie sat in amused silence on the bench, watching as Nurse Mildred hurriedly trotted back toward the wayward group. Her right arm waved in the air as she brought down a multitude of unpleasant circumstances the deviant women would face if they didn't fall into order. None of them gave any sign they were even aware of her approach.

They were swimming in a sea of forgetful laughter, awash with their own hilarity.

His attention was diverted from the pandemonium breaking out at the ladies' pavilion by Nurse Bea, who was making double-time now as she bolted wildly across the cricket oval. Long, wiry black hair springing ingloriously loose from a once-tidy bun, she quite encapsulated the look of one of the patients sprinting for the gate. Arriving down to the lake in an apologetic, wheezing heap, she then proved herself twice useless to poor, exasperated Nurse Mildred, who had still not regained any true sense of order. Her panting face a bright, stricken red, the young woman collapsed onto the bench inside the pavilion, croaking loudly at the concerned patients to quickly bring her a drink of water.

Jakie dropped his head into his hands and chuckled. Rolling his head sideways, he peered over at Myrtle and grinned. In spite of her ever-present pain, she grinned back, a narrow black gash forming her mouth until an embarrassed hand flew up to cover it. As if the grin had triggered something deep within, she suddenly doubled over herself, trembling, white-knuckled fists punching deep into her abdomen.

Jakie reached out to put a soothing hand on her shoulder, but she struggled away from him, rising slowly to her feet.

"Nooo...it hurts too much. Too much. I have to move. Can't stay in me skin no more," she gasped as she stepped around herself in small circles.

He stood up beside her, wandering slowly along as she made her shuffled way back down to the reforming group by the lake.

"Can you not do something for me? Bring me some more of that stuff? Seemed to help you know."

"I'll try, Myrtle," he promised. "Season's mostly over for the mushrooms now though."

"And me chompers."

"Chompers?"

"If I could least chew me food right for once—"

Promising Myrtle he would do his best, Jakie deposited her into the double line the walking group was forming as they prepared for their journey back up to the wards.

Hurrying ahead of the group, he made a beeline across the asylum grounds toward the old woman who sat alone on a stone bench in the shade of a magnificent maple. She had long since become too frail to continue on outings with the walking group. In an effort to at least expose her to some light and fresh air, she was instead helped down the stairs of Cottage Four by the other ladies and settled onto the hard bench to await the group's circuitous return. She rarely moved or wandered from her place, seemingly lost in a world that was hers alone.

Jakie approached her slowly, talking softly as he assessed the vacant stare in her gray eyes. Some days she was there to join him, chattering away as freely as a chipmunk—others not. Today, she blinked and smiled encouragingly, hurrying him along with a little wiggle of her parchment-paper hands.

"Wherever have you been?" she chided gently. "I've been waiting all night for you. Sitting here...all by myself. Listening to the ocean. You can't see it, you know. It's much too far away. But I can feel it. Feel the impetuous, restless waves crashing over each other in their ceaseless struggle with the restraining shore."

She smiled up at him through the mist of her eyes. "As a child I was frightened of it, you know. Frightened its constant pulsing would one day creep in through my door and fill my room. I'm not afraid anymore though," she said proudly. "Not since they've moved me up to the fourth floor.

"Mother will come to see me soon. We will have a glorious day! It seems ages since she was last here. I still remember her though. Her face. It's a smile, mother's face is. No ears, no nose, no eyes. Just a smile. Mother never knew a cloudy day.

"Father is cloudier. Stormy. Or perhaps I just remember him that way because of all the smoke. He loves his pipe. He's almost quaintly old-fashioned, Father is.

"Apricots!" she exclaimed suddenly, placing a wrinkled hand on Jakie's sleeve as she looked off into the vapid air. "The smoke of his pipe smelled of apricots. It was everywhere. Clung like gloom to the inside of the house so that even when Father was not there, he never truly went away.

"Father is difficult. To remember, I mean. Scattered throughout my mind. I almost put him together sometimes, but then he fractures and spins off at right angles. Like the four elements—polarized. I love Father. I do. He is a good man. I can remember other things about him as well. Other times—" She drifted off into solitary thought for a while, and Jakie waited quietly for her return.

"We went to the seashore once. Father and I. I remember crystal splashes of light and water. And gulls, soaring high above the waves—calling. And when we were walking home, I heard a bird—singing. People were walking by and smiling at its beautiful song. But I thought maybe the bird was not singing at all but crying but because of its beautiful voice they couldn't tell." She peered over at Jakie, her face a great chasm of sadness he could not know and then continued on.

"Tan leather slippers with lamb's wool peeking out around the edges. That is how my father's slippers looked. They made a shussing sound as he slipped down the waxed wooden floor of the hallway. Oh! Now, there you go. He's gone again. Just the smell of apricot remains. Can you smell it?" she asked earnestly.

Jakie shook his head.

"Well!" she said brightly. "What a glorious place to sit isn't it? They've put me under the maple tree again today. In the shade so I don't damage my skin. They're so lovely to me here. Always fussing. Look at all of these wonderful hydrangeas. How their creamy bonnet-heads bob in the breeze. I almost feel among friends.

"Do you see that weed over there?" She pointed off randomly to a place Jakie's eyes could not follow. "The one against the fence? The one with sharp, angular leaves. Serrated almost. Weeds seem averse to softness don't they? Well. No matter. I'm cheering for it anyway. Does that surprise you?" She turned to look up at Jakie with a coy smile. "That I would cheer for the weed?"

He rubbed his tired eyes and smiled vaguely. Most times, it didn't seem to matter whether he responded or not, her soft litany continued on undisturbed anyway, more or less verbatim each time.

"I'm not *always* such a good girl, you know. I have a secret. I will share it with you if you promise not to tell. If you tell you will lose it. You can't have a secret if you give it away," she admonished sternly.

"It's not quite perfect, my secret. It bends to one side. And the rain has fallen on it and rusted it in the most beautiful way. Would you like to see it?"

She had his attention now. She did not usually veer off course like this. He watched with mild interest as she worked a flat rock beside the bench loose with her slippered foot. A tiny treasure-trove of glittering hair ornaments sparkled into the sun.

"This is my favorite." She giggled as she bent over stiffly and pulled one free. "Would you kindly put it in my hair please?" she asked, pressing it into Jakie's hand. "It's very special. Mother gave it to me for my birthday, you know."

Jakie quite doubted that, but he said nothing as he fumbled the pretty pearl comb into place. It looked like a butterfly.

Bending down again, she reached back into the hole and withdrew the remnants of an old knife. "Shh! This is my secret. I suppose a workman must have dropped it," she murmured. "It's not very sharp, but I think it will still work. I've tested it. Twice. Not a lot. Just a little. Along the inside crease of my leg. You *must* keep that part a secret!" she implored fiercely, and Jakie nodded his head in quick, bewildered agreement.

"Father is a good man. Mother will tell you that. He doesn't come to visit. I think he is still too sad that I had to go away. But Mother will bring me his love and take mine back to him. She's thoughtful that way, Mother is. Of course, Father should know how deeply I love him. After all, all love originates from the Father and he *is* a religious man.

"Fierce untamed eyebrows. Fragile blue-veined skin," she whispered, her little hand clawing at the top of Jakie's rough sleeve. "I'm remembering him now! Just there! With the moonlight streaming across his animal back. The bristling burn of his skin.

"Oh! My!" she started, shaking her head the tiniest bit. "The sun is getting hotter isn't it? Too hot for the hydrangeas. Poor things. They look like they're weeping, don't they?

"I don't weep. *Tears are the blood of the soul.* Who said that?" she asked, not looking at Jakie now, but off into the haze that had claimed her. "I can't remember who it was—I think maybe it was me.

"There's something untrusting about this place, you know. I can feel it in the air. The regimented buildings. The tightly clipped grass. They cut all the trees down yesterday. All the beautiful orchard trees. They were useless, I suppose. They've been dead for years. But still, I found them so enchanting. The way their gnarled blackness scratched at the sky. Such beauty is abysmally hard to find.

"This stone slab we're sitting on is just wondrous, isn't it?" she exclaimed, clapping her hands with childish abandon. "The iciness of it against my skin even though the day is uncannily warm. If I were to lay myself across it, which do you think would claim me first—the sun on my face or the rock at my back?" She looked up at Jakie expectantly, even cheerfully.

"Oh!" she exclaimed, suddenly looking up at the walking group crossing the cricket oval as they made their way toward them. "Excuse me. They're coming for me now.

"You know, I would love to come back to talk with you more—but I don't know who you are." She looked over at Jakie, blinking congenially.

"I'm Jakie Hewitt, ma'am. We've talked before. Remember?"

"Of course I remember, Mr. Hewitt," she said formally. "You were going to bring me some dye for my hair. Correct?"

"Uh...correct," Jakie agreed slowly, again spun by her imperceptible transition back into the land of clarity. "I have it right here for you."

He reached into his jacket pocket and extracted the only gift that hadn't been taken from him earlier that morning. The old woman shivered with excitement as he handed it to her. "Now, you make sure Nurse Mildred helps you with that stuff, or you'll make an awful mess of your hair."

"I know...I know." She giggled, impatiently taking it from his hand. "My hair's gone and got itself to be quite an awful mess already hasn't it?" She tipped her head forward to reveal a garish strip of white down the center of her scalp.

"It's getting a little bit white, ma'am," Jakie hedged.

"How white? As white as St. Nicholas' beard?"

"Almost."

"As white as Frosty the Snowman?" She giggled into her lace handkerchief.

Jakie smiled down at her. "Not quite."

"As white as Snow White's hair then?" she asked playfully.

Jakie frowned. "Don't think Snow White had white hair, ma'am."

"No? What color was it then?"

"Black. If I recall correctly."

"Oh," the old woman said, her whole being slouching in disappointment. "I must have forgotten that."

Jakie turned on the bench and lightly took her hand, alarmed at the depth of her despondency over this simple fact.

"It's of no matter anyhow, ma'am," he declared emphatically. "In this here hospital...Snow White's hair can be any color you *want* it to be."

"Can it be? Truly?" She brightened, just as a still-exasperated Nurse Mildred—followed by the chastised and sullen walking group—slowed to a stop beside the stone bench.

"Yes. It can." Jakie grinned coltishly. "Isn't that right, Nurse Mildred?"

"I'm sure it is, Jakie," she agreed wearily. "Whatever it is that you've said."

CHAPTER 8

D
r. Davidson was livid. More livid than Jakie could ever remember seeing him. Gone, the tranquil veneer. The slightly arrogant façade. This was the man beneath the gray suit. Naked in his rage. Enraged by his nakedness.

Jakie entered the boiling cauldron of the doctor's office slowly. Aware that any abrupt movement might provoke the trigger that would set the simmering man off. He couldn't be absolutely sure why he had been summoned to the doctor's room, but he could fathom a pretty good guess.

"Sit *down*," the doctor seethed, rising to his feet as Jakie eased onto a stiff, ladder-back chair. "Well—what is all this I've been hearing?"

"Don't rightly know—"

"Don't—you—play—dumb—with—me," Dr. Davidson spat explosively. His long knobby forefinger accentuated the words into the air. "You know exactly what I mean. Don't you?"

Jakie dropped his gaze to his folded hands, working a look of compliance onto his face.

"S'pose so, sir."

"What were you thinking? Trying to bring that stuff into my hospital."

"No different than I've done before, sir. You even said yourself some of it seemed to help—"

"Nonsense! I was merely placating you. You do know what placating is—don't you, Jakie?"

"'Course."

"Besides, the new attendant said you had mushrooms. That they looked poisonous."

"Weren't poisonous. Just some reishis."

"I don't care what they were. I'll not have you bringing your witchcraft into my hospital, poisoning my patients—"

"*Witchcraft*, sir?" Jakie said, looking up at the doctor with concern.

"*I'm* the doctor here, Mr. Hewitt. I alone will decide the treatments. This is *my* hospital. *My* patients. You understand?"

Jakie nodded, not looking up at the man unfolding before him. This was not the Dr. Davidson he knew. Not the doctor who, in spite of his overglaze of condescension, had always been willing to at least give the herbal treatments a fair shake. Who had even studied up on some of them, adding to Jakie's knowledge a few things he had not already known. A man with a keen, inquiring mind. Who had duly noted corrections in temperaments brought about by the forest's remedies, observing improvements in physiological symptoms.

"Yes, sir. I understand." Slowly, Jakie raised his eyes to meet the doctor's. The pupils were dilated, the trembling face, furious.

"Feeling okay, sir—"

"*I'm* the doctor here!" Dr. Davidson exploded into Jakie's surprised face. "You are just a patient here. A patient. Remember that—"

"Yes, sir. 'Course, sir. I just—"

"You just leave it alone, Jakie Hewitt. You hear me? You just leave that girl alone."

CHAPTER 9

T he aborted tunnel was ragged. In actuality, it was now little more than a black gash carved into the side of the hill the asylum had been perched upon. Originally, the tunnel had been intended to provide transport between the open fields surrounding the hospital and the large root cellar buried in its bowels. The cellar had been constructed for storage, employing the last of the basement rooms. It was vented through an outside wall. Inmate labor had been cheap and the fields fertile. The asylum's creators had envisioned a productive and efficient harvest. Eventually, however, their vision had been forfeited, an unrelenting patch of marshy bog leading into the tunnel insistently suctioning wheels, and hooves, and rubber-booted feet to a standstill.

The year after Jakie's committal, alternate arrangements had been made. Salvaged from the rubble of a local hotel, an archaic dumbwaiter had been modified and fit into the side of Cottage Four, which sat directly atop the cellar room. Jakie had been commandeered to help, his mental dexterity at figuring and reconfiguring the humble contraption proving invaluable. For the next few autumns, as the fields had been gleaned, a groaning parade of wagons had sidled up to the heavy wooden door offering their bounty of potatoes, turnips, beets, cabbages, and onions. Inmate hands off-loaded the vegetables and lowered the straining dumbwaiter into the cellar room below, where it was unloaded by more of the same. It had been several years now since the practice had been discontinued, vegetables trucked in from town, the fields sold off for profit. Jakie remembered the harvest times fondly. They had all pulled together then, inmates and staff alike, working as one to beat the weather. Sleep had taken him early each night, satisfied to have felt again the exhaustion of a hard-earned day.

The overgrown cave of the tunnel entrance had appeared again to him early one dawn as he tracked the red fox back to her lair. He had been astonished that he could have forgotten about the place for so long. Its possibilities had instantly captivated him. Like most of the patients in the asylum, he was well aware of the rules. If any of them were to go missing for longer than thirty days, they would simply be *written off of the books*. At first, those words had sounded like a golden promise. Now, they filled him with an unspeakable terror.

He had seen the faces. Of the runners. The ones who found their way back. Vapid. Or panicked. Begging at the main gate to be allowed back in. He had averted his eyes and pretended deafness, trying to block their fear from entering into him. They had run away full of adrenalin lust, fueled by illusions of merging back into life. But they could never run far enough or fast enough, and the reality of their situation had chased them like a relentless shade. They returned. Broken, humbled, shaken. No money. Few skills. Devoid of family or friends. And now homeless. Islands of desperation. But they were free.

Jakie's forest home had long ago become lost to him. He could not remember when or how. He was not a man then but just a boy. Wild. Hopeful. Parts of him that he could no longer find. He wondered silently where the pieces of a man went when he began to disappear.

The city he remembered well. Oh, yes. She had beckoned to his brokenness like a whore. Flashed and dazzled him with her false love, her broken-glass smile. Bit by bit, she had consumed him. And he had let her. Had not known what of himself might be worth saving. One night, he sought out the soothing caress of the creek. But, although even she was defiled in such a place, her wisdom still ran ancient. She spit him out on the coarse bosom of her banks. *They* had found him then and brought him here. In time, he had forgiven her.

Pulling himself present, he closed his eyes and surveyed the lay of the land. A mental visual, showing the labyrinth of tunnels and rooms emerged with articulate grace on the screen of his mind. The slight swell of the hill, the asylum rising from it like a deceptive fortress. Austere basement rooms housing the kitchen, morgue, laundry, isolation rooms, and the operating theater. The root cellar, a room never devised to hold a human soul. Listening to the careless chatter of the nurses, he had easily ascertained that it was there the young girl was being held. He floated his thoughts back to the night he'd stumbled upon her, bound beneath the tree like a wild beast.

Jakie felt a deep ghost of sadness sweep through him as he imagined the girl incarcerated in the cellar room. Vast, bare now, the remaining rot of vegetables cleared out, their must and stink left behind, still permeating the floor. The nurses had laughed at their own hysterics upon finding a dead rat in the room, screeching like banshees and jostling the girl for a spot on top of the iron bed. Remembering their words and off-tilted by a swell of dark emotion, Jakie held his breath. It had been a long, long time since his heart had known such ache. The intensity frightened him, and he struggled to regain his emotional footing. Taunting voices started up in the back of his mind. He pulled himself forward and silenced them. He would be useless to the girl, useless to himself, if he allowed them to continue.

Pushing through the bramble that obscured the opening, he entered, a burlap sack swaying heavily from his shoulder. His head lowered, he waited, the flustering of hundreds of wings taking flight overhead as a colony of brown bats exited the cave, startled by his stealthy approach.

A sudden flare as he scratched a match awake and lit the thick stub of a candle. Soft light draped the dirt walls, the gentle sway of the flame engaging them in a sensual dance. He liked it here. A place that felt as close to home as the womb of the forest he'd grown up in. He had wanted to ask the doctor if he would let him live here. In the cave. He could still tend the asylum gardens. And bury its dead. Bring his gifts of healing to those in need. But living here, perhaps *he* could begin to heal as well. Away from the constant degradation of living under lock and key. Not that his physical body could be so easily constrained. That was almost laughable. At least to him. But away from the restraints, that constant assault against his mind.

Sighing, he lowered the bag and himself onto a makeshift bed hollowed into the wall. He knew he would never ask the doctor, because he knew the doctor could never allow such a plan. He was already most uncomfortable with the few nights Jakie chose to spend at the cemetery cabin. Jakie understood the fear. People's desire to feel a modicum of safety. Sanity separated from craziness. Crazy from sane. They would not thank him for telling them it did not work that way. That each of the patients wandered in bewilderment, finding themselves adrift on the far shore, searching vainly for a bridge that did not exist for them anymore. Or, if it did, to find that they were no longer trusted to step upon it. And then the wounded-animal glaze would begin to cataract the eyes, each night that lock clicking them one more turn toward beasts, hostile and raging or, more often, dumb and docile.

Jakie shook his mind free of such thoughts. He would have to be careful of his mind. The way it took him to other worlds and places, telling him things others said were not true. He thought about the girl. Her delicate face. The way the trail of her leg had disappeared shyly beneath her nightgown. At night, sleep had evaded him. He wanted to be close to her. Not close enough to frighten her but just to be able to look in on her. To make sure she was okay. Bring her some gifts from the forest that he knew would help her body and mind recover from the abuse they had suffered. Maybe bring some sense of comfort to her just by breathing the same air for a time. The plan had come to him in the cold aloofness of late night. As he'd tried to sort out how to help with the girl's healing without further antagonizing Dr. Davidson. He would tunnel toward her. His caretaker's duties afforded him a bevy of tools. And those he didn't have, he could make. The idea had delighted him. Having worked on opening up the wall and installing the dumbwaiter years before, he knew the cellar room's structure better than anyone. And—if the rats were finding their way in there—so could he.

CHAPTER 10

I t was cold, the day unreasonably rainy. Jakie pulled one of the gray blankets he'd pilfered from the supply room into a square around his broad shoulders. Looking down at the forty-five gallon drum he'd fashioned into a fireplace, he resisted the temptation to light up a few sticks. He knew the telltale trail of smoke would alert someone to his presence here. It was a risk he could not take. And besides, he also knew it was only a matter of time before the hard work of digging into the hillside would have him cursing and wiping the sweat from his body. The fireplace could only be lit under the cover of night, a rickety old car exhaust funneling the smoke to the outside world. Pulling a Roger's Golden Syrup can toward him, he pried the lid loose with his knife. Reaching in, he pulled out a handful of knobby walnuts, positioned them carefully atop a flat stone, and hopped his farrier's hammer agilely across them, splitting them open with expert precision.

Rummaging deep into his burlap bag, he pulled out a variety of tools: a small spade, a metal rasp, a bucket, a small tin can with a long thin chain attached, and a hand-held drill. Popping a handful of walnut meat into his mouth, he stepped across to a rack made from barkless branches and searched familiarly through a nosegay of dried roots and herbs. Crumpling his selection of goldenseal, ginseng, valerian, and wild reishi mushrooms inside his calloused fist, he stuffed them into his mouth and chewed horsily. His efforts to forge a tunnel into the girl had proved exhausting. His muscles had quickly remembered themselves but he was weary. If he were to get it done at all, he knew it would require far more sustenance than the daily rations the hospital required him to eat.

In reality, his new tunnel was little more than a man-sized burrow, leading from the cave opening straight through the hillside toward the cellar room. Dropping his suspenders, he shimmied out of his pants and shirt and folded them neatly onto the bed. He felt a little tingle of embarrassment creep over him. He knew it was silly, but he also knew there was now very little earth remaining that actually separated him from the girl. A grin crept goofily across his face, and he wiped it away quickly. The relentless digging was getting to him. Playing nasty with his mind.

Slipping each night from the cold comfort of his bed, he vanished with ease from Cottage Five's grasp, weaving his way noiselessly through the sullen watching of the asylum grounds. At night, the place lay beneath a morose blanket of thick melancholy. Deep night was when the true spirit of the place tended to have its way. Jakie did not mind. Did not fear it as did the doctor whose hand trembled as he quickly tried to inject calm up through the corridor of his vein into his frantic mind, all the while unaware of Jakie standing inside the dark abyss of shadows—watching.

Fastening the metal chain of the tin can in a loop around his neck, Jakie picked up the metal rasp, raised his arms and slid headfirst into the rough opening, kicking and squirming his way forward. Eventually, a firm resistance against the rasp indicated the end of his journey and the beginning of his night's work. He was hopeful that tonight would bring his reward. Although, perhaps not quite as hopeful as he had been for the previous three weeks.

Sighing, he mustered his determination once more, stretching his arms forward, scraping blindly into the dark. Scrape, scrape, scrape. Fill the tin cup. Wiggle free from the tunnel, empty the cup into the waiting bucket and begin again. Each night the cadence and rhythm of it eventually lulled him into something like a productive trance, moving effortlessly as imaginings of the girl urged him on.

Tonight, something hard in the alluvial soil assaulted the forward thrust of his hand. His heart jumped and then shrunk. It was probably just more rock. Boulders of granite seemingly placed directly in his way. Dropping the rasp, he stretched his aching body deeper, raw fingers impatiently scraping the dirt, demanding answers. A large, rectangular stone emerged beneath their groping. A thin seam and then another, almost identical stone. A smile lit his blackened face. Placed stones. Frantically, he picked up his rasp and gouged deeply into the dirt bordering the side of the stones. Fragments of splintered wood immediately rewarded him, piercing his hand into an ecstasy of pure joy. He had not confused his way. He had traversed to the exact spot where, years earlier, the slow hands of tired patients had dug a shaft deep into the ground for the installation of the makeshift dumbwaiter. Something akin to joy and pride enveloped Jakie. They felt like strangers.

Pushing back out of the hole, he picked up the long-handled hand drill from the cave floor and re-emerged into the dirt opening. Twisting and kicking his way forward, he strained to position the drill as high up as he could on the dumbwaiter's wooden frame. If his calculations were correct—and it seemed as if they were—then the drill should be positioned against the thick oak header, which had been installed to bear the load of the heavy rock wall above it. Carefully, he tilted the drill on a slight downward angle and began to work it into the wood.

Sweat wetted him, a thin covering of dirt metamorphosing him into a muddy cocoon. Exhaustion beat against him. Each revolution of the drill seemed an eternity. Abruptly, he stopped. A voice, ethereal but muted, had found him. Rubbing the dirt aside, he opened his eyes to try and see if the voice was true. Countless times he had imagined this moment. Now, he was confused. Was he really here? Or had he once again traveled too far down the pathway in his mind that led him beyond himself and out the gateway of his soul? Such moments had stumbled him before.

Summoning himself, he focused intently on the melodic singing. Suddenly, shrugging his head toward his shoulder, he bit his raw, soiled flesh—hard. Welcoming the steely jolt of pain, he ground his teeth fiercely as a river of connection drew him back into himself. Forcing his trembling hands to obey, he withdrew the drill from the short, tubular hole it had made. He was close. Too close. And now he had to be certain of his every move.

A violent whirlpool of emotions began to spin him out of control. He had no choice but to shut himself down. It had never ended this way. He was unprepared. In all of his oft-imagined plans, he had never arrived to the sound of her voice singing. He had always found his way into her world while she and her room were darkened inside sleep. Wooing his mind toward stillness, he drew a great draught of air deep into his lungs and then slowly exhaled. He would not move until he was able to do so calmly. The girl had suffered enough. He reviled the thought that his actions might frighten her further. Hated himself for even possessing the possibility of such a thing.

Time was not, and he didn't know how much of it had passed before he slowly allowed himself to raise the tool and resume his drilling. Fine curls of wood spit down into his face as he worked, his whole body aching for him to stop. Abruptly, it now seemed, the wood gave way. A bright splinter of light dove in at him. Instinctively, Jakie ducked his head and froze.

The girl's song continued undisturbed. Dreamily, she sang of hills and flowers and far-off lands, her voice bell-like now, no longer muffled by the barrier that had existed between them. Her innocence erupted Jakie's heart to rage. He wanted to kill those who had allowed such purity to suffer such pain. Overwhelmed by the intensity of such emotion, he wrestled to contain it. Windows of memories flew open, and he quickly snapped them shut.

Small movements, requiring extreme exertion, eventually succeeded in turning him over onto his stomach. Squinting against the unaccustomed light, he furtively raised his eye up to the hole. She reclined on her bed against the far wall. Curled around herself like an early flower, she sang freely, the expression on her face accompanying her song. The filthy quilt was gone, an institution-gray blanket scattered across the bottoms of her thin bare legs. She hugged against a stained pillow, the case taken off and fashioned into a little blanket for her baby doll. The sweater she had worn when he found her down by the creek was nestled tidily at the foot of her bed, clean now, the gaily embroidered flowers providing a riot of color in the stark room. Jakie noticed her tangle of hair had been tamed, cut shorter, but not shorn as was the usual custom for one so unkempt when admitted. Lilac bruises still littered her face, softer now, like shadows. Weaving and unweaving her slender fingers, she played with them absently as she sang.

A thud of panic seized him. Perhaps she no longer required his healing. Certainly somebody had been looking after her care somewhat adequately. He had even noticed an extra blanket stuffed beneath her cot. His body stiffened, preparing to drag himself free from the hole, his mind starting up with a barrage of insults. Resisting their taunts, he looked deeper at the girl. Unmistakably, a resident fear still flickered inside the quick blue fire of her eyes, the green cotton bed-dress, clearly a hand-me-down, unable to fully conceal the deterioration of her young body. Squinting his eye to see clearer, he could just make out a tiny black dot that seemed to run in rapid randomness across her hands as she wove her fingers in and out. Slipping from the side of her palm, the dot seemed to hover in midair. Realizing it was a spider, Jakie smiled. She still held a fascination for this small friend and he was glad. The dehumanizing isolation had altered but not deformed her as it had to some.

Closing his eyes, he allowed her music to bathe over him. It soothed him in a way he had long forgotten possible. A foreign pressure began to squeeze around his heart, disabling his breath until a ragged sound escaped him, almost like a sob.

An awful silence answered back. Snapping his eyes open, he looked at the girl, trying to ascertain whether the sound had erupted inside or outside of him. Wildness had reclaimed her. Cowered deep into the corner, blanket pulled into a tight armor around her, she clutched her doll furiously. Head jerking about fearfully, panic flashed in the vast openness of her eyes as she searched desperately for the source of the sound. Ragged breaths jumped from her as her face collapsed from bewilderment into pure terror.

Had Jakie been able to move, he would have stabbed himself with the drill bit. Silently cursing, he berated his stupidity. Maybe the records Dr. Davidson referred to were correct after all. Maybe he was a moron. Or insane. Shaking himself, he quickly dislodged such thoughts.

The remembrance of a voice filtered to him. An old voice. Older than the ones he knew here. Older still than the ones that had chased him into the asylum in the first place. A guttural voice, rising up and bursting into Cardinal's song. Coyote had calmed him this way many times. In the deep of night when the screams and pictures would not let young Jakie sleep.

Licking his lips to free them of encrusted dirt, he pursed them and then gently called a bird to life. "Cheeeer-a-dote, cheeer-a-dote-dote-dote, purdy, purdy, purdy...whoit, whoit, whoit, whoit." The sharp notes reverberated around him. A rush of exhilaration danced through him dangerously. He shrunk back from the eyehole as her eyes darted toward him. He feared for a moment that he'd been exposed. But as he peered again through the hole, he was rewarded as the strain on her face slackened its grip and then disappeared into a cautious smile. Mesmerized, she stared wondrously up at him. Seeing nothing but a graffitied patch of stone wall, she delighted in the bird's song.

CHAPTER 11

E veryone was excited. Not just the patients but the doctors and nurses as well. Even the attendants, who held the unenviable task of keeping the event in order, could not contain their enthusiasm.

Idle chatter had centered around little else for weeks. The promise of a fancy tea and dance social had fragranced the monotony of institution days like a bouquet of sudden roses. Everyone who had been issued a pass to the assembly hall had been on their best behavior. Smiles broke out quickly, and silvery peals of laughter occasionally rang out like beacons of hope.

Jakie had been keeping his head low, intently inspecting the flowers, eavesdropping on the air as the women's walking groups had passed him by. Rapidly chattering, they busily formed alliances of trade: hats for shoes, hairdos for seldom-used corsets, secret intrigues for the telling of who-stole-what-kiss-from-whom at last year's big gathering.

In the weeks prior to the dance, Jakie had felt just as excited as the rest—confident even. He knew from the nurse's chatter that Dr. Davidson had decided to bring the girl upstairs in an attempt to socialize her a bit. The thought of it had caused Jakie to go all gooey inside. In fact, when he had first overheard the nurses opining about the doctor's decision, he had whooped out loud and jumped a punch into the air, garden spade still held in his fisted hand. Reprimanded by Nurse Mildred's scowling face, he'd quickly recovered, theatrically feigning that he had been stung by a bee.

Now, his initial excitement had abandoned him, having morphed itself into a serious case of anxiety. What little remained of his fingernails had been further gnawed down far below the quick.

Standing up from his bed, he again chased stubborn wrinkles down his pant leg with the palm of his hand. Bustling with agitation, he strode back and forth through the ward several times before being hollered at to stop. Settling in front of the heavily barred window, he made a quick study of himself. It always surprised him how he looked. He felt years older.

A rub of dissatisfaction nudged him when he glanced down at his shoes. Years had gone by since he had used up the last of his shoe polish. He had no money to buy more. Surreptitiously, he scanned the room, eyeing up boots and shoes that sported a fresh polish. An expensive-looking pair of tooled-leather dress shoes caught his attention. Puffing on a rolled-up wad of newsprint, the retired barrister, Mr. Seymour, stood erect and unapproachable next to the supply room door. He stared vacantly at the impeccably folded, yellowed newspaper he read each and every afternoon at precisely four o'clock. Prominent red circles on the front page rallied deliriously around the bold black date: October 28, 1929.

"You going to the dance this afternoon, Mr. Seymour?" Jakie asked as he sidled over.

The older man's walrus face clamped down menacingly. "Who wants to know?"

Jakie swallowed thickly, impotently extending his hand. "It's Jakie, sir."

"Well, you can tell that nincompoop it's none of his business!" Mr. Seymour bellowed.

Jakie jumped. "Sorry. I was just wondering—"

"Wondering what?"

"If ya were going...to the dance?" Jakie replied carefully.

"Then why not just ask?"

"Uh...I did ask."

"Objection!" Mr. Seymour thundered. "Judge! The witness is blatantly lying on the stand."

"But...I *did* ask," Jakie protested.

"Overruled! Now what do you want?" He glowered down at Jakie expectantly.

"Uh, I was just wondering, sir, if you are going to the dance?"

The whiskery face pulled around to look at Jakie as if he had just materialized. "The dance?"

Jakie nodded slowly.

"Oh, I'll go if there's no way around it. Why do you people insist on pestering me about such things? Damn inconvenience on my time. I'm a busy man if you must know. A busy, busy man."

Seeing the course of the conversation was working Mr. Seymour into an uncomplimentary lather, Jakie tried a different turn.

"That is a very nice jacket ya have on, Mr. Seymour. New, is it?"

"Same's I wear every day," the old barrister replied, eyeing him suspiciously.

"No! The same one?"

"Doubting my word then, are you, boy?" he challenged back.

Jakie shrunk. "Not a word of it, sir. Never! It just looks quite new."

"It's not, you ninny!"

"Maybe," Jakie ventured tentatively, "maybe you've been slimming a bit then."

Mr. Seymour brightened.

Seeing his break, Jakie quickly pulled a rickety chair toward him, raised up his knee and placed a foot upon its seat. Hiking his pant leg up, he pulled it unnecessarily high in order to better expose the shabby disposition of his footwear.

Mr. Seymour, inquisitively patting both hands around his ample girth, remained entirely oblivious to Jakie's shoe's obvious need. He inclined his head to the side and whispered, "I suppose I *have* dropped down a few pounds."

Jakie withheld a grin as he elaborately refastened his laces several times. Finally, Mr. Seymour quit patting and looked down to see what Jakie was doing.

"I say! You're a right awful mess there, aren't you?"

Working a look of confusion across his face, Jakie looked up.

"Your shoes. God-awful mess."

Jakie rubbed the heel of his hand over the toe of his shoe, as if to erase the well-embedded scuff marks. "Not so bad, really. I've only just polished them."

"Rubbish!" Mr. Seymour spluttered.

"But I did."

"Overruled! The evidence against it is overwhelming."

Looking down at the offending shoes, Jakie shook his head shamefully. "S'pose you're right. Well, it's too late to do anything about it now. I'm clean out of polish."

Mr. Seymour leaned over the bulk of his belly and perused Jakie's other foot. Setting back against the wall, he puffed heavily on his paper cigar.

"It seems quite evident to me that you cannot go to the dance dressed like that, can you?"

Jakie opened his mouth to agree, but Mr. Seymour continued on.

"At any rate, those shoes will have to be polished. Otherwise—" He dropped his voice. "Otherwise, all the young ladies are going to think you're a loony-loon!"

Splitting into a fit of hysterical laughter, he drew a battalion of stern stares as he strode past the nursing station. Making his way over to his bed, he shoved the frantically restuffed Bible sitting on it onto the floor. Riffling through his tiny bedside table, he impatiently waved Jakie over with his free hand.

"Well, hurry up, will you. I'm not a shoeshine, you cabbage-head. I've better things to do all day than sit about shining your shoes. I'm a busy man if you must know. A busy, busy man."

"I'm sure you are," Jakie replied, smiling lightly as he sat atop Mr. Seymour's bed, Mr. Seymour taking a seat on the one across from it. Taking up Jakie's foot, he meticulously set to work with the polish.

"Represented Jesus once, did you know?"

"You don't say."

"I just *did* say, you ninny!"

"Right. I believe ya did."

"Pleasant enough man. But see here..." Mr. Seymour leaned forward menacingly and shook a meaty finger in Jakie's face. "Now that in no way means that I'll be vouching for the fellow's character, you understand!"

Jakie leaned back slightly, shaking his head. "No, sir. I hadn't thought ya were."

"Well, I'm not! If I recollect correctly, I think he may have been my last case before I moved in here."

"Seems likely, Mr. Seymour," Jakie agreed. "Quite likely, in fact."

CHAPTER 12

Thanking Mr. Seymour for his kindness, Jakie made his way toward the ward doors. Ignoring white-stockinged, beefy calves, he solely admired the new look of his shoes. He joined a group of impatiently agitated men milling about. Some muttered against their misfortune, others smiled secretly to themselves, and still others stared off silently into their memories. Several sported fresh haircuts, having successfully coerced the younger nurses into unsuccessfully trying to update their styles.

After what seemed an interminable wait, the nurses began herding the rest of the patients toward the door like a group of scattered cats. A reasonable line was formed, the riot act again pronounced and—finally—the key unlatched them. Toe-to-heel, they trundled across the asylum grounds. Jakie could see that each of them was individually lost in a cloud of elation or fear, expectation, or trepidation.

Appropriately festooned with a rainbow of balloons and flowing purple streamers, the assembly hall opened up heartily to greet them. For weeks, the women of Cottage Three had taken it upon themselves to fashion puffy white flowers from sheets of crepe paper. These hung from the high ceiling like softly exploded stars. Beneath them, swarms of patients clustered about in tight groups, staying close to the protective familiarity of those they knew. A few still clutched their hall passes, a little insurance should anyone choose to question the validity of their presence.

Various occasions arose throughout the year where the residents of the Cottages were encouraged to comingle— plays, recitals, religious ceremonies, funerals—and yet even so, a pervasive mistrust prevailed.

As usual, the men from Cottage Five were ushered in last. Peals of nervous laughter squealed out from the women's groups. Flashing eyes and quickly turned heads revealed quite clearly that some of the women had been eagerly anticipating the men's arrival. Rumored to be slightly dangerous and quite remote, their approach ushered an element of excitement into the hall.

Wheezing itself toward the right key, the band was still warming up. Fingers fumbled off frets, and the big horns went dry as the Cottage Five men silently filed in. An ebony-colored stringed instrument, propped up on a side table, caught Jakie's eye. Stopping to pick it up, his hands echoed the fine lines of its peculiar shape. A stiffly starched little man wearing a red bowtie interrupted himself from the piano and glared at Jakie.

"Be careful with it. Please. It's quite old."

Jakie pulled his eyes away from the gold embroidery of inlaid wood decorating the instrument and slowly looked up. The man's bald cantaloupe-head quivered in a rapid nod.

"It's a zither, you know. And quite old. It's very, very fragile."

"Oh? I thought it was firewood," Jakie teased.

"Oh, my goodness. No! It's not firewood you...you..." the little man burst out, a substantial spray of spit exploding across the stage.

Holding the man's eye for a gentle moment, Jakie sighed, then looked back to the instrument. Even with his head down, he could feel the agitation growing around him, knew the quick, furtive looks being glanced around between the band members. He had seen it all before.

Fascinated by the vast arrangement of strings covering the strange instrument's face, he busied himself studying it.

"Familiar with it are you?" A voice, rich and deep now, and Jakie followed it to a heavyset man comfortably reclining against the far wall, a massive stand-up bass guitar resting at his side.

"Naw," Jakie returned, as he laid the instrument back down on the table, his flat fingers finding the strings and beginning to plunk awkwardly.

The man watched him curiously as he picked up his bass and followed the rest of the band into a frolicking Vienna Waltz. Jakie was enraptured as the music swooned over him. Half closing his eyes, he let the music speak to him. An energy, unbearable in its intensity, began to swell into his fingers. Plucking at the maze of strings, the memory of the rhythm began to fill him, the unexpected voice of the zither rising expertly into the air.

Astonished looks were exchanged between members of the band and those patients and staff who stood close enough to notice what had happened. Their amazement passed over Jakie only partially noticed. Lost inside a solitary moment, he swayed with ecstasy.

A rousing trickle of applause brought him fully back to himself, confusion replacing the contentment on his face. Jerking his hands from the instrument, he quickly stepped away from it. A warm hand patted him on the back.

"Well, well. Who would have known we had us a famous musician living in our midsts?"

Jakie flushed hotly.

"And whoever taught you to play like that anyhow?" Nurse Mildred asked—loudly.

Ducking his head, Jakie smiled vaguely, then slipped into the crowd. Seeking out the comforting shadows in the back of the room, her question seemed to follow him as he went. Standing alone, he struggled with the music as it threatened to overwhelm him. It had reached into him, unbidden and unadorned, then flowed back out riding a river of deep desire. It had flowed as natural as a glacial spring. Its depths frightened him. Nurse Mildred's question reverberated in his mind. *Who had taught him how to play like that?* In truth—he had no idea.

≡ ≡ ≡

Jakie's discomfort was distracted as a flurry of excitement sparkled past him on her way toward the door. Scarcely six steps into the assembly hall, extreme dismay rewrote Dr. Davidson's face as Mary Larson accosted him, demanding his first dance. Brusquely shrugging her off, he took a moment to collect himself before returning his attentions to the delicate flower who adorned his side.

Jakie's spirits soared. He had feared the girl might not come. That the doctor would rethink the wisdom of bringing her into such a swirl of activity. Or that she might struggle free of his grasp and run off into the woods. But no such thing had happened, and now she was here, her frail body whispered close to the familiarity of the doctor in the onslaught of such a cacophonous place. Tucking his head into his chest, Jakie pretended interest in his hands, sliding his eyes across the room and filling them full of her. She looked almost well. He allowed himself a small smile, pleased to see the gifts of herbs, roots, and berries that he'd been delivering through the hole in her wall were beginning to reveal their desired effect. Her hair had grown longer, a luminous shine highlighting its burnished gold. Still decimated, her white skin stretched painfully thin over the sharp angle of her cheekbones.

Without a doubt, Jakie knew she was the most beautiful girl he had ever seen: her shapely nose—graceful, her wild blue eyes—luminous with wonder. Her movements were that of the deer, dreamlike in their softness, quick in their alertness. He wanted to wrap himself around her, taking her with him into a depthless slumber. A pain, far more excruciating than a merely physical one, tortured him as he watched her nervously shadowing the doctor's every move.

Head bowed, her eyes sought refuge in the floor as Dr. Davidson mingled around the room, occasionally introducing her to nurses, attendants, and a select few of the other patients. Cowered beside him, her tiny shoulders rounded in on themselves as if she were trying to fold herself away. Her hands clutched the brightly embroidered sweater around her, a pretty pink-chiffon skirt billowing out below it. Jakie eyed the pink skirt suspiciously. It looked by far newer than anything most of the other patients were wearing.

Suddenly roiling into a rather raucous number, the band increased both its volume and tempo, startling the girl. Flinching, she leaned in closer toward the doctor. Jakie burned as he watched a knobby-fingered hand settle protectively over her lower back.

Leaning down to speak to her, Dr. Davidson took her reluctant hand and proceeded to lead her across the room, closer toward Jakie, stopping at the heavily laden and festively arrayed banquet table. Plucking a white daisy from the center display, he offered it to her. Looking up timidly, she took the flower and held it awkwardly. The doctor's face lit up with a pleased smile, a habitual hand flying up to cover the sight of uncomely teeth.

Jakie watched darkly, directing sullen thoughts toward the doctor and the easy privilege he assumed with the girl. Every sinew in his body ached to propel him forward. To seize that flower from her hand and push the doctor away. But, with great effort, he held himself down. One burst of aggression and he knew he would be instantly buried beneath an avalanche of white-coated attendants, a quick injection slipping him into a useless, drug-induced haze.

The banquet table had originally been intended to be self-serving, but a hunched older woman buzzed around it like a bee over clover, making herself busy. By all accounts, she was frightful to look at. Frizzy white strands of hair seemed to shriek out in every direction from her half-bald head. Small scabs, some still fresh and oozing, littered her face and arms. Overfilling a small plate with a kaleidoscope of geometrically shaped tea sandwiches, she talked rapidly to herself, as if oblivious of the doctor and the girl standing in front of her.

"Three plus three plus three equals four," she chanted. "It's all very simple really. One only has to do the math."

Still mumbling quietly, she put the plate of sandwiches aside and began to meticulously separate out nine strands of her broken hair. Twirling five of these around her gnarled ring finger, she forcefully yanked them out, twizzled them into a tiny ball, and stuffed them into the pocket of her apron.

Loudly, Dr. Davidson cleared his throat. Looking up wearily, she began to hand the plate to him then abruptly she stopped. Eyes flaring owl-wide with astonishment, she stared at the girl's sweater. Jakie watched with rising interest as a wave of supreme hurt flushed across the old woman's face, then was swept quickly away by a storm of catastrophic anger. Flashing her livid eyes back toward the doctor, she glared at him, dropping the plate full of sandwiches just short of his outstretched hand. Dr. Davidson and the girl jumped back as one being as the plate exploded noisily at their feet. Shaken, he wagged a furious finger.

"See here, Anna! I do think you did that quite on purpose."

Eyes narrowed into defiant black slits, Anna held his glare, looked one more time at the girl's sweater, then spun on her worn heel and stormed away.

"I do apologize, my dear," Dr. Davidson fussed, as he attempted to soothe the girl's alarm. "It was a very regrettable way for Anna to act. Most unusual."

Mrs. Anna Mason's aggression had unsettled the girl further, and Dr. Davidson was visibly annoyed. Impatiently gesturing for an attendant to clean up the mess, Dr. Davidson wrung his pert blue-and-white striped bowtie through six degrees of crookedness before satisfying himself that it was actually straight. Fishing once again for the girl's soft hand, he artfully dodged her through a parade of dancers as he led her toward two vacant chairs at the edge of the dance floor. Scowling, Jakie could see that he was going to have to come up with a plan if he ever hoped to get anywhere near the girl. Jabbering excitedly, Dr. Davidson was glommed onto her like an insecure octopus.

Scouting around the hall, Jakie's eyes found Mary Lawson shimmering alone in a back corner, looking very sorry for herself. She wore a fuchsia caftan that attempted to drape itself in a Grecian fashion over her ample curves. A small tiara adorned her head. Jakie had overheard the asylum gossip that Mary had managed to use familial connections to secure one of the basement treadle machines for her exclusive privilege, then ordered her mother to buy her a bolt of expensive silk damask. Apparently, she had then proceeded to orchestrate the help of several Cottage Three ladies, having them encrust her self-styled gown with a full pail of cheap silver sequins. A plan birthing itself in his head, Jakie hid a grin as he nonchalantly made his way over to her.

"Hello, Miss Lawson," he greeted cheerily. "Would ya like to dance?"

"It's Angel Queen."

Jakie eased back, swallowing dryly.

"Uh, okay. Miss Angel Queen, would *you* like to dance?"

She glared at him as if he had lost his mind.

"Of *course* I'd like to dance. But it seems my Gerald just never has time for me anymore." She exhaled forcefully.

"Uh...I meant with me."

Mary glanced him up and down. Jakie firmed up his posture, smiling encouragement.

"No, thanks," she sniffed. "I'm saving myself for Gerald."

Catching himself halfway through an eye roll, Jakie awkwardly switched it into a rather convoluted smile.

Mary wrinkled her nose up unattractively. "What's wrong with your face?"

"Nothing." Jakie shrugged self-consciously.

"Well, why did it just do that strange thing?" she demanded.

"Oh. That. Spasm. Happens sometimes."

"*Well,*" Mary puffed, "you shouldn't let it. Makes you look like your fruitcake is a little nutty."

Jakie nodded vaguely.

"And you're really not such a bad-looking chap," she teased, breaking into a sniggering giggle.

Taking a half step back, Jakie studied his freshly polished shoes as he mustered up the courage to continue.

"I'd like to talk with ya, Mary."

Mary's lip sprung a prominent pout. "*Talk* with me? I thought you wanted to dance with me."

"Oh. Yes. I do want to."

"Want to what?" she accused. "Talk...or dance?"

Having pulled her formidable self together, Mary's whole countenance seemed to spark like an impending lightening storm as she awaited his answer.

"Uh...*both?*"

"Oh! You men!" she erupted. "Make up your mind. Next thing I know, *you'll* be wanting to marry me too. Won't you?"

Holding his head absolutely still, Jakie smiled ambiguously.

"Well, come on then, silly," she purred, linking him by the arm and whirling him onto the dance floor.

For all of her confirmed bulk and extravagance, Mary Lawson was a surprisingly articulate dancer. Spinning him first one way then the next, she was an expert lead. Feeling somewhat like the unfortunate fish that had taken the lure, Jakie shouted out to her as she played him around the dance floor.

"He's really very fond of ya, ya know."

"Who is?" Mary demanded, snapping him prematurely out of a turn.

Wincing, Jakie reached up to rub his wrenched shoulder. Inclining his head toward Dr. Davidson, he gestured heavily with his eyebrows.

"Oh, Gerald? Yes, I know. He's in love with *meeeee...*" she sang, fanning her glittering, fuchsia arms out like butterfly wings and spinning around ecstatically.

Losing the step completely, Jakie shuffled around self-consciously as Mary Lawson morphed herself into some sort of maniacal merry-go-round. Suddenly snatching him up by both arms, she resumed the dance without missing a beat. Leading them across the floor in wide, swooping arcs, she managed to negotiate a turn right in front of the doctor, fluttering her lashes robustly.

"Gerald doesn't like me dancing with other men," she said loudly, too close to Jakie's ear. "He's insanely jealous that way."

Jakie slid a covert glance at the doctor. Preoccupied with the girl, he seemed quite oblivious of them as they cavorted on by.

"You know, Mary. There really is something I need to tell you," Jakie began seriously.

Seductively grinning over at the doctor, she leaned in far closer to Jakie than was necessary, colliding her tiaraed head full square into his face. Grinding to a stop, her two bejeweled hands darted up to pat the assaulted spot.

"*Ow!* Watch what you're doing, will you," she cried out. "Did you break it?"

Reaching up tentatively, Jakie attempted to modify the now-bent, little crown.

"Not that!" She slapped his hands away. "My noggin. Did you break it? It's made of glass, you know."

Jakie looked at her with open surprise. She met him with wide, earnest, fear-filled eyes.

"Did you?"

In spite of himself, Jakie carefully leaned forward and checked.

"No. Looks good to me."

"Are you sure?"

He nodded, peripherally aware of the attendants' ever-watchful eyes. Gently, he coaxed Mary back into the dance.

"You mustn't tell anyone what I just said. About my noggin. Gerald doesn't like it when I say that. He says I'm just trying to be like all the other patients." She huffed her hair back over her shoulder, looking up for Jakie's support.

"Well, your secret is safe with me, Mary. Can you keep one?"

"One what?"

"A secret. Can you keep a secret?"

"No."

"Oh, good grief!" Jakie groaned under his breath. "Well, just try, okay? It's about the doctor."

He'd snagged Mary good now, and even though the music and most of the dancers had dribbled to a stop, she was immovable in the center of the dance floor, refusing to be led off until he'd divulged the promised goods.

"He doesn't know how to dance," Jakie whispered.

"Who doesn't know how to dance? My Gerald? Well, that's absurd. Everyone knows how to dance," she espoused loudly.

Ducking his head, Jakie urged her toward the edge of the dance floor as white coats began to turn their way.

"Well, the doctor doesn't. He said he would be much too embarrassed to dance with ya."

Mary drew herself up. "Embarrassed?"

"Because *you* dance so well," Jakie hastened.

"Oh." Pity softened her features as she looked longingly over at the unsuspecting doctor. "My poor little pookie-poo. I had no idea he was so shy."

"*Horribly* shy," Jakie encouraged, underscoring the word with a remorseful wag of his head. "But—"

Mary glittered up at him hopefully.

"But, he did mention there was one dance he could do quite well—"

"What one?"

Leaning extra carefully in toward Mary, he whispered into her ear.

"Haw! That's an easy one," she guffawed.

With one eye on the doctor sitting happily beside his girl, Jakie smiled at Mary.

"So, here's what we'll do."

CHAPTER 13

Jakie thanked Mary for the dance and made his way toward the band, tenderly rubbing his shoulder. The gal could certainly dance, but she was a bit of a bull in ballet slippers.

Seeing Jakie headed his way, the priggish piano player abandoned his music, snatched up the antique zither, and clutched it protectively to his concave chest. Working up his best gargoyle scowl, Jakie eyed the little man cuttingly as he walked by. Slouched comfortably around his instrument, the hefty bass player watched and grinned.

"What'cha up to, young fellar?"

"Do ya take requests?" Jakie asked.

"Depends," the other man boomed slowly, effortlessly continuing to strum along as he talked. "Is it a song?"

Jakie twisted his face up, confused.

"Well, last fella came by, had a request I smuggle him out of here tonight in my case. Not anything like that is it?" He chuckled freely.

Jakie shook his head. "No, sir. Nothing like that. Just a song. For my friend."

"That I can do," he replied, nodding his head in time with the waltz he was playing. "What song would that be?"

Jakie made a discreet check over his shoulder. Shielding the side of his mouth with his hand, he passed on his request.

"Haw!" laughed the big bass player. "That's an easy one."

"So I've heard said," Jakie agreed. "So I've heard said."

"Say," the older man ventured, his deep voice reaching out over the music. "How is it you learned to play that zither so well?"

Jakie looked at the floor.

"Well, don't you be worrying yourself about that none. I'm sure once the docs get you fixed up, it'll all come back to you."

Winking, he gave Jakie a solid wallop on his abused shoulder. Grimacing a smile, Jakie turned and began to slowly make his way over to where Dr. Davidson sat encompassing the girl. In the dark corner behind them, Jakie could just make out the solid outline of Mary Lawson, hovering impatiently. The band spit out the last of its waltz. Switching gears, they began to toy with a few new notes. Mary's shadow became more animated. Jakie grinned and, as if his grin held the power of the conductor's baton, the band exploded. Pouncing free of the shadows like a mammoth cat, Angel Queen physically hauled the doctor out of his chair and onto his protesting feet. Paralyzing his upper body in a sweaty, fuchsia-armed straightjacket, she manhandled him onto the dance floor, happily tossing him side to side in a lively polka.

Chuckling as he pretended not to watch, Jakie seamlessly slipped himself into the doctor's newly vacated chair. He grinned over at the girl. She looked away. Instantly, the air went out of him. He clamored futilely for breath. The room had disappeared. There remained only himself, the girl, and the translucent bubble that enveloped them. He felt obscenely large. His freshly polished shoes had become horrendous, clownish, poking out everywhere at once. He stuffed them under his chair. His legs became deformed, cut off at the knees. He wiggled his feet forward so he could just barely see the very tops of his shoes. Feeling an urgency to breathe, he pulled in, a grotesque sucking sound filling his ears.

Bodies bobbed before him like a drunken sea full of flot-sam. He pretended great interest. But it had all ceased to truly be. There remained only the girl who sat at his side. Peripherally, he noticed everything about her: the graceful wave her hair made as it swept like a waterway to one side and cascaded over her frail shoulder; how her faint breath expanded and contracted the lively colors of her flowered sweater; her perfect eyebrows—the graceful arch of a gull's wing in flight; the painfully sweet curl of her dark lashes as they temporarily shuttered the blaze of her blue eyes. He felt, more than saw, the fibrous trembling in her body. The slight way she shadowed herself away from him when he moved. Gutted with emotion, he restrained his longing to cover her soft tiny hands with his large calloused ones. To hold them gently until she understood. Until she calmed to a knowing that he meant her no harm. The way he had done countless times with the young birds of his home, returning them to the safety of their nests, far above the forest floor.

He knew he could make no such movement toward her. Of all the things that remained unclear to him in his life, this was a certainty. Her silent horror of him was palpa-ble. Hidden behind a rock wall, he had felt he had gained her trust. Withdrawn from her a type of friendship. Now he realized that he had merely gained the effigy of such things. Her friendship and laughter had been bestowed to another. To a tiny winged creature that had brought her gifts of herbs, roots, and berries. That had shared its song with her and filled the vast loneliness of her days with something more. A tiny winged illusion that he had cre-ated into her life.

Suddenly it occurred to him that in her world he was not a friend but merely the dark mask of a man. Not a man like Dr. Davidson, who seemed to bring a protective con-cern for her well-being. But rather, a brute of a man. One who, upon finding her chained and helpless beneath a tree, had calmly unsheathed his blade and attempted to cut her throat. The realization shredded him.

Thinking quickly, he moved slowly. The polka was in its final chords. Easing his hanky from his jacket pocket, he gently inclined it toward her. She shrank from his hand, startled eyes flying to his, then back to the hanky. Following her lead, Jakie saw his mistake. The white cotton bundle had turned a nightmarish red. Quickly he hastened the topknot free, revealing oozing, plump raspberries.

Drawing an audible breath, the girl flashed her eyes back to Jakie's and searched deeply. The red flush that overwhelmed Jakie's face rivaled the raspberries, and he tried to look away, mortified. He found himself unable to do so. Her intense gaze was unflinching. He was utterly absorbed within it. Hers was a depthless power that belied her minuscule form.

Desperate to cool the mercurial moment, Jakie fumbled with the raspberries. Securing one between his thumb and forefinger, he put it self-consciously into his mouth. Then, with exaggerated slowness, he dared to take another one. With a vaporous tremor of his hand testifying against him, he offered it up toward the ripe fullness of the girl's lips.

She watched him warily. The last hurrah of the polka grew louder. To Jakie's vision, the whole assembly hall had faded into a sepia hue. Only the shimmer of the girl's soft mouth and the brilliant burgundy raspberry remained. He began to feel profoundly stupid as he sat turned slightly toward her, his inadequate offering still held up to her unreceptive mouth. Then, just as he was about to draw it away, she parted her lips ever so slightly, a little silver doorway into heaven. Her eyes burning lucidly, she hesitated, then allowed the proffered fruit.

Jakie could accept the intensity of her gaze no more. She stole straight into him. Through secret passageways and beyond locked doors. He felt she knew him in a way no one else ever had. And what she didn't know, he could feel her gleaning from deep within his soul.

The dance finally at its end, a furiously disheveled Dr. Davidson extricated himself from Mary Lawson's fused embrace and fumed his way toward them. Jakie dove his other hand quickly into his pocket, withdrawing an exquisite red feather. Tentatively he held it up toward the girl. A cloud of confusion crossed her face, replaced by a slow recognition. She stared even harder into Jakie, as if she could penetrate his silence with her mind. Aware of the doctor's imminent—and unhappy—approach, Jakie wet his dry lips and began to whistle Cardinal's song. "Cheeeer-a-dote, cheeer-a-dote-dote-dote. Purdy, purdy, purdy...whoit, whoit, whoit, whoit."

The girl's eyes flew open even wider as an informed intelligence transformed her face. Slowly, she took the feather from Jakie's trembling hand then, looking away, she began to whistle softly. Repelling the violent gesticulations of the doctor with his stained, blood-red hand, Jakie strained desperately to hear the sounds emitting from the girl's lips. "What-cheer, what-cheer...wheet, wheet, wheet, wheet."

CHAPTER 14

A huddle of nurses, patients, and attendants hovered around Mary Lawson's bed. She lay inert, her flossy, golden silk eiderdown quilt cocooned up over her head.

"Is she dead?" whispered Delores tearfully, swiping at her pained, withered face.

"Heavens, no!" chastised the young student nurse, Jenny. "I've only just checked her vitals." Still, she reached in under the quilt, withdrawing Mary's limp hand, and checked once again.

"Best you be getting up now, Queenie," Delores pleaded, lightly shaking the corner of the bedding. "Before the other one comes along."

The shimmering heap held immovable, save for a quick movement thrusting a white envelope, sealed with a gold star, in the general direction of Delores' voice.

Curtsying slightly, Delores stumbled over herself in order to grasp the proffered note. The full front of it was inscribed over and over again with black block letters: **Dr. Gerald Isaac Davidson.**

"Oh—" she wailed as she gingerly held the envelope in her trembling hands. "Not another one, Angel Queen. Nurse said she won't give him no more—"

"Delores—" Mary's muffled voice surfaced from beneath the covers. "You are to ensure Gerald receives that note."

"But Mary...Mary, is it a...a *suicide* note? Like the others?"

"They were *not* suicide notes!" Mary exploded, thrashing the quilt off of her. Her face was scarlet, perspiring profusely.

"Oh my...look, nurse. I told you she was having a fever—"

"I'm *not* having a fever!" Mary snapped, slapping at the hands of the nurse who had quickly stepped forward to examine her. "It's just wretchedly hot under there."

"But Mary, this note—" whimpered Delores. "It scathes my hands to even hold it. I can't bear the thought, Queenie. I can't bear it if you bring harm to yourself."

"Oh, for pity's sake, Delores. I told you. It is *not* a suicide note."

The older lady's crumpled face brightened. "Honestly, Mary?"

"Honestly." Mary Lawson yawned loudly. "It's a dying note. There's a big difference."

"Oh no!" Delores resumed her wailing. "Queenie, there is no difference. In the end, there is no difference at *all*."

"Of course there's a difference, you dope. A suicide note is for when you don't want to live anymore. Very pedestrian really. I, on the other hand, have written a *dying* note—for I am dying of a broken heart." Mary feigned a Juliet swoon, laying a bejeweled hand across her bosom as she reinterred herself beneath the comforter.

All heads except Mary's suddenly popped up, throwing a collective nervous glance at the ward's door. The familiar rubber squeak of Nurse Bea's shoes striding down the corridor toward them sent the majority of the onlookers quickly back to their various duties.

"What is *this*?" Nurse Bea hissed as she approached the scene around Mary's bed, somewhat less than happy about being called away from her morning tea.

"Mary's written a *dying* note," the younger nurse whispered fretfully.

"A what?"

"A *dying* note, ma'am. And then she took to her bed and nothing I say seems able to get her back up."

"Oh, for God's sake!" Nurse Bea fumed, glaring over at the other nurse with uncompromising, slate-gray eyes. "Don't they teach you girls anything over at that nursing school? You'll not get far in here just using your please-and-thank-yous all day, I'll have you know."

"Get up!" she yelled, forcefully grabbing a handful of golden silk and peeling the blanket from Mary like a banana skin. "Good Lord, Miss Lawson! Where are your underthings?"

"I'll not wear them, you brute," Mary fumed, wrestling her quilt back from the startled nurse. "I want him to see me this way. When I'm dead—"

"Oh for goodness sake, Mary. You're not going to die. There's not a single thing wrong with you."

"Well, if there's not a single thing wrong with me—what am I doing in this wretched hospital then?"

"It's not *that* kind of hospital—"

"Oh, what would you know? You're just a worker lady here anyhow—"

"You—" Nurse Bea indicated to the slightly overwhelmed, younger nurse. "Don't just stand there like a dodo. Go get me an attendant. A big one. I'm warning you one more time, Mary Lawson. You get yourself out of that bed!"

"No, I'll not get out. Ever again. I'll lay here until I die. And then when they come to take me away, *he* will have to see me—just as I am."

"What are you babbling about? Who will have to see you?"

"Gerald."

"Who?"

"Dr. Gerald Isaac Davidson, ma'am," Delores cut in importantly.

"Now, why on God's green earth would you want Dr. Davidson to see you stark plum naked?"

"So he'll know what he's *missed*! That's why," choked Mary, as she wound the quilt even tighter around herself.

There were a few audible gasps and moans as the ward door crashed open again, Oswald and the young nurse barraging through it with a determined sense of purpose.

"This is your last chance," Nurse Bea warned. "You get yourself up out of that bed."

The golden silk mound remained motionless. Delores started to whimper.

Oswald and Nurse Jenny approached the bed. His breathing was heavy, winded from the exertion of climbing the ward stairs. The nurse inclined her head slightly away from Oswald as they stood together, awaiting orders. The man's breath was grotesque. His few remaining teeth rotten, at least one clearly abscessed.

"Miss Lawson is to be up, dressed, and waiting outside with the rest of the walking group by the time I finish my tea," Nurse Bea said pointedly, spinning on her heel and squeaking loudly back down the corridor.

"Oh, Queenie, please—" Delores started before Oswald glowered her mouth shut.

Contrary to the young nurse's previous suggestion, he did not wait to form a plan. Hurling himself on top of the bed, he grabbed at Mary's quilt, engaging her in a rough wrestling match as he breathed foul expletives into her face.

"Stop—please stop," wailed Delores. "You're hurting her." Heroically, she attempted to subdue Oswald's wildly waving, hairy arms. A stiff backhand to the mouth sent the older woman stumbling back over herself until she collapsed into a heap on the cold floor.

"See here, Mr. Oswald," Nurse Jenny ventured timidly. "I don't think—"

"What you don't think don't make no matter to me," he growled. "Now get making yourself useful here, and pry this fat heifer's hands free of these bedposts."

Cowering under his glare, the young nurse promptly forgot the authority her training had bestowed on her and acquiesced to his dark directive. Gently, but firmly, she attempted to pry Mary's hands from their place. Although young and able, she proved little match against Mary's surprising strength.

"Ah, get outta my gaw-damned way," Oswald spat. Grabbing Mary's hands forcefully, he yanked her violently up and down like a ragdoll, the back of her head cracking several times against the iron bed-frame before she finally released her grip.

"Quit now! Quit," she pleaded frantically. "Before you end up breaking it."

"I'll break every bone in your bloated body if you don't get the hell out of this bed—"

Struggling herself free of Oswald's sweaty body, Mary shuffled herself up to a half-sitting position, clutching possessively at her quilt. The quilt, which had been disordered and torn during the tussle, fell short of her, revealing the great heaving swell of her white bosom.

"Not for you!" she sniped at Oswald's leering eyes. "Nurse! Get this hog-humper off of me. Delores! Bring me my purple robe."

Swaddled tightly inside her mangled quilt, Mary maneuvered herself carefully from the bed, then waddled her way to the bathroom to change, accompanied by Delores and the perplexed nurse.

Oswald hovered just outside the door, overtly listening to the women's private functions, as he repeatedly hollered at them to ask what was taking so long.

Finally they re-emerged, Delores fretting over a stain on the purple robe, Nurse Jenny attempting to massage away a blazing headache from her temples, and Mary— regal and composed—again wrapped in all her false splendor.

≡ ≡ ≡

She descended the ward stairs slowly, expectantly. As if she were waiting for an uproar of exultation to rise up and greet her.

"So nice you could finally join us, Mary," said a manly-looking woman patient. "Not that we haven't already been waiting half the fuckin' day—"

"Language!" screeched Nurse Bea. "You see, Miss Lawson. You will not be making yourself any friends in here—keeping the other ladies waiting."

"That's their job," Mary droned dryly. "Waiting—is what ladies-in-waiting—*do*."

"Mary's the Queen," Delores rushed to explain.

"The *Queen!*" Nurse Bea spewed. "You're no queen, Mary Lawson. You're just a fat, spoiled little girl whose daddy doesn't want her to come home until she learns herself a thing or two."

Mary gazed elegantly off, past Nurse Bea and the walking group, over the cricket oval, and out toward the murky gray lake. Her face was composed. As if she stood all alone on top of a high mountain, caressed by a gentle breeze.

"You just go right ahead and try to ignore me, Mary Lawson. I've got plenty of ways to fix that. You understand?"

Again receiving no answer—or even the courtesy of a quick glance—Nurse Bea contained her outrage, funneling her frustrations into an industrious three-mile walk.

Fussing over the defiled hem of the purple robe, Delores firmly attached herself to Mary as the walking group started off. Before a hundred yards were stepped off, the collage of ladies had fallen into a bedraggled, marching order. Stubbornly, Mary held back, resisting the impulse of their synchronistic thumping. Such reluctance to join the group was unlike her. Usually playful—and highly energetic—she relished nothing more than usurping the lead nurse's position, detouring the dully cooperative ladies down alternate paths and through the deep denseness of the surrounding forest.

Today, she seemed to move forward only on account of some invisible cord binding her to the group. Her head hung low; rarely did she cast a glance at where they were going. Her eyes were gated, keeping private a turmoil all her own. Delores brightened as they crested a hill. Chipping away at a section of earth, several of the men patients were preparing the way for yet another sidewalk. Her wrinkled face scrunching into a smile, Delores grinned over at her morose queen. Mary always enjoyed an impromptu visit with the men. She was like an artesian well of flirtation, bubbling up and out of herself with spectacular ease. Today, she wandered straight on by, not even noticing their looks of concern and consternation.

"Oh, my poor Queenie. Are you feeling quite okay?" Delores asked, to which Mary did not reply.

Mary and Delores continued on in silence, straggling along behind the walking group, which seemed to have become infected by Mary's dispirited mood, having considerably slowed its pace.

Above them, the sky growled out a sudden spattering of rain, hastening them all forward a little quicker to seek refuge in the ladies' pavilion. Huddled in a circle, they trembled against the cold wind chucking itself up from the lake. Their eyes avoided contact, dusting around at nothing in particular, or down at their own feet, each one lost without the gaiety of Mary's jokes to carry them along. Quickly tiring of their abject company, Nurse Bea decided the group should push forward back to the wards, braving the inclement weather before the storm truly broke.

Impatiently shuttling the group down from the pavilion as a torrential rain began to fall, she attempted to order them into two rather scraggy lines to be led by herself and the junior nurse. Promptly losing control of one group, then the other, anarchy prevailed as several of the women sprinted off in a Mad Hatter's dash for the comparative comfort of the Cottages.

Fuming with outrage, Nurse Bea began chasing after the runaways until a manic yelping behind her pulled her to a stop. Shielding her eyes from the driving rain, she squinted back toward the lake. Running toward her was Delores, arms waving, mouth shrieking, the words inaudible, whipped away in a whorl of wind.

"Oh, whatever is it now?" she directed to herself, not for the first time severely regretting her career choice. "I can't hear a word you're saying, Delores. What—"

Then—with a shock that felt like a blow to the stomach—she saw beyond Delores and down to the lake. The group of men patients formed a loose cluster on the fore shore, the discarded spectacle of a purple robe lying at their feet. Beyond them, a splashing commotion of movement churned the already churning dark water.

"Oh, good mother of Mary!" the frustrated nurse seethed, as she started running across the sloppy ground, back toward the lake. She looked down at her new white shoes as she squished along. The oozing mud had completely obliterated them. Well. She knew just who was going to get them cleaned up again.

Desperate voices frightened her a little bit as she arrived—breathless—down to the drenched crew pacing about by the pavilion.

"Ah, nurse is here now. She'll get her out."

Nurse Bea watched, appalled, as a bobbing murmur of heads seemed to agree.

"Miss Lawson!" she hollered out into the turbulent storm. "Miss Mary Lawson—you just get yourself right back here this very minute."

The flailing of limbs and water that had become Mary swam on toward the distant horizon in a lake that looked like a sea. Evidently, she was not a particularly good swimmer—more of a regular spasmodic explosion of body parts—but she was managing to create a respectable distance between herself and those onshore just the same.

"Nope. Looks like you're going to have to go in and get her yourself."

"I'll not," stammered Nurse Bea, eyes roving frantically for someone who could help.

"And just why not?" bellowed Mr. Seymour, bushy eyebrows beaded with rain. "In my estimation, *that* would be your job, nurse. Would it not? Speak up now. I've not got all day."

"Doesn't matter if it's my job—"

"Oh, but it does! It most certainly does," the old barrister challenged, puffing his belly out dramatically. "And I think the jury would agree."

The dripping, frazzled nurse threw her hands up in despair as the group of men around her murmured themselves toward a consensus.

"Be quiet! All of you," she yelled. "I can't go after her. I don't know how to swim."

"Pity," replied Mr. Seymour. Taking out a stubby pencil and damp paper from the Bible he had tucked inside his jacket, he unsuccessfully attempted to jot down a note.

A quiet figure from the back of the group stepped forward, shovel still in hand.

"I'll go in and get her," Jakie said.

Nurse Bea felt almost able to kiss him. She looked out again at the still swimming Mary.

"Will you?"

"Well—I can give it a try," he replied, already stepping free of his rubber boots.

"Just a minute, Mr. Hewitt. Can you swim?"

Hesitating, he considered the question.

"Here now—" Nurse Bea said in exasperation. "I can't have you going after her if you're not a good swimmer—"

"No disrespect, ma'am," Jakie said. "But—in case you haven't noticed—neither is Mary."

The gaggle of men turned their attention back to the now tired—and less animated—splashing in the water, then collectively inclined their heads to agree.

"Well, well," piped Mr. Seymour as he made his way over to the pavilion to get free of the insistent rain. "Someone will have to do something pretty soon and it won't be me. I'm a busy man I'll have you know. A busy, busy man. And it looks to me like she's almost in over her head already!"

"*Almost* over her head—" Nurse Bea screeched incredulously. "*Almost?*"

Hats and heads—all drenched equally—turned to survey the water and the surrounding shoreline, nodding in unison.

"Why—" spat the ballistic nurse. "Why. Did. Someone. Not. Tell. Me? I thought she was long in over her head—"

"Oh, she'll get there, eventually." Mr. Seymour chuckled. "She's not much farther to go now, I reckon—"

"Mary Lawson!" the nurse screamed hoarsely across the murky black water. "I'm warning you now—"

"Objection!"

"Oh! You! Shut up! Just shut up the whole useless lot of you."

"Well...Jakie *did* offer to help—" Phillip pointed out.

"Help *what!*" Nurse Bea exclaimed, completely coming unraveled now. "Help me end up with two suicides on my hands?"

"Objection. Leading—"

A flurry of yelling up by the cricket oval diverted their attention. An excited group of patients and nurses hurried their way. They were followed by a burly attendant whom Delores had alerted to the cause. Beyond them, tripping over himself with agitation, his dripping umbrella popping up into the air with each step, was Dr. Davidson. He did not look pleased.

A hearty hurrah went up from the soggy group of men around her, and Nurse Bea turned to see them pointing out to the lake and clapping.

"Well, that's capital," Mr. Seymour said, thumping the railing of the pavilion with his Bible for good measure. "Just capital."

All eyes were fixed on Mary now as she paddled herself into the reverse direction and began to splash toward shore. Nurse Bea, along with Delores, sunk onto Mary's soaked purple robe and started to weep.

Oswald waded out to retrieve the exhausted Mary, hauling her ignobly from the water and depositing her like a pale, shivering jellyfish at the doctor's feet.

"What on *earth* are you trying to prove, Miss Lawson? Just what on *earth*?"

"I'm not trying to prove anything on *earth*," she contradicted without looking up. "Only that which is in heaven. And that—my darling husband—is my undying love for you."

"Don't be ridiculous—"

"You're right. Maybe it is ridiculous. Having such love for you, pookie, when you only have eyes for the new girl—"

Dr. Davidson's face flushed as an agreement of consternation murmured around him.

"Such madness, Mary! Hush up now, before you embarrass yourself any further."

She looked up at him longingly, her whole body shuddering from the cold, hot tears searing down her face.

"Embarrassed? Oh no, Gerald. I'm not in the least embarrassed—"

"Well, you damn well should be, Miss Lawson. You damn well should be. Can you even begin to imagine the scandal you would bring down on your family—and this institution—if you were to have drowned out there? Good god, Mary! What were you thinking?"

Aided by Jakie's hand, Mary struggled slowly to her feet. Her sand-soiled dress clung to her body, the long streams of her flattened hair hanging like seaweed from her trembling head. Standing as straight as the cold wind would allow, she stared Dr. Davidson directly in the eye.

"You *want* to know what I was thinking, Gerald? I was thinking it would be easier to drown than it would be to stay living and watch my husband be in love with another girl. And—when the weather gets warmer—I intend to come right back down here and do just that."

All eyes flickered between Dr. Davidson and the defiant Mary.

"Very well, Miss Lawson. Very well. If you're so terribly fond of the water—it'll be an ice bath and then the cold pack for you."

Visibly staggered under the threat of his words, it took her a moment to collect herself, a choir of horror singing out around her.

"You *can't*," she challenged back. "Daddy would never allow it."

"Daddy will never know."

"Ha! I'll tell him."

"And *I'll* tell him differently. Your word against mine, Mary. How far do you think that will take you?"

"The doctor has a valid argument there," Mr. Seymour offered from the pavilion. "A *very* valid argument."

"Well...well," fumbled Mary. "All these people here will back up my story." She tossed Dr. Davidson a haughty smirk as she gestured her hand around the witnessing party.

"*Patients*, Mary. Patients—not people. Patients much like yourself, who are incarcerated in this asylum with delusions of the mind. Do you really think your father will take their word over mine?"

"Ruddy good point!" Mr. Seymour exclaimed excitedly. "You simply can't get a reliable statement from a bunch of ninnies like us, Miss Lawson. You're doomed, I'm afraid.

Nurse! Take me back up to my office. I want to change into dry clothes before my lunch meeting."

"You wouldn't *dare*," Mary blustered back at Dr. Davidson, her voice breaking with a lack of conviction.

"Oh...hush now Queenie. Hush. You're not making things get any better—" Delores wavered frantically as Dr. Davidson's angry glare drove into Mary, his outer veneer of calm infiltrated by a furious rage visibly welling up inside. He looked over at the eagerly awaiting Oswald and nodded.

"This one is yours. Nurse Bea! Get the rest of these patients back up to their wards before we end up with a rash of pneumonia."

"Please, sir. Not my Queenie," Delores pleaded, throwing herself like an octopus around Dr. Davidson's feet. "Take me instead—"

"Get off of me, woman," he hissed, kicking out with his knee as he attempted to dislodge her. "Get off—or it will be an afternoon of ECT for you."

"Oh, good Lord!" the frantic Delores whimpered as she slid free from the doctor to attend her queen, who had collapsed heavily back to the ground. "Why do they persecute us so? Why—"

Ξ Ξ Ξ

When Mary Lawson next opened her eyes, she cursed the gift of sight that God had given her. She had been transferred to a tunnel room, the dim, flickering bulb, and her still-groggy mind slowly unveiling the space around her as she lay prone, strapped to some kind of bed. She felt crushed with exhaustion and fear as she struggled to remember what they had done to her. She recalled fragments of fragments. Snippets of conversation with the bossy nurse. A monstrous oaf of a man who had handled her roughly, grinning at her obvious terror. The humiliating and massive betrayal at the hands of her cherished Gerald. Nothing

else. The rest was gone. Thankfully so. But clearly, somehow they had maneuvered her back to Cottage Four and
down the stairs into the small oppressive treatment room.

Her other senses flowing back to her now, she realized she was trembling internally. She reached to find her
quilt. Her arm, her hand, her fingers, the whole of her body
remained motionless. Frightened, she attempted to lift her
head to reconnect herself by at least gaining a visual of her
unresponsive body parts. Her head would not move. Could
not move. Frantic, she searched down over herself with her
eyes. She was a great swaddled corpse. Mummified within
reams of icy, wet sheets.

Panic overtook her as she realized what they had done.
Cold packed. She'd overheard the whispered nightmares of
other patients who had endured the treatment. By their
remembered counsel, she knew she should try not to move.
That fighting against the sheets would only cause them
to tighten up further. But—try as she might—she simply
could not help herself. A dam of terror burst through her,
and she pressed out against the wrappings, which seemed
to have become an immovable tomb around her. She
heard—from a far distance—her own screaming. Her own
frenzied wailing as she struggled to free herself, feeling the
blackness descending again like a bucketful of thick pitch
as she was finally suffocated back into darkness.

☰ ☰ ☰

A bright stream of light eventually pulled her awake into
incredible pain. The wet sheets had dried, binding her
impossibly tight. Every fiber of her body ached for release.
Horrified, she became cognizant of an urgent, insistent
pressure demanding her to get up and empty her bursting
bladder. Tears rolled sideways off her face as she struggled
vainly to squeeze off the flow, hot pee trickling, then soak-
ing her immobilized inner thighs.

"Aw, ya filthy pig. You've gone done and pissed your-self," a voice growled right beside her, startling her free of her silent sobbing.

The bright light left her in sudden darkness as Oswald swung his flashlight up toward an abrasion of sound. Mary watched in immobilized terror as the brief light illumined a scruffy rat scurrying along the ceiling pipe. She moaned pitifully as a surge of adrenalin—meant to free her—was met with an unrelenting reminder of just how impossible it was for her to do just that. Emotionally collapsing, mor-tified to be lying wrapped up in her own urine, she again began to cry.

"*Please.* I've had quite enough now. Please call my daddy—tell him I want to come home."

Oswald snorted, returning the blinding light to her face.

"Your daddy don't want you to come home, princess—"

"Well...tell him I want to come home anyhow. I'm not having fun here anymore. Daddy said it would be fun."

Oswald's vicious laughter disrupted the empty quiet of the room. "Well, imagine that. Poor little Miss Lawson ain't having fun no more. Well, I got news for you, princess. This here's a gaw-damn nuthouse, not some poshy summer camp. It ain't supposed to be *fun*—"

"I'm *not* a princess, you peasant!" Mary exploded. "Now, go and phone my father—"

"Don't be ordering me around, you bloated cow!" he yelled back into her face, rapping his flashlight solidly against the side of her head.

"*Ow!* Don't hit me. Don't hit my noggin. It's very frag-ile, you know—you'll break it."

"Damn rights I'll break it. Break it right in half if you try ordering me around again. You got that?"

Mary nodded without movement.

"Please. Please, could you please just loosen the sheets a bit. *Please?* The pressure is unbearable—"

"Naw. I like you this way," he mumbled, taking the palm of his hand and sliding it up over the massive swell of her bosom. "That's what I like about you fat girls. Your big titties."

"Don't touch me—" Mary pleaded hopelessly, as he deadened the light, both hands now rummaging hard over her bosom as he half-mounted the bed and began grinding his groin into the side of her.

"No—please, no," she whispered as Oswald's huge head approached her own, his hot sloppy mouth eagerly sucking up a handful of her chin fat and masticating it wetly.

A wad of Mary's spit caught him just above the left eye, and he pulled back sharply. Flicking his flashlight back on, he wiped away the gob sliding down his face—then slapped Mary hard.

"So. That the way you want to play? Okay. I got more than one way to make you behave."

He reached into his pocket as Mary lay sobbing for mercy and pulled out the remains of a sandwich.

"Hungry, Mary? Been a long time since you had something to eat."

Mary said nothing, just lay defeated, praying for the darkness to descend upon her once again.

Oswald horked up a huge ball of spit and phlegm, spat it into his hand, then proceeded to slather it all across her face.

"Know who else is hungry, princess? That rat—that's who. Not much to eat down here in these tunnel rooms you know," he hissed as he crumbled the sandwich apart in his hands, then rubbed it roughly into the spit covering her.

"No! Please, no—" Mary blubbered up at the grinning leer of Oswald's impassive face. "Don't leave me like this. Please. I'll be a good girl now. I will. I'll do whatever they say—"

"Oh, I'll be sure to let them know that, Mary. The good doctor wants me to be sure to let him know when I feel you've responded well to the constraints of your therapy."

He shone the flashlight over her breasts and again kneaded them—painfully rough.

"And, I'm sure the doc will be *very* pleased to know that you're not having yourself so much fun here anymore... *princess*."

Looking down at his watch, he cursed foully, then spat into the corner behind him. Raking his watery eyes once more over Mary's chest, he turned and followed his flashlight back toward the door.

"Please!" she pleaded pitifully. "Please God, have mercy—"

She felt a swoop of musty air as he pulled the door open, then slammed it shut forcefully as he departed, again leaving her cloistered—an abject heap of misery—senses detaching from her rapidly in the vacuum of darkness. She began to lose touch with the ability to discern if she still lay firmly on a bed—or perhaps floated abstractedly—drifting within a sea of sewage. Her heart pounded relentlessly in her ears, thundering so forcefully it became all that she was. She ceased to be anything else. Just the steady rushing thump of her own wounded heart.

Panic alerted her to a presence in her gut. It wound around like an evil thing. A caustic tendril, moving up through her intestines—ignoring the mad beating of her heart—fixated on crawling up and out of her throat. Birthing its awful fear into the false night.

Whimpering for her darling, mistaken Gerald, she struggled to keep herself calm. Surely, he would not allow this. For herself or for any of his patients. It was merely a lover's quarrel. A silly threat gone wrong. Oswald was to blame. That brutal beast of a man. She would tell on him. Straightaway. She felt sure that once her Gerald realized the error of his ways—searched high and low for her—he would remorsefully beg for her forgiveness. And this hoped-for moment of his future anguished apology, she could see now. A vision as clear as a new-dawning day. His tentative kiss. The touch of his hand. The depth of his pain as he asked for her continued love. And of course, she *would* forgive him. She already had.

Sharply, her mind mutinied, offering her up a screen not of a sweet reconciliation, but rather vivid, lurid images of the watching rat. She squeezed her eyes shut against the vile tormenter but it continued on. That filthy rodent watching. Oswald's base hungering reflected in its beady eyes. Her breath stopped as an unmistakable, distinctive sound, scratched the air above her. Scraping little steps—small claws making their way along the ceiling pipe—closer and closer until they finally stopped, right above her head. Then the slow, cautious, sliding descent as they made their way down the wall beside her bed. Launching itself through the air, guided only by its quivering scent, the rat landed just above her, scrambling and scratching its way over her face as she boiled into a fit of screams.

"Go away! Go—" She gasped. "Please. Daddy. Oh, please, Daddy. I'll be a good girl now. I'll be a good little girl. I'll be anything you want me to be—"

Sobbing herself into a despair of silence, she focused every ounce of energy she had left, listening for the whereabouts of the rodent. It was not gone. She was sure about that. She could feel its greedy waiting. Its animalistic patience as it anticipated its eventual, morbid feast. Below her, a faint sound. Barely perceptible. Terrifying in its faintness. A rapid, eager crunching. The consumption of the crumbs that had fallen from the plate of her face.

Brutalized. Exhausted. She lay in complete submission to her fate, listening as the sounds came less and less often, the space between them growing longer and longer, as the starving creature cleared the floor of crumbs. Soon—she knew—it would expire all the easy offerings from below and then—emboldened by her weakness—it would again make an attempt for the more bountiful pickings still stuck to her skin. Utterly beyond hope, she was too tired to resist. Devoid of even the energy to issue a response, she waited in mute horror as she felt a mad scrambling tugging up the edge of her sheets and over her body. The scream would not come. Pressing her eyes shut once more, she welcomed the dark void of obliterating blackness that met her as the quick, jagged claws began to make their scurried way across her face.

Ξ Ξ Ξ

She awoke to something hard, pressing sharply into her clavicle. Beyond caring what fresh nightmare had arrived to greet her—she half-opened her eyes. She saw an apish hand, the bright glint of metal. A knife. No—not a knife—but scissors. An oversize pair of scissors being clumsily maneuvered, burrowing insistently into a narrow channel between the bulk of her bosom and the sheets.

A loud ripping sound filled the room as the taut fabric half-cut—half-tore beneath the scissor's sharp teeth.

"Thank you. Oh, thank you." She gasped with tangible relief as the center sheet split open suddenly from her neck down to her belly button, finally allowing her a full breath of air.

Oswald snickered as he stared down, fixated on her fully exposed, heaving breasts. Once more swept of hope, she blankly watched his hollow face. Floating away from her flaccid self, she meekly awaited whatever it was he was going to do.

His breath coming hard and irregular, he groped his rough meaty hands full of her, pinching and pulling the soft pink nipples until he finally succeeded in making her cry out in pain.

"Milking cows. Best job I ever had. Big, fat old Guern-seys. Just like you. No one could milk those gaw-damn tit-ties dry fast as me—"

Suddenly—the room was black. For a brief moment, Mary thought it had simply come for her again. But this blackness was different. Charged with a foreign, electric energy—a swift phantasm of unseen movement.

"What the—" Oswald cursed as he ripped his inter-rupted hands from Mary's chest, smashed on his flashlight and started toward the light switch.

He did not make it. Accosted by a storm of dark momen-tum—swirling around him as he flailed out—crashing into him, it bowled him over backward like a midnight tidal wave. Shaking his head, he scurried quickly to his knees grasping for the flashlight, which had been knocked free of his hand, rolling closer to Mary's bed. Something kicked his hand away just as his reaching fingers settled over it, then another stealth blow came from his other side, catch-ing him squarely upside the head. Propelled onto his feet, his arms swung wildly into the whirling blindness around him. The blows came again. One—two—three. Increasing in their intensity until they rained down over him like a waterfall of boulders.

Frozen with fear, Mary lay on the bed—eyes wide—watching the dance of shadows above her. She moaned qui-etly as Oswald's great bulk hit the wall behind her, then careened off the side of her bed, before collapsing heavily to the floor.

Her mind was a mess of conversations past. Patients' whisperings of demons and possessions. Of evil things lurking in the God-forsaken labyrinth of tunnels below. She hadn't believed such nonsense—had laughed arrogantly at their tales. She was not laughing now. The belief had mate-rialized around her. And the belief was so ghastly—that it was impossible for her to believe.

Ξ Ξ Ξ

When Mary Lawson once again awoke, the room around her was empty. Above her, the same meager light bulb flickered wearily, but valiantly. And yet, something had changed. She felt herself breathing, her lungs once again full and elastic, no longer bound by the encasement of sheets. She was naked but warm, tucked beneath the covering of a thick flannel blanket. The sheets, that oppressive, awful cage of fabric, flailed out below her, hanging limply from either side of the bed. They had been severed from the death grip they had held on her. Someone—or something—had shred them completely down the middle. She had no recollection of when that may have happened. All she knew was that she was no longer bound but that she was still alone. Alone and hidden below the hospital in a desperate room that had been visited by unspeakable horror.

Struggling to right herself, she slowly worked her body up to a sitting position. Her head felt woozy, the waves of nausea and inky blackness traveling through her. Waiting for it to pass, she anxiously perused the nightmarish room. It lay stark and bare, replete in its emptiness. The heavy wooden door was unlocked. Widely ajar. Gathering the warm blanket around her, she slipped off the bed onto her bare feet. The shock of the cold stone floor violated her senses, drawing back the memory of her abuse with such overwhelming intensity that her body almost collapsed her to her knees.

Whispering encouragement, she riveted herself together, forcing one foot and then the other to begin the journey toward the door. She gained the frame of it, then hesitated. The tunnel was a dark void. Behind her, the dim light bulb seemed like a source of infinite comfort. Panic welled in her throat as she fought to move beyond its illumined grace. She had to be strong. Gerald needed to know what was happening in the bowels of his beloved hospital. He would be sure to put a stop to such things immediately. She knew there was only one way out of the wretched basement rooms and that was to enter the blackness, following the intestinal contours of the tunnel until she eventually came upon a stairway leading upward. Leaning against the doorway in the hollow of a shadow, she rationalized with her non-rational mind. Scarcely able to breathe, she strained to listen into the darkness deeper than night. No sounds came to her, save the creaks and groans of the old building itself. Perhaps they were all dead. All of those above her—gone. Or, perhaps they had never even existed. Elements of her own fantasy. She could not bear the thought. She needed them to be real. All of them. For the world to hold gaiety, laughter—a place for her to know love. Crippling loneliness edged her feet forward, through her terror, toward a small glimmer of hope that someone—a special someone—would be relieved to see her again. Bravely, she stepped beyond the edge of light into the dark abyss.

Curiously, she felt at once less scared, more empowered the moment she let go of the circle of light. The realization occurred in her that the light had merely held her there, tethered to that miserable room by its false promise of safety. She moved forward quicker now, patting out the invisible floor and walls, trusting her senses to show her the way toward a portal that would elevate her back into the world above. Stretching forward like an accordion, she explored the rough-hewn brick of the corridor with searching fingers and toes, occasionally pulling back in raw disgust as they encountered something unrecognizable.

Eventually, the sequence of the tunnel became familiar to her: a long expanse of bare brick wall, an abrupt interruption of elevated doorframe, and then the door itself. Beyond that, another expanse of bare brick. Another doorframe. Room after mysterious room, passing by just beyond her searching hands. She could not allow herself to wonder what went on in them. Once, the stolid walls yielded a mutation beneath her touch. She hesitated, puzzled by the thick curve of leather cuffs, the stub of sturdy chain bolting them to the wall. Concluding that they must be some sort of animal collar, the abrupt epiphany of her error startled her forward again.

She began to plead that a stairway to heaven would open up. That a narrow ladder of light would descend down to her and call her back to the land of the living. It was all far, far more than she could endure. It felt like eons since she had last eaten. Flashes of a horrendous nightmare drove relentlessly into her. And yet, deep within, a Mary no one knew whispered to her to find her way free.

Her hand slid yet again over what now seemed like a ubiquitous doorframe. Anxiety praying on her over-whelmed nerves, she wondered hysterically if she had been wandering futilely—going in circles all along. Drained by even the thought of such a possibility, her head sagged, resting against the metal door. Yielding beneath her, it opened and she drew back, breathless.

It silently swung half-open, partially revealing the shadowy cavern of a large room. Mesmerized by the emotional warmth wavering from a candle's glow, she remained still, squinting into the room as her eyes accustomed themselves to the sudden light.

The room was not empty, as she had first assumed, but rather occupied by a large figure reclining on a small bed. Not able to ascertain whether she should flee or ask for help, she did neither. Frozen in indecision, she stood silent and merely watched. When her vision adapted to the inconsistent light, the shadows slowly separated the large figure on the bed into two smaller ones. The taller one reclined, back supported against the wall behind it, the other one held—childlike—across its lap. The small figure curled around over itself as if it were asleep. A gentle hand petted over long, silken strands of hair, which floated like

gossamer in the dreamy yellow light. Slow, loving—caressing strokes—the fingers trailing from the hair to lightly
trace over the delicate angles of the supine face.

Mary stood invisible. Staggered by the sacred scene
of such unrestrained, candid love. Holding the small body
with cherished adoration, the petite head was lolled carefully backward, an intimate kiss received on the unresponsive lips.

"Oh, Gerald...my darling Gerald—" Mary cried out
silently before vanishing again back into the darkness.

CHAPTER 15

By the time the maintenance man found her the next morning, Mary Lawson had degenerated into a blackened, babbling mess, hiding in the furnace room behind the coal chute. Laying a quick shame into an audience of gawking eyes, Nurse Mildred firmly ushered the still-distraught girl up out of the tunnel room and into a warm cleansing shower in Cottage Four.

"There, there, Mary. Do calm yourself," she reprimanded gently as Mary's emotions continually crested, then collapsed over themselves in waves of despair. "Whatever were you doing...trying to drown yourself in the first place?"

"Gerald...he...didn't mean...couldn't move...breathe..." She sobbed as Nurse Mildred slipped her into a fresh robe. "Barn boy milked...like...a cow..."

"Shoosh. Shoosh now, Mary."

"It came down from the ceiling—"

"What came down from the ceiling?" Nurse Mildred asked, checking her watch. It would be time soon enough for morning meds to be issued.

"The rat—"

"A rat?"

Mary nodded, her expression frozen in the memory.

"It ate my face—"

"Oh! Mary! Don't be so absurd. Your face is just fine."

"And then...the demon came...fighting...and I ran. I ran...and then...no, oh no...I can't bear it. I can't—"

"Can't bear what, girl? You're not making a stitch of sense."

"He kissed her, Nurse Mildred. He held her in his arms...and he kissed her."

Putting her own arm around Mary's bowed, shaking shoulders, the nurse slowly steered the sobbing girl back down the corridor.

"Hm-hmm...who kissed who, Mary?" she asked absently as she pulled the newly mended, golden silk quilt back, patted up the pillow, and settled Mary onto her bed.

"Gerald did," Mary whispered. "He kissed her. The new girl. She was sleeping...and he kissed her. I got lost in the tunnel...but I saw—"

Nurse Mildred pulled back fiercely, straightening as she closely studied Mary's trembling face. Finally, she shook her head resolutely. Grabbing Mary's compliant arm out from under the covers, she efficiently prepared to administer her a calming shot.

"There, there child. Don't fret yourself so. Not a bit of it is real, dear. Not a bit. You've just gone and made it all up in your silly little head."

Ξ Ξ Ξ

They didn't find Oswald until quite some time later. But then, no one had even known he was missing. He'd had the weekend off, and when he didn't show up Monday morning, everyone just assumed that he'd missed his shift—again. When they finally did stumble across him—shackled to the wall, bound and gagged in the remotest reaches of the far tunnel—he was just a quivering shadow of his cocky former self. The attendant Don had been quickly summoned, arriving with a pocketful of old keys, hoping one of them would still unlock the rusty chain shackles.

They brought Oswald into the dining hall just as the patients were lining up for their noon meal. Pushing his way through the line, he eyed the men with suspicious contempt. Waving away the plate of hash Phillip offered him, he poured himself a mug of strong black coffee, then made his way back over to the table where Don sat.

"Three of them for sure. Probably even four—"

Phillip's hands worked sluggishly over the food as the parade of men slowed down, each one straining to catch a word or two, which might explain the nasty attendant's battered face.

"Whatcha doing down there anyhow?" Don asked innocently. "I thought you worked the early shift on Friday."

Oswald spilled his coffee, burning his lip as he tried to drink too fast.

"Ah...fuck it! Did work the early shift. Went back down to make sure that fat girl was doing all right."

"You mean Miss Law—"

"Jumped me from behind. Shackled me up so I couldn't go after them, the crazy bastards."

"Patients? You sure it was patients, Oswald—"

"Patients—or the gaw-damn devil, Don. Take your pick—"

Jakie stepped forward in the line, eyes averted to the floor as Phillip playfully pushed a plate of hash toward him, then whisked it away again. Quickly grabbing the edge of the plate as Phillip teased it his way again, Jakie looked up, catching the grinning man's eye.

"Bet it was a devil," Phillip whispered. "Probably a black one. Right, Jakie?" he giggled as he fluttered his eyelashes, stroking a delicate touch across the top of Jakie's fisted knuckles.

Snapping his hand away, Jakie buried it deep in his trouser pocket. He fired Phillip a steely glare.

"Glass of something bubbly then?" Phillip grinned as Jakie turned and stormed toward the dining hall's door.

He bolted down the stairs and away from Cottage Five. He moved with an uncharacteristic quickness, so perturbed that he momentarily forgot to enact his habitual limp. Gathering himself back together as he crossed over toward the cricket oval, he slowed his gait and unsteadied his countenance.

The stone bench beneath the large maple sat empty, and he was glad for it. He needed to be alone. To be alone and sort out the pieces of what had happened to him. He approached the bench and wearily lowered himself onto it. His eyes roved off over the lake, resting on the gray horizon that formed the south wall of his world. Both hands remained firmly entrenched deep within his pockets.

Closing his eyes, he offered the sun his face, hoping its illuminating rays would somehow infiltrate the cobwebs and corners of his mind. Help him see more clearly the faded sketches of memories from the life he'd left behind.

Slowly, he withdrew his hands from his pockets and rested them on his lap. They were bruised—bashed. It was evident they had been bleeding. The accusing sight of them frightened him. This he could not pretend away. Could not deny their existence with a convenient mental fog. The fog was thinning anyway. He *knew* he had been the one lurking like a nightshade in the tunnel corridor. Waiting for an opportune moment to surprise the unsuspecting Oswald. Knew that he had flown into a fury, knocking the big man to the ground, punishing him with a flurry of expertly executed blows. All *that* he knew. What he did not know— what still escaped him—was *how* he had done it. How had he been able to so easily incapacitate that brute of a man? Where within him had those finely enhanced skills—skills that made weapons out of his own hands—originated?

Clearly, the time had come. The time to open the doors into himself and investigate. Allow all the unallowable questions to finally have their day. Who was he? Beyond the cartoon caricature he had allowed to emerge here— in the asylum—where such notions covered over a multitude of unknowns and kept him safe. Safe from what—or whom—he truly did not know. But he had a feeling that the things he most had to fear were the memories frozen deep within himself.

Sighing, he tugged the sleeve of his jacket up to reveal the tattoo. He gazed down at the black lettering. The names of two countries: one standing vertical, the other etched like the top of a *T* resting above it. Resentment arose in him as he studied the image. It unnerved him a little, having the meaningless emblem embroidered into his arm. It was like looking into a mirror, only to find yourself facing a stranger. He'd seen the distinctive arrowhead design before. Many times. In fact, he'd filled his life with replicas of the mysterious likeness, etching it onto the rocks and walls of his cave, imprinting it deep into the logs and planks of his cemetery home, carving it into the bone handle of the peculiar, double-edged knife he had forged for himself. Yes, the emblem was a familiar—almost intricate—part of his every day. And yet, he had no idea as to its significance. Or why it boldly defaced his muscular forearm.

Letting his sleeve slip back down, he half-turned and stared back at the high, crested peak of Cottage Five. Its attic—he knew—possibly held some of the answers he was silently seeking. Whether it would yield up those treasures still remained to be seen. But, he thought it might be worth a try. Years earlier, he had heard it mentioned that he'd also arrived with a suitcase—a drunkard dragged from the creek—clutching onto his few belongings, as if his very life depended on it. It was only a story he'd once been told. He had no idea if there was even any truth to it. But, in the search back into himself—it was all he really had to go on.

CHAPTER 16

Everything sensible was still asleep when Jakie slipped away from his cabin that night. Even the little red fox was not there to greet him, burrowed contentedly around her pups, deep within the slumber of her den. He smiled as he thought of her.

The moon held her haughty head high. A bright cascade of light tumbled a path across the cemetery, but Jakie steered clear of it, preferring the anonymity of the tree's shadows. Invisibly approaching the back wall of Cottage Four, he was seized motionless by a spasm of trepidation. The prospect of getting caught did not concern him. He'd freely roamed the institution right from the time he was first incarcerated, no one ever discovering him during his nocturnal jaunts. The poison bead of trepidation arose solely from what he was about to do. An exploration into the attic may yield an exploration into himself. It was not yet something he was convinced he was ready to do.

Strangely, a sense of duty overrode his wavering sense of desire, and he pressed forward, jimmying loose the door of the coal chute and quietly prying it open. Untying the burlap potato sacks from around his waist, he stepped into one, pulling the other one up and over to cover his head. Rolling into a ball, he disappeared down the waiting mouth of the chute. He came to a stop on top of a lumpy mountain of coal. Kicking free of the soiled burlap sacks, he edged them off into a far corner, then slipped like a shade into the grim maze of tunnels.

Following the map superimposed on his mind, he easily connected his sightless way over to the basement door
leading up to Cottage Five. When he'd first been committed
to the asylum—in the months before they had determined
him a harmless moron with amnesia—Cottage Five had
been his home. Several times there had been talk of moving him into one of the more appropriate wards, but busy-
ness and a shortage of beds had always waylaid such good
intentions, and he had remained housed with the severely
insane. His hope was that—if indeed he had arrived with
some semblance of a connection with his past—then perhaps he would find it here. Stuffed away in the attic, items
and mementos deemed useless by anyone else but for
him, in the long search back for his past memories, possibly providing triggers of remembrance that could prove
invaluable.

He entered the stairwell uber-slowly, the old building
set to complain over every step. Slowing his movements
and breathing down even further, he floated into an ethereal space deep within himself, assuming now the feather
touch of the cat—effortless and undetectable. Continuing
to ascend the stairs like a thin breeze, he moved through
but remained disconnected from all that surrounded him.
For a time, the self of him simply disappeared into this
space, floating higher and higher through the building, his
encasement of bones dutifully following along behind.

Finally, the top floor approached him and beyond it a
narrow passageway of rough steps leading up to the attic.
The entrance was blocked by a paneled door. Pulling a long,
slim metal tool from a seam sewn into the lower inside leg
of his jeans, Jakie prepared to pick open the lock. To his
surprise, the knob turned effortlessly in his hand.

Pushing the door open, he stepped into a wide swath
of moonlight peering in through a high transom window.
Before him stretched row after row after row of sturdy
lumber shelves. Stacked haphazardly upon them were

hundreds of suitcases, boxes, crates, each one of them a forgotten time capsule of the pre-asylum lives lived by the patients below.

The moon warned down at him with her bright light. It was not too late. He could still turn around, wind himself back down the stairs, disappear back into sleep inside his cemetery home. He closed his eyes and tried to force her free from his mind. This was not easy for him. Not here. Not surrounded by the promise of these lost ghosts. Her voice had grown too loud—he had ventured too close.

Opening his eyes again, he surveyed the space surrounding him, accustoming himself to the sounds of the old building's breathing. The fir-timbered floor beneath him was littered with droppings. Bat or rat, it was impossible to tell in the melancholy gloom, but he suspected it was a mixture of both.

Unhooking his flashlight from the thin cord around his neck, he pressed it on, shielding its tattletale light with his cupped hand. Reverently, he guided its cool beam over the stacks of luggage and belongings. One, a most rudimentary case, had a jumble of baling wire in place of a handle. He flipped it open. Empty save for reams of rope, and what appeared to be a half-deck of cards. One could only guess what sort of voyage they had been packed for. He closed it up again quickly. Some of the luggage had names—identifying their owners—boldly printed across their fronts. Others did not. Many of the names were familiar to him. Those he had known, intermingled with for a time, or made a concerted effort to avoid. Occasionally, he had received notice that one or the other of them had passed away. Then, he had busied himself with the digging of their graves, the names sometimes transposed from the hope of a transient suitcase, to the permanent desolation of a meager wooden cross marked only by an anonymous number.

He shifted his attention down toward the floor. A modest suitcase, black with silver hinges, lay crookedly at his feet. Its lid was ajar, random contents spilling out from it. Sinking into a low crouch, he opened the lid up completely and looked inside. Several delicate, embroidered lace doilies—one half-finished. A dainty flowered tea cup, a minuscule chip out of its florentine handle. A tea towel, clean and starched. A hosiery mending kit marking a page in a leather-bound book on anatomy. The crackled and faded photograph of a large family—none of them smiling. And, secured by two elastics sewn onto the inside of the lid, a pretty, ivory-handled hairbrush, its soft bristles still wound full with long strands of amber-brown hair.

Jakie searched across the front of the suitcase, eventually locating a barely readable name tag. Mrs. John Mason. He looked back at the photograph with a growing sense of sadness. Anna stood proudly at the helm of her family. A beautiful, if somewhat exhausted-looking young woman. Her hair, woven into a thick braid, wound its way over one shoulder, hanging down just past her waist. She wore a gaily flowered sweater over a simple dress, her arms full of blankets, which presumably held a small baby. Jakie moved the flashlight closer over the picture, inspecting with interest the sweater Anna wore. He could clearly understand now why she had become so furious at the dance when she saw the sweater the young girl had been wearing. It would have been easy for anyone to have mistaken the sweaters to be one and the same.

A glint of silver caught his eye as he edged the suitcase away from the shelves. A petite, beaded purse lay open and empty on the floor behind it. Scattered around lay an assortment of mundane items. Evidently, someone had rifled through the suitcase, presumably looking for something of value, their feral looting either interrupted, or their conscience simply not concerned with the prospect of being caught. Slowly gleaming his flashlight over the walls of luggage surrounding him, Jakie suspected most of them had probably been searched through as well.

The thought angered him. Immensely. Forcing himself to remain on his knees, he drew deep draughts of air into his lungs, applying his deliberate breathing like a soothing balm over the hot rage awakened within him. Never before since he'd been put into the asylum could he remember feeling so swept up by his emotions. Considering this, he wondered if he too had *flattened* over the years—the expression used by staff to identify those patients whose emotions had tampered down to a barely flickering pilot light. Those who had turned inward, becoming adrift in a sea of lost hope.

He had never thought of himself this way—flattened. Detached from his own life cord. Now, after encountering the seismic jolt of the beautiful, delicate girl interrupting his life, he was not so sure that the label might not have been apt. She had effortlessly infused color into the monochrome landscape of his world. Suddenly, he felt, spoke, and thought in color; everything was imbued with a new sense of purpose. It was as if her mere presence in the asylum had completed the circuitry of his soul.

Calmer now, he replaced the items back into Anna's suitcase and placed it high up on the shelf. Turning, he made his way softly toward the window, his eyes and fingers tracing over the fronts of suitcases and boxes, searching out names he knew, apprehensive and a little fearful of discovering his own. The cavernous room wore a solemn hush as he moved through it. A graveyard of lives. Each one of the containers a small casket bearing the remains of lives lived—left—but never completely forgotten. Many of the owners of those lives were now interred here, outside in the asylum cemetery—people twice dead.

He chased the morbid corpse of thought from his mind and along with it the taunting choir of voices rising up to join in. He realized that he had to be vigilant. Vigilant in this battle for his mind. It seemed strange to him now that in some ways he had so readily accepted the ill-fitting jacket of insanity the staff had insisted he wear. Although, he had to admit, the frugal comfort of having something to identify himself with had felt like a warmer companion than existing in the complete cold void that denied him any earthly connection at all.

His eyes and fingers continued to slip over the named and nameless suitcases, trunks, and boxes, touching briefly on several, then letting go as he continued searching for the one he was looking for. Finally, they came to rest on the broken-down remnant of a cardboard box. Written in a flawless cursive across its side was Myrtle's name.

Opening up what remained of the lid, Jakie glanced down at the contents, then awkwardly looked away. He had not expected this. This deep emotional wrenching as he encountered for the first time evidence of the older woman's pre-institutional self. Had it not been for the promise he'd made to try and recover her much needed dentures— he would have gladly resealed the box right then and placed it back on the shelf.

Forcing his eyes to once again probe its contents, a Myrtle he'd never known—nor could he have even imagined ever existed—began to emerge. Several small, elegant books of poetry rested haphazardly interspersed among a jumble of loose photographs. Picnics and travels. Weddings and christenings. A handmade doll—half-stuffed. Two serviette rings—well tarnished, and a stained and scorched purple tea cozy.

A tidy rectangle of postcards, tightly secured with a red velvet ribbon reposed off to one side. The top one displayed a pretty scene. Pastoral with spring blossoms. Swept up in a moment of curiosity, Jakie turned the stack over and quickly scanned the beautifully penned message on the underside.

The message was addressed *To My Beloved*, the eloquent words that followed along underneath an outpouring of such unbridled profound desire that Jakie blushed to read them. Fascinated, he struggled against his own shame, loosening the red velvet ribbon and letting the remaining postcards fall free. One by one he turned them over. None of them bore an address, nor the name of a recipient. Undated, unstamped—each one an eternal silent cry of unrequited love.

Moving with the type of slow reverence usually reserved for church, Jakie gathered the postcards back up and reaffirmed the role of the red velvet tie. Clearing a pile of loose cotton hankies from a corner of the box, he settled the tight rectangular pile beneath them. Aware again that the time was passing him quickly by, he rummaged loosely through the remaining belongings. Myrtle's dentures did not appear to be among them. Almost ready to concede that Nurse Mildred was correct and that the dentures had simply never found their way into the asylum in the first place, he hesitated as a small ceramic ornament caught his notice. It was oriental in design, the round bottom topped by a fat saggy little man, half-naked and laughing like all of life was some sort of splendid joke. Jakie had never seen anything like it before. He didn't much care for it. Eyeing the fat little man's protruding stomach, Jakie allowed himself to follow a hunch brewing in his own gut. Reaching into the box, he squeezed the laughing head between his thumb and forefinger, tipping open the top of the container. There, smiling up in a grimacing greeting, were Myrtle's false teeth. Disconcerted by their grinning entrance into his dark space, Jakie snapped the lid back down, scooped the container up, and suffocated it into his jacket pocket.

Happy with his slightly gruesome find, he was preparing to reclose the cardboard box when one of the sepia photographs found its way into his hand. Shining the yellow beam of the flashlight over it, he closely inspected the figure forever held there. A commandingly confident woman—handsome rather than beautiful.

Clearly, the facial features belonged to a much younger Myrtle. And yet—as much as he tried—it was simply impossible to string a bead between this forward-reaching image and the fitful, fearful, humped and bumped, jabbering mess that Myrtle had become. A woman reviled even by the other patients. An outcast among outcasts. Ostracized from the group because of her outlandish tendency—complained about so publicly by the other women patients—of defecating freely on top of their beds. Shaking his head slowly, Jakie put the photograph back into the box.

A deep blue steamer trunk over by the wall drew his attention, and he stepped over to examine it. Larger than most of the boxes and suitcases, it had been pushed back into the dark corner, out of the way. Its black straps were unbuckled, hanging down like limp arms. Jakie eyed the brass lock face centered in the sturdy lid. It was a well-made lock, stamped by its maker, expensive and, Jakie knew, not easy to pick.

Running his hands over the contours of the trunk, he admired its superior craftsmanship. It bore a myriad of colorful, exotic labels, each one proclaiming with gay visibility the many locations the trunk had once traveled to. Constantinople. Marrakech. Lisbon. Paris. Jakie's curiosity grew as he continued to peruse the elegant piece of luggage, inspecting its back and sides, discovering a virtual globe of place names, some that he recognized and others that he did not.

He knelt back to the floor. Whoever had been the owner of the trunk had certainly led an adventurous, well-traveled life. How had they ever ended up here? How was such a thing even possible? That someone with such wanderlust of spirit and evidently the means to support it, could have ever found his or her seeking cut short, tapped down and compressed into the tiny cubicle of asylum life.

The impossibility of it haunted around his mind as he sifted through a list of names and faces, trying to grasp out one that could possibly bridge the gap. None were forth-coming. He considered whether the owner of the suitcase might have become so deformed by insanity and asylum life that he or she might be beyond recognition, even to his or her former self. Or perhaps—more agreeably—whether the viral piece of luggage had merely once belonged to a patient whom Jakie had never met; someone long dead and forgotten. This thought was just beginning to mollify him when a thin silver script, etched into the base of the lock, called to his eye.

Glancing his flashlight across the letters, a name appeared with abrupt suddenness. J. K. Hewitt. A disbe-lief of air expelled itself from his lungs as he physically recoiled. Scrambling backward away from the trunk, he sat down heavily on the floor, his back supported by the timbered wall as he stared over at the illumined, cursive name. He studied the whole trunk through different eyes now, his mind aflame with questions. What secrets might it contain? And if it did contain secrets—did he truly want to know them? Even though it boldly proclaimed his own name, the blue box remained a stranger to him. Its procla-mations of travel and privilege were as foreign to Jakie as some of the unfamiliar label names that announced where it had once visited. Closing his tired eyes, he tried to coax forward a thin trail of remembrance between himself and the austere, worldly trunk.

Eons of visions streamed by him, but he couldn't dis-cern if they were fragments of fractured memories or just his own frantic attempt to create a semblance of personal history. Uncomfortable swirling in the confusion of his mind, he opened his eyes again. The sturdy steamer trunk stared back at him expectantly. This finely crafted strang-er's luggage that unapologetically bore his own name. The whole event rattled him in a way few things had.

Faced now with the sudden possibility that he might finally be able to access some clues about his former self, he hesitated. Did he really *want* to know? Here—in his asylum life that the girl had become a part of—he had found a type of contentment, a modicum of happiness. Obviously, his former life—for all of its veneer of pomp and elegance—had not ended well. Had ended here, a broken man, devoid of memory, eking out his days in the morose drudgery of asylum life, digging the graves of his more fortunate friends.

He tried again to pull himself back together. He was anxious to glean any tiny bit of information. Anything that might help him to discern how much more he may want to know. His mind remained shut. His memories locked up as tight as the suitcase holding his tangible former remains. He lingered for a moment, hovering in indecision, pondering the complexities of his mind. How it was able to just steal away every remembrance of his former life, locking it away in a room so deeply buried he could not hope to find it. A crypt of memories held within him, yet denying him access. A room without windows or—as far as he could tell—even a door.

A whole lifetime neatly absorbed and sealed away. Every moment still there, hidden within his psyche. Every love. Every loss. A multitude of materials. The building blocks that form a man. His essence. Each lost moment eternally repeating. Just beyond his conscious awareness. The realization tore at him. He knew the memories were still there. He always had. All of them. He felt them like night shadows of buried shades moving restlessly just beyond his grasp. He could not even begin to fathom why they had been taken from him. But he suspected the contents of this unfamiliar luggage, so surprisingly bearing his own name, might serve him as a means to begin bringing them forward once again.

Taking a deep breath of musty air, he settled his nerves, then moved back in front of the distinctive blue trunk. Again extracting the long, hooked piece of metal from its hiding place in the seam of his pants, he guided it quickly and efficiently into the brass lock. The lock released its hold so easily that were it not for the telltale click of the tumblers falling into place, Jakie would have wondered if it had actually been locked at all.

He stopped and studied his hands with an acute sense of bewilderment. Picking locks was but only one of the many skills that seemed to come to them so naturally. He'd never really given their effortless abilities much thought before. Now, his mind was raging with all kinds of possibilities. Had he been a thief? A bank robber who'd taken a knock to the head, forgetting his own life and waking up here in the asylum—a just purgatory worthy of his own sins? But, if that were so, what of his seemingly innate knowledge of wilderness survival? Who had taught him to burrow down deep into the snow, curling around himself like a dog atop a mattress of spongy pine boughs? Or how to discern the difference between a mushroom that could heal a heart from the one that would effectively silence it? What of the tattoo that mocked his ignorance? The old wounds and scars that littered his body? And Coyote? Was he from the forgotten past, or only a figment of the disturbed present? The questions swirled around him relentlessly. A cloud of unknown accusations, all pointing in the same direction. Who was Jakie Hewitt? Beyond and before this façade of self he had accepted for himself here in the asylum? For, if he indeed was the owner of this piece of well-traveled luggage—as the scripted name proclaimed—then the Jakie Hewitt that he had allowed himself to become bore absolutely no shadow of resemblance to his illustrious former self.

He pulled in another deep breath of stagnant air, and with no small degree of apprehension, he began to edge the big trunk open. He was greeted by the scent of a heavy perfume, a plethora of compartments, and several smallish drawers. The inside of the lid was upholstered with dramatic navy-and-gold striped silk, a little wooden dowel fitted across it, presumably to hang fancy wear.

None of it looked particularly familiar and Jakie felt disappointed. Feeling like an intruder, he picked a drawer at random and slid it open. It held few contents. A couple of scarves, a belt, a pair of butter-soft tan gloves. Everything intricately folded and neatly tucked away. Jakie eased back, then gently rooted among the items. None of them made any sense. More rapidly now, he began to pull the remaining drawers open, searching with desperate abandon. Hankies, perfume bottles, hairpins, a tiny diary— empty, soft lace underthings, a garter belt, and three sets of seamed silk stockings. Aghast, he tore open a larger bottom drawer. It was full of carefully folded clothing. *Women's* clothing.

A horrifying thought shuddered through him. Had he been like Phillip, whose proclivity for stealing the female patients' clothes was well known? Shaking his head wildly, he looked again at the delicates then down at his own body. He breathed a sigh of relief. Even if he had been a size or two smaller, there was absolutely no way the petite garments would have ever fit him.

Swinging the lid back toward him, he reshone his flashlight at the name. It responded as before. J.K. Hewitt. Dropping his head into his hands, he rubbed his eyes. He felt tricked. Confused. Like he'd been given an equation without a sum. Absently, he pressed down with his hands on top of the stack of cool blouses. Something hard beneath them refused to yield. Slowly, he edged up the corner of the fabric to reveal the gilt frame of an old black and white photograph.

He pulled it free, examining the immortalized faces of a group of sternly posed ladies. One of the faces looked vaguely familiar. Whether the familiarity arose from his memory or just because the face may have born a similarity to someone else he'd once encountered, he had no way of knowing. Flipping the frame over, he found a handwritten caption fastened to its back. Three rows of names—presumably corresponding to the ladies in the photo. Some sort of women's club. Jakie scanned over the names. One jumped out at him. Jacqueline K. Hewitt.

Emitting a low whistle, Jakie sank back down against the wall, his eyes already searching out the lady whose position would line up with the name. And indeed, when he found her, she was the woman with the slightly familiar face. Feeling a trace of optimism, he snapped the photograph over and rechecked the name. There was no mistake. He shone his flashlight back over to the silver name plate. J. K. Hewitt. He laughed a little, shaking his head with amazement. The suitcase did not belong to him at all. It was *hers*. Jacqueline K. Hewitt. Whoever *she* was. Had she been his mother? Or his wife? And why had he been found clutching onto her belongings in the first place?

For the first time in years, Jakie wished for a drink. He'd hoped against hope that his nocturnal searching would unveil some answers about his vanished past. Instead, it had stirred up a virtual slough of more unanswered questions. And then—suddenly—something significant occurred to him. The steamer trunk had never been opened since his nefarious arrival in the asylum. The structure and quality of the lock would have assured that. Deposited into the admitting staffs' busy hands, they would have had to discern what little they could about him without the benefit of prior paperwork or even a functioning memory. Evidently, his name had been carelessly transposed from the initials on the lock face. J. K. Hewitt conveniently becoming none other than his new self—Jakie Hewitt. He did not know if he wanted to laugh or to cry.

Rather than having regained some clarity about himself, he had only succeeded in erasing his identity further. Now, along with his former memories, even his name had disappeared. *Well, too damn bad*, he thought. He wasn't going to give the name back. At least not until he'd found himself a new one. He glanced up at the high window above him. Dawn was beginning to blush the night awake. He had little time and even less hope, but he was determined to at least find a glimmer of explanation to help justify having had the steamer trunk with him when they pulled him out of the creek. If, as he now suspected, he was not J. K. Hewitt—then what was his tie back to this woman who apparently was? A lover? A brother? Or had she simply been some innocent he'd brutally murdered and then stolen away with her belongings? In the great vast void of his existence, anything seemed possible.

He directed his hands back under the clothing in the large drawer, searching again for any elusive, covered clue. A strange sense overwhelmed him as his fingers began to travel along its edges and bottom, seemingly guided of their own accord. Beneath them emerged an unusual, hard ridge. Without knowing how, he knew exactly what it was. Jakie Hewitt grinned.

Ξ Ξ Ξ

He pressed down on the bottom of the drawer, then slid it forward a minuscule movement. He was rewarded with a satisfying release that he had somehow expected. Expelling the pretty blouses almost joyfully onto the dusty attic floor, he began to work with a certain fluid familiarity, easing the bottom of the drawer through an intricate series of motions until it gave way. Suddenly, the whole piece lifted up into his hands, the narrow, concealed false bottom of the steamer trunk revealed.

Jakie sat back on his heels, emitting a soft slow whistle of disbelief. Attached securely to the trunk's actual bottom were several shockingly unfeminine items. A small tin cup—well used. A severely battered silver flask. Several polished pins. Each one bearing an insignia that now looked eerily familiar. And—perhaps most shocking and unexpected of all—a flat leather case sheathing a long dark knife.

Unfastening it carefully, he withdrew the weapon—and it was most obviously a weapon—running his finger almost reverently along the fine blade. His loose fist curved comfortably around its rounded black handle, his thumb resting naturally on the grooved imprint just beyond the cross-guard. An odd piece of metal secured the base end of the handle. It looked like a small hard-pointed hat. Decorative and yet no mere decoration. He could tell that applied with force, the shapely turned end would easily crack a man's skull wide open. Turning the dagger toward him, Jakie inspected the long stiletto with his eye. It tapered gracefully to a delicate, deadly point.

Mesmerized, he was also acutely aware that the knife he held was an exact replica of the one he had long ago hand-forged for himself in the asylum's farrier shed. And then the awareness twisted, and he realized it was actually the other way around. The knife he held was not a replica at all. It was the original. The original of *what*—that was the question clawing its way up through Jakie's swirling mind.

Unaware that she was being shadowed, Nurse Mildred huffed her way up four flights of stairs, down a slick-polished corridor, arriving unannounced and unapologetic into Dr. Davidson's private office.

Jolted unceremoniously from his silent sanctuary over by the window, the doctor surreptitiously slipped a little vial of pills back into his pocket. Gagging slightly, he swallowed the one he'd just deposited into his mouth. Clacking the tip of his pipe hard against his bottom teeth, he glared at Mildred as he awaited an explanation for her intrusion.

"Brought the doll," she said, dropping it onto the desk as she presumed herself into Dr. Davidson's worn leather chair. Loosening, then rerolling her messy hair, she reached into the desk's top drawer, pulled out his best fountain pen, and secured it through her bun. Dr. Davidson's face switched rapidly between scowling at her intrusiveness and looking with bewilderment at the ratty doll she'd dumped on top of his papered desk.

"What?" she asked brusquely. "You wanted me to get it for you, didn't ya?"

Dr. Davidson nodded unconvincingly.

"Yes, of course," he stammered. "Was it difficult?"

Nurse Mildred's eyebrows shot up like flags in a hurricane.

"Not much more difficult than separating a couple of Siamese twins I reckon."

Ignoring her tone, he walked over to his desk, picked the doll up by an arm and pushed it off to one side. Thankfully, the pill he had taken was already beginning to administer its effects, making any encounter with Nurse Mildred so much easier for him to ingest. A bubble of caution surfaced among his newly floated ease, however; he knew his head nurse could be just as wily as she pretended not to be. Averting his eyes away from hers, Dr. Davidson pulled up a bare wooden chair and attempted unsuccessfully to find a comfortable position. His eyes glazing, he stared across the desk at Mildred's tightly fastened top button. Miscalculating the angle of his gaze, she eased back slightly, puffing out the massive heave of her bosom even farther.

"What you want it for anyways?" she asked, pointing at the doll with a pencil she'd been using to pick at her teeth.

"To gain the girl's trust."

"Gain her trust!" Nurse Mildred guffawed loudly before catching herself. "Come now, doctor," she teased back coyly. "What's your plan? Really? Most likely, I can be of some help."

"Oh, assuredly. You already have been, Nurse Mildred. You've been most helpful, in fact."

She batted her short lashes across at him. The gesture translated as more of a spasmodic twitching rather than a romantic lure.

"And how did I do that, doctor?"

Suddenly feeling overly pleased with himself, Dr. Davidson repositioned himself once again on the unforgiving chair. Forgetting completely that he was in a lady's company, he absently massaged the base of his lower gums with the tip of his unlit pipe.

"Look," he began. "It's most evident that the girl can speak, and yet to my knowledge, she still hasn't uttered a single word to anyone..."

"Yes, she's a stubborn one she is..."

"Stubborn. Or maybe just frightened. Perhaps she feels herself among strangers here..."

Stretching her arms overhead, Mildred yawned noisily.

"I thought it might be helpful if she could look on me as a confidant. Perhaps if I gained her trust..."

"Gained her *trust!*" Nurse Mildred yelped again, exploding into robust laughter. Eventually noticing that the doctor was evidently not sharing her amusement, she quieted herself down and shook her head with disbelief.

"Go on with you, Gerald...uh, Dr. Gerald. You can't mean to gain her trust by stealing away the only thing in the whole world she holds precious..."

Straightening himself on the chair, he extracted the pipe from his mouth and looked firmly across at her.

"But I didn't steal it, Nurse Mildred."

"Well, of course you did," she replied forcefully as she threw an expressive hand up in the air, indicating the obvious evidence lying between them.

"No," he smiled gently. "*I* did not steal it, Nurse Mildred. *You* did. I will merely be the good soul who brings it back to her."

Stymied, Nurse Mildred pushed back heavily into the chair. She chewed rapidly on the side of her trembling lower lip. Anger. Humiliation. Pain. Each one of these swept in turn across her face. Her bright bravado exposed and gone. For a brief moment, Dr. Davidson feared she might actually begin to cry.

Distancing himself once more over by the window, he struggled to compose himself through the thick fog clouding his brain. He felt a deep pull of remorse, and this he quickly identified, isolating it off much like one would a dangerous shard of sharp glass found on a busy street.

"Is there a problem, nurse?" he asked, far more sternly than the situation warranted.

"Yes, well no..." she flubbered. "It's just that, well...well, I...I thought maybe the girl was just beginning to take a liking to me, that's all."

His tightly rounded shoulders releasing, Dr. Davidson exhaled loudly.

"Nurse Mildred, what I have consistently found in this institution is that we are most successful when we keep our focus on treating the dysfunctional minds of our patients, rather than on trying to become their friends."

"And what I've found, doctor, is that sometimes it takes the one to do the other," she leveled back quietly.

Not eager to agitate her brew into a storm, he turned away, smiling sardonically at his reflection in the window. He would relinquish her this blow.

"It's not just me, doctor. She seems more comfortable with the whole place now. Probably time to move her upstairs anyhow. Maybe she would start to talk if she was with..."

"No! Absolutely not."

"And just why not? Seems perfectly well. The company would do..."

"Please," he hissed, turning back toward her abruptly. "Remember your place here. The girl is *my* patient. Mine. And she will not be transferred upstairs until *I* say so. Have I made myself abundantly clear, Nurse Mildred?"

"Not. At. All," she articulated, then shrugged. "But, have it your way. *You're* the doctor."

Her narrowed eyes searched into him in a way that rankled him intrusively.

"It's just..." he stumbled. "It's just, that I want to ensure that she's more accustomed to living in all of that light and noise and commotion before I move her upstairs."

"Oh, phht! She's perfectly fine with all that. I had her out for a walk just last week, and she was as happy as a bee in broccoli."

"A bee...in *broccoli*?" the doctor repeated, his brain short-circuiting over the image. "What on earth does that have to do with..."

"Mm-huh. Spent the whole time whistling at the birds... then giggling."

"Birds? What kind of birds?"

"Well I don't rightly know...the kind that fly I guess."

Dr. Davidson shot her a violent look.

"I truly haven't a clue. I couldn't even see any around. But there *was* one somewhere 'cause when she whistled at it...it almost seemed to answer her back."

Rattling his pipe tip over his yellowed teeth in agitation, Dr. Davidson moved back over to his desk, pushed some papers aside and leaned up against it.

"She shouldn't be out walking unescorted, anyhow."

His nurse scrunched her spongy face up at him unbecomingly. "She *had* an escort, doctor. She was with me."

"Not enough," he fumed. The anxiety had slipped free of the pill's constraints, and he could feel it driving up inside of him. He eased himself slightly away from Mildred so that she couldn't examine his face.

"From now on, the girl is only allowed up for walks if she's with me."

Nurse Mildred arched her eyebrows, obviously sizing up his gaunt six-foot frame.

"'Shore, doctor," she drawled. "Whatever you say. Shouldn't be any problem for you to find time in your busy schedule to take her out for a walk every single day."

"Don't be ridiculous, Nurse Mildred. Of course I can't take her out every day."

"Well," she puffed up defensively. "You can't just be leaving the poor girl stuck down there alone in that room."

Dr. Davidson bristled at the imposition on his authority.

"Of course not, nurse. You and the others can walk her in the tunnels on the days I can't get to her."

"Hardly. Not one of the staff is very keen on going down there after what happened to Oswald."

"Attendant Oswald is a drunk, Nurse Mildred. Surely you know that. Chances are he simply fell down the stairs and tried to cover it up with that preposterous story..."

"Well, could be. But on top of that, ol' Angel Queen's got half of my nurses scared beyond their wits with the stories she's been telling..."

Dr. Davidson's bony fingers massaged at his temples, attempting to stave off the massive migraine he could feel coming on.

"She keeps talking of rats and devils. Even says she saw you down there that night..."

"Well...that is completely preposterous!" he burst, exploding from the desk and striding forcefully across the room. "Why would any of you listen to such nonsense? It's obvious the woman is insane..."

"Well yes, it does appear that her crackers got a tad crumbled after that last bit."

"A tad crumbled? A *tad*? She's completely insane, nurse. *Completely!*"

"Hmm," Nurse Mildred intoned noncommittally.

Dr. Davison remained at the window, his back blocking her as he worked to regain his composure. His mind grappled against the possibility that he may have been seen. He grew livid at the thought. At the invasion of his privacy. Right now, he greatly desired to be left alone, but he instinctively knew he had but this one chance to suffocate his head nurse's nose of suspicion. He could feel her unanswered questions hanging in the silence of her too-quiet waiting.

"I've been speaking with Dr. Uldrich, Nurse Mildred," he said, turning back toward her. "We've come to an agreement that Miss Lawson might benefit greatly from his Sleep Therapy treatments."

Nurse Mildred ceased picking at her teeth, her mouth hanging open in a rare moment of silent disapproval.

"Oh, but...Dr. Davidson...surely you can't be serious."

"Of course I'm serious. What else would I be?"

"Yes, well, right," she conceded. "I only meant that perhaps the course of action might be a little extreme. Mary's not usually so much..."

"It's *not* extreme, nurse. It's timely. Obviously our current approach is not doing well by her."

"Ah, but doctor...she's only gone and acted up a bit and got carried away with herself. I don't think she..."

"What you think, Nurse Mildred, is not of any particular interest to me." He watched her face warily to see if he'd undercut her or merely riled her. Sensing the former, he continued on. "It is my position, as the head of this institution, to treat my patients in the most effective ways possible. And Dr. Uldrich has assured me that he can almost completely wipe out her memory, then reprogram her thoughts..."

"But she'll no longer be our Mary!" Nurse Mildred objected, raising herself up off the chair and thumping both fists heavily on top of the desk.

"Of course she will be. Just...tidier, if you please. Think of it. The absolute freedom of such an outcome for Mary. She'll no longer be held captive by her silly fantasies and delusions. Perhaps...if she fares well enough...it might even be possible for her to return home again."

"Well—I won't say I much care for the idea."

They held each other off with a mutual glare.

"And what of her father? Surely he doesn't..."

"Ah...yes. Well, he took some convincing as I well guessed he would. But after I related to him the potentially embarrassing events of her last escapade, he was wont to finally agree with me."

"That last bit?" Nurse Mildred struggled. "I really don't think that should be held against her, sir. She was just being a silly young girl. She was only vying for your attentions, doctor."

Dr. Davidson flushed as he stabbed his pipe back at her.

"She almost succeeded in drowning herself in her silliness, Nurse Mildred. And she could have very well taken down anyone fool enough to try and save her. I'm afraid Miss Lawson has become a danger to others, as well as to herself. It's simply my duty to prescribe a more viable form of treatment, is it not?"

He turned back to the window and settled his gaze aimlessly in the clouds.

"But she won't be our Angel Queen no more. I seen what it did to the others, doctor. Mary's always been one of the few that could make all the ladies laugh. She's always been harmless enough..."

"She's *not* harmless, Nurse Mildred. Not anymore. You've said yourself she's disrupting the ward. Upsetting the patients and your nurses with her fanciful stories."

"Aye," she agreed reluctantly. "I don't know," she said shaking her head. "I just don't know. Something about those treatments won't settle in my gut. When I see what happened to Mr. Headly..."

Dr. Davidson frowned. "What happened to Mr. Headly?"

"Well, about twelve courses of electricity firing through his brain...and that on top of enough Thorazine and Curare to stumble a horse. That's what I heard. Knocked him right out for days."

"Oh, that. Yes, well he's done quite well since..."

"Done *well?* The man was completely befuddled when I saw him last."

"Oh, well...that's temporary. To be expected."

"He couldn't even count..."

"No, not well. But have you seen him bat? Swing is as smooth as it ever was."

"Maybe so. Still can't count."

"What on earth does it matter if he can count, Nurse Mildred? Norman Headly is a batsman not a banker. And now, thanks to Dr. Uldrich's therapy, he can once again do just that."

Ξ Ξ Ξ

Pushing the broom he'd seized from an immobilized patient stuck in an inertia of thought on the second floor, Jakie shuffled up and down the gleaming corridor outside Dr. Davidson's office, eavesdropping, the conversation through the partially opened door. Twice he'd had to slow his pace and increase his limp as the disturbing words floated to him, igniting a volcano of protective fire within. Fueled by a vision of the girl's anguished weeping at the loss of her doll, he raged against a desire to boil into the doctor's office and dangle him from the fifth-story window by the stuffy tie that noosed around his scrawny neck.

Of course, he knew he could do nothing of the kind, and his helpless acceptance made him feel like a coconspirator in the girl's pain. Then, with a sharp clarity, an idea sprung loose within him. The doctor's plan—though hideous in its execution—was actually not such a bad idea after all.

His thoughts were cut short by Nurse Mildred's unexpected appearance in the doorway.

"Jakie...what on earth are you doing out here?"

"Uh...I'm sweeping, ma'am."

"Yes, I can see that," she said as she walked over to him. "The question is—*why* are you sweeping? You've no business in this building."

"Just helping out where I can," he charmed.

She eyed him suspiciously.

"Actually, ma'am, I brought you Myrtle's chompers," he said, conveniently remembering the false teeth he still had in his pocket and digging them out. "Here," he said as he snapped open the little ceramic container and offered them to her. "I told Myrtle I'd get them for her."

"Get them from *where*, Jakie?" Nurse Mildred asked pointedly.

Obviously caught out by his own admission, Jakie chose silence as his best defense.

"Well, at any rate, she won't have much need of these anymore—"

"But she does, Nurse Mildred. She asked me—"

"Aye. So you've not heard then?"

Jakie looked at her blankly.

"Myrtle left us yesterday, Jakie."

"Left us? What happened?" he asked quietly, looking down at his feet. Over the years, he'd grown rather fond of the strange old bird.

"Autopsy showed stomach cancer. Couldn't have been helped, Jakie. No one knew."

He looked up sharply.

"*Someone* knew, Nurse Mildred. Myrtle knew. It's what she's been trying to tell us all along."

Nurse Mildred dropped her head and nodded wearily.

"You might be right, Jakie. You just very well might be right."

CHAPTER 18

☰ ☰ ☰

Jakie moved swiftly, feeling along the rough walls of the tunnels, the meager light spilling from the sporadic bulbs insufficient in their reach to truly illuminate the musty gloom. He listened around him. He didn't bother to strain. If there were anyone else traversing through the tunnels, they would be sure to announce their presence—loudly. Even those few who claimed no fear of the dark spaces below became transformed into jabbering fools as they made their way along. Often, those who claimed the least fear jabbered the loudest.

Stopping far short of the heavy door that guarded the girl's room, Jakie sank to one knee, withdrew a pebble and a slingshot from his back pocket and aptly picked out the light. He waited for a moment as the fine glass shattered to the floor, then slipped through the perfect darkness toward the cellar.

Easing himself once again to his knees, he hesitated just long enough to remove a small pack from his back and fuss with something inside, before lowering his head down to the thin band of light pushing out along the bottom of the doorway.

At first, no sound traveled to him. Closing his eyes, he stilled his breathing. A gentle sob, soft and muted, reached out, so forlorn in its languorous timbre that he feared the sound of it would crush him. Flashing his eyes open, he attempted to renegotiate his senses. Suddenly, Jakie Hewitt felt very unsure of his plan. The girl awaited him only a few short feet away. The door was all that separated them. A door he was confident he could unlock. And yet, a caution sounded within him. The door remained as a tangible physical barrier. He knew there were other ones as well. Ones that could not be so easily gained.

He thought back to the dance and questioned himself. Had it actually happened exactly the way he remembered? Was his defective memory even capable of such a task? Inwardly, he stumbled harshly over his inability to be able to trust himself. Such permanence of mind seemed a God-given right. Somehow, he'd lost even that.

Scraping the self-effacing thoughts loose from him, he closed his eyes and felt his way back to the glorious moments at the dance. If he could not trust his memories to inform him, then he would simply bring back the events of the dance through his feelings. *One cannot always trust their feelings*, Dr. Davidson was fond of claiming. But for Jakie, sometimes in the absence of trusted memories, feelings were all that he had. Feelings, unlike memories, didn't lie. Often, they were the only things left he *could* trust.

He remembered now his feeling of jubilation when the girl had first entered the dance hall. The lightness and joy that had floated through him as he noted how much healthier she looked. A feeling of satisfaction over how well his offered gifts of wild medicinals had worked. And then a dark cloud of resentment and protective concern as he watched Dr. Davidson's hand touch her small back. The slightly smug feeling as he brewed a plan with the cooperative Mary, and the hilarity riding euphoria as he watched it play out even better than he could have hoped for. The confusing blend of excitement and fear, confidence and inhibition, as he'd sauntered over and sat down in the doctor's chair, the girl—finally—sitting lightly by his side. Yes, the feelings were all still there. Vibrant. Vivid. Fresh. And with them, they called forth a dazzling Ferris wheel of memories. He chose to believe they were all one and the same.

The discomfort in his leg forced him to his feet. The discomfort of hearing the girl's sorrow pushed him back down. He couldn't pause to think any longer. To console himself or cajole himself, bolster his courage, or whatever it was he was doing. He had her doll—her precious baby doll—in his pack. It had been playfully easy to slip it out of Dr. Davidson's office the very night after Nurse Mildred had brought it in. He could only imagine the doctor's surprise the next morning when he'd arrived to find his bargaining piece inexplicably gone. Jakie felt a little for the poor nurse. Undoubtedly, she would end up taking the blame. Or, perhaps the doctor would keep the vanishing and sudden reappearance of the doll to himself. It was the sort of story that, when spoken aloud, made one seem like they might be bending a tad to the inside. And, Jakie could tell, the good doctor was not finding himself on particularly solid ground lately, anyway. The increased dosing to enable him to spend more and more time in the claustrophobic tunnels was eroding his grip day by day.

Jakie returned to his position in front of the door. Fear vacillated him between inertia and action. He reminded himself that he had her most precious possession. Indeed, almost her only possession. And, if somehow that were not enough to mollify her, he reminded himself that he'd brought along a backup plan that surely would.

He thought back again to their brief encounter at the dance. Was there a chance he might have misjudged her reactions? His own thoughts he could reach back and feel. But hers were an enigma. He had to admit his conclusions were little more than a hopeful guessing. She had *seemed* to warm to his presumptuous company. At least once he'd managed to overcome her understandable fear when he presented his berry-stained hands. But could he have mistaken the brightness of recognition when he whistled Cardinal's song? Had he seen what was really there? Or had he seen only that which he had so wished to see?

Rapping his bruised knuckles hard against his fore-head, Jakie knocked his awareness loose from the twisting thoughts. Breathing deeply, he sought to reassure him-self. It was true that he'd felt her obvious discomfort when he'd appropriated Dr. Davidson's seat and had so poorly attempted to introduce himself. But then too, he'd also noticed the softening of her features, the little drop of her shoulders, the sudden bright burn of understanding glow-ing in her beautiful eyes as he'd shared Cardinal's song. And then, there was the moment of her whistled reply. He wanted to trust that it had all actually happened that way.

Jakie smiled through his fears. He was surprised to find his heart racing, his breath coming in little jagged gulps. Reaching up, he held his head with both hands. He had to be diligent. These depths of emotion altered him somehow. Dislocated him from himself. For a moment, he'd lost sense of where he was—and why. Straining now, he searched into the quietness surrounding him. Something was gone.

Suddenly, he felt the void of the girl's strangled weep-ing. She was silent. Silent and, he instinctively felt, listen-ing back at him. Quickly composing himself, he wondered if he'd uttered a sound. If she'd heard him mumbling out-side her door or—God forbid—sobbing. Time was pressing in on him, the cold of the floor aching deep into his knees. He lowered his face once more to the ribbon of light.

"Cheeeer-a-dote, cheeer-a-dote-dote-dote. Purdy, purdy, purdy...whoit, whoit, whoit, whoit."

He waited without breath. No sound returned to him and his spirit tumbled like Lucifer. If he didn't know the room was a virtual prison, he would have tried to convince himself that she had left it. Pressing himself forward, he tried once again.

"What-cheer, what-cheer...wheet, wheet, wheet, wheet."

This time he whistled louder, a note of desperation sullying the song. The sharp noise exploded eagerly off of the barren brick walls and echoed down the tunnel.

Folding around himself, Jakie held perfectly still. He was sure that he'd gone too far. That surely someone in the far rooms would have heard and would be along to investigate. Then a thought occurred to him. None were eager to walk through the tunnels for any reason. Many had sacrificed their jobs in order to avoid doing so. How silly of him to think anyone would choose to do it just to rescue a way-ward bird trapped within.

He took a deep breath and steadied himself. Being so close to the girl, anticipating her reaction to his bringing the doll back to her, had off-kiltered him. Like gaining the extraordinary, monumental summit of a high mountain, only to discover the air is too thin to be sustainable.

Suddenly, a brief shadow crossed the light—then drew back. Jakie grinned wide. He wanted to jump up, pound on the door and beg her to let him in. Instead, he dug his fingernails roughly into his palms, allowing the sharp pain to refocus him. Bowing his head once more to the floor, he whistled once again. Gently—with feeling.

Sitting back on his heels, he waited—triumphantly—for the answer he was sure would come. Time inched by. He grew puzzled once more. Surely Dr. Davidson hadn't won her over with his clever ways. But no, even the doctor had said he too was still trying to win her trust. *She's just afraid*, Jakie thought. *Wary at hearing Cardinal's song outside her door.*

Jakie rested his forehead on his knees and contemplated the situation. He was adamant about presenting himself a little more graciously this meeting. He simply could not just jimmy open the bolt and barge into her room. Even if he were able to overcome her terror for long enough to offer her back her baby, he refused to do it. He would not again have her mistake him for some murderous beast. Too many episodes like that could prove impossible to overcome. Besides, he wanted her to trust him into her room. To see that he meant her no harm and offered only his humble love.

Again reaching into his backpack, he withdrew a few tools and settled them in the dust. Rummaging deeper among the contents of the pack, he extracted a large feather that plumed beautifully under the stroke of his hand.

Raising it up to his forehead, he kissed it ceremoniously, then placed it gently down, pushing it halfway under the door. It lay there undisturbed—half-illumined—half in darkness. A minute edged by, five, ten. Half an hour, maybe more. Jakie knelt in motionless patience, waiting to see if his entry would be accepted. His mind began to fret. Dinner meals would be served soon, and he knew an unhappy orderly would be along with hers.

He focused all of his attention on the remaining half of the feather still sheathed in darkness, willing it gone. And then—suddenly—it was. Almost forgetting his surroundings, he barely stifled a wild victory whoop from ringing its way down the lost corridors.

Standing in front of the door, Jakie worked to steady his hands. His tools felt large. Rough and awkward in his grip. Sweat crystals beaded his forehead. His whole body actually trembled with trepidation. None of this was helpful in unencumbering the lock, and it took him far longer than he knew it should until he finally heard the tumblers falling into place.

Crouching down, he hurriedly shifted the contents of the pack into place, then slung it over his shoulder. With one hand already on the door ready to enter, he suddenly remembered himself. Living so long in the asylum, it was easy to forget about society's little decencies and manners. Very gently, he knocked. So gently in fact that he couldn't even hear the sound himself.

He pulled back and took a deep breath. Ran his hands over his dusty pant legs. Licked his fingers then pushed the hair back from his face. Shifting a little, he took a swipe at his nose. Why hadn't he brought a handkerchief along? What if something unacceptable was burrowed in there? He rubbed at it brutally with the back of his sleeve. He felt an urgent need to pee.

Clearing his throat noisily, he tapped again. She did not come to the door to answer, nor had he expected that she would. He merely wanted to indicate to her his intentions. Carefully, he twisted the big knob and pushed open the door. The gloomy light escaping the cellar room seemed as vibrant as the noonday sun to his light-deprived eyes. He stood still for a moment, open to her searching, blinking blindly until his eyes had time to adjust.

She sat over by the wall on the edge of the bed. Upright and erect, her large glassy eyes stared into him. Jakie smiled widely, generously showing all of his teeth. She did not smile back. A thin, furtive frown troubled her brow. Concerned, he quickly dropped the smile from his face. Perhaps she read him as the animals did, not seeing a smile at all, but rather just a strange man bearing his teeth.

Lowering his eyes from hers, he softened his countenance. He closed the door in tiny increments, sympathetic to any sign of fear arising in her. Detecting none, he gently clicked it shut and turned back to face her. She'd curled into a tiny ball on the bed, one hand dangling down into the corner, absently strumming at a gauzy spider web. A spirit of extreme melancholy invaded the room. Jakie wondered how she had not gone stark raving mad, locked away with nothing to keep her company save for the spiders and shadows that crawled across her walls.

Finding himself unexpectedly self-conscious in her presence, he looked at the inscribed walls, pretending great interest in the mournful writings. *Surely, it was yet possible that she is the Madonna*, he thought. Such a thing would so easily explain the monumental effect she had on his carnal heart. *And so would love*, whispered another voice, and he swung around fast to see if Coyote had followed him.

The sudden movement startled her, and she pulled herself up against the wall at the far end of the bed. She watched him warily, her wide eyes like vibrant orbs of seeking.

She did not seem particularly scared, but when he stepped toward her, she drew back. Stopping, he sank to the floor, halving the distance between them. Although still watching, she noticeably relaxed. Jakie searched around for the bright red shock of the cardinal's feather he had offered her under the door. He could detect no sign of it. Hidden from view and who could blame her?

They sat in mutual silence, the girl staring at him with frank interest, Jakie sneaking occasional furtive glances her way. These she calmly captured without providing any indication back of what she might be thinking. A shifting movement in his pack alerted him back to the scope of his original mission, and with careful, busy movements, he took the pack off of his shoulder and drew down the sides.

Snapping lizard-quick off the bed, the girl pulled her doll free of the bag. Collapsing back onto her bed, she wrapped her frail body around the doll, convulsing with sobs as tears flowed like the Ganges down her trembling face.

"My baby...my baby..."

"Whoa," Jakie said into the suddenly broken silence. "You talked."

The moment felt mystical, born out of a peculiar form of high magic. Like some eternal spell had been broken. For, even though he'd known she was capable of speaking, it struck him as other-worldly to actually hear her do so.

Jakie watched her tender ministrations with unhindered fascination. The light fell soft on her long hair, a mysterious cleft of shadow swiping below her high cheekbones. Encouraged by the look of happy relief on her face, he again smiled over at her, careful this time to not bare too many teeth. She glared at him. Huddling the doll protectively inside her open sweater, she turned aside.

"Oh...no, no..." Jakie stumbled. "*I* didn't take your baby. The doctor did. I only brought it back—"

The girl cut him short with her violent stare. Even without words, it was more than obvious she did not believe a word he had said. Desperate to redeem himself, Jakie tottered on.

"Well...I guess Nurse Mildred actually took it...*her*. But only because Dr. Davidson made her."

Still studying him, she stroked the hard plastic face, then hugged the doll for a very protracted moment.

Forcing himself to be quiet, Jakie tried to assess the situation from the way she might see it. Of *course* she was not going to believe that Dr. Davidson had stolen her doll. Why would she? He had cleverly managed to keep any defilement from tarnishing his own hands. The only hands the girl had actually seen on her precious baby were those of Nurse Mildred, and now his own. Jakie realized, far too late, that of all the few people the girl had interacted with in the asylum, perhaps Dr. Davidson seemed to her like the one she could trust the most. The thought infuriated him. But he had to admit, it was not the doctor's hands that had violated the patients with sharp needles or pushed pills that they were forced into taking. No, for the most part, the good doctor's hands remained pure from all of this that happened daily at his behest.

Jakie felt momentarily defeated. Then he remembered that the doctor was not the only one who had managed to gain a bit of the girl's trust. A small red bird had done the same. A feathered friend that had spent countless hours outside her room, singing her songs, offering her company. Bringing her healing herbs. Berries from the forest floor. And now, since their meeting at the dance, he trusted that she understood that the bird was also himself. Bolstered by this remembrance, he looked into her eyes earnestly and tried to win her over once again.

"I...I only ask that you...that you—*trust me*," he stammered. "The doctor had your doll taken away. Honest. I only wanted to bring her back."

Without changing her position or the intensity of her gaze, she stared into him as if she were reaching back through the ages of his soul. He wondered if she was able to read his mind. He swallowed dryly. His eyes started to burn as they sat locked in a mutual eye-hold. The internal innocence of her shone through like radiant light. Illuminating her from the inside. Jakie felt he could just sit and gaze upon her face for days. Swim deep into her eyes, her large pupils dilated like dark full moons floating in a clear sky. He knew he was losing himself in the diaphanous rays of her beauty. Caution told him the only way to save himself was to look away. *Impossible*, he answered back.

He became aware of their synchronized breathing. The rapid fire of his heart. Slowly, he began to allow the love he felt to soften through him. In the void of their words, he began to feel he understood. That he *was* understood. The feeling was a delight. A strong tide pulled feelings of relief from all the dark corners of his psyche. Softly, he smiled a small smile to acknowledge it.

A vaporous smile glanced across her face as well and—almost shyly—she looked away.

"They've all gone," she whispered, blinking up at him. "She's all I've got left."

Jakie reeled. Lighthearted and giddy. He felt the sound of her spoken words were so melodic that even winter trees would be forced into bloom upon hearing them. He resisted an urge to wrap her in his arms as she did the doll and roll with her gently across the bed, tickling her into a river of glorious laughter.

"Who's gone?" he whispered gently. His voice sounded harsh and gritty riding on the echo of hers.

She stared into him searchingly.

"Your family?"

Tears brimmed, almost spilling.

Jakie nodded gently. He wrestled between his desire not to cause her any more pain and an insatiable urge to uproot and absorb everything that he could about her.

"Where'd ya come from?"

A ghost of confusion crossed her face.

Falling quiet, they sat in a comfortable silence. Jakie tried to ascertain whether her reluctance to talk stemmed from the intrusiveness of his questions or whether she simply didn't understand his requests. Studying the intelligence alive in her face, he was surprised to find her also making an analysis of his own. It was quite plain to see that her hesitation arose from something else altogether.

"Are you a loony?" she asked.

"A loony! What? Me? No...I'm no loony."

"You sure?"

Jakie nodded quickly.

"How do you know?"

Well—she had him there. Gathering himself together, he boldly looked as sanely as he could into her unflinching stare.

"I just *do*," he said emphatically.

"Why is your face all dirty then?"

He hadn't known it was. It seemed to happen often—when he ran in the forest or stole invisible through the dark night. Embarrassed, and distinctly aware of how it must make him look, he attempted—unsuccessfully—to wipe the dirt away.

She continued to eye him sharply for a minute more, as if attempting to analyze the truth of this. Finally, much to Jakie's relief, she nodded.

"I thought maybe you were. They said they were taking me to the place where the loonies live. Have you seen any?"

Jakie considered this for a long moment, then sorrowfully shook his head.

"No. Alls who live here are just folks like us. Sometimes some of them do things that seem a little strange."

"*You* tried to kill me," she sparked brightly.

Jakie flushed hotly over the spoken remembrance of their first night. He could barely feel his way back to the broken man he had once been. Nor was he eager to give it much effort. Having the girl enter his life, even from a distance, had irrevocably altered all of that. She had inspired within him the hope of change.

"I'm sorry I scared you when I found ya down by the creek that night," he apologized. "I thought you were a fawn."

She blasted him with a look of such consternation that he wished he could cut out his own tongue.

"A sick fawn, I mean...a hurt one..." he fumbled, acutely aware—too late—that each word proved to be a finger pointing him out as the loony he'd just denied to be. Forcing himself to a stop, he drew a full breath, then exhaled. Before attempting to speak again, he sorted through the thoughts storming his mind and this time, selected carefully.

"I thought it was suffering."

This she seemed to recognize, and the concern lifted from her face.

"Then, when I saw it was you...I thought you were the Madonna," he blurted. Now he felt he could forgo the knife altogether and just pull the wagging uncontrollable beast straight out.

She looked at him, puzzled.

"You know...Madonna. The holy mother."

"I'm not Maw Donna," she said, sounding slightly offended. "I'm Lily."

"*Lily!*" Jakie sprang back, far too loudly. Thrilled to have finally gained her name, he was also relieved to have the conversation spin off on another course. "That's a beautiful name. My name is...well...Jakie, I guess."

"I know your name," she giggled, her hands rising up to cover her mouth impishly.

He shifted a bit on the hard floor, feeling a bit the fool. Of course she knew his name. She'd have heard others address him by it the day of the dance. His heart skipped a little, flattered that she had remembered it. Separated by the wall of her silence, it had been easy to forget that she was still observing everything around her, drawing in every word.

"So," he ventured. "Where do ya come from, Lily? Before here...where did ya live?"

Her face brightened. "In the barn."

"The *barn*?"

She nodded cheerfully. "With Ol' Brown."

Jakie guarded his heart, trying hard not to over-imagine what sort of depravity this delicate, soulful being may have been subjected to.

"I used to live down in the house. With the others. But then Maw said she had enough of that. Said I scared the little ones. Sometimes I fall—"

The lightness dropped and even a dead man could see the extreme burden of pain that descended upon her.

"My brother said not to mind her so much. That the little ones were only scared 'cause she told them I got the devil in me. Said she weren't never my real maw anyhow. But she was the only one I ever got—"

Softly maintaining eye contact, Jakie cautiously moved from the floor to sit on the other end of the bed. She didn't seem to mind.

Suddenly, a delighted squeal pealed out of her, and she sprung from the bed, her attention captured by something furry wriggling free of Jakie's pack. Chuckling heartedly, he joined her on the floor, watching with enamored enjoyment as her graceful hands blossomed with a tiny black-and-white bundle that she nestled up against her face. He'd completely forgotten about his unneeded backup plan.

"What is it?" she asked.

"Skunk. A baby one—"

Concern instantly clouded her face, cutting him short.

"Where's its mama?" she demanded.

"Dead...wasn't me!" Jakie hastened to explain. "I've just been feeding it until it can go off on its own again."

She narrowed her eyes at him protectively. Jakie stifled a smile. He hadn't expected her to be so fierce.

Cradling the little skunk gently, she scampered back onto the bed and gathered up her baby. Bubbling with joyful enthusiasm, she worked to contain the squirming ball of fur as she attempted to hold it up against the faded cheek of her doll.

"Oh...look. She loves it." She giggled. "Can I keep it?"

Jakie sat back, swallowing hard as he lightly frowned. He had not considered this. His only thought had been of her surprise and delight when he presented her with the irresistibly cute creature. In his pleasure imagining that, he'd given no thought at all to the disappointment she would feel when he inevitably had to take it away again. He sighed heavily, angry with himself.

"Forgive me, Lily. But I can't leave it with you. The doctor would be none too pleased if he found out I'd been visiting with ya. And I think a baby skunk suddenly appearing in your room might be a bit hard to explain. Never mind your baby doll coming back all on its own."

"Okay," she agreed easily. *Far too easily*, Jakie thought.

Watching intently, he marveled at the way the light sparkled, playing lightly across the silver, silken gauze that feathered her arm. He longed to stroke his finger along it. To caress her with a generous, open love—the same way she did the tiny kit.

Instead, he waited, his heart feeling heavy and bad, as she nuzzled the skunk for a brief moment more with the tip of her nose, then relinquished it back to him. Clearly, she was well accustomed to disappointment. As if she had no access to the well inside of her that held demands. No wonder she was so protective over her baby doll. Besides the sweater, the doll was the only possession she truly had. Even the spiders and shadows that occasionally crept out to play with her eventually receded back beyond the thick walls.

Jakie knew his heart was in a perilous place. He had to break the magic. To let go of his hold on this newly found pleasure in the same accepting manner as she had done. He resisted doing so. Strongly. His foundation of wants and needs had formed differently than hers. He held within him the knowledge and memory of standing hard for what he believed in. For what he wanted. And every fiber in his being wanted happiness for this girl. This beautiful, gentle Lily.

His will had been formed by tasting the satisfaction of gaining his heart's desire. It was apparent the girl had known none of this. Her heart was a huge, open ocean of love, delighted by each small bit of flotsam that floated through her day, relinquishing it easily to the eventual—perpetual—changing of the tide.

Every morsel and muscle in him sought to change this. He ached to tell her that she was worthy of such wonderful things. That she need not accept so little for herself. But he didn't know where to begin. The seeds of her self were evident to him. But they were stunted and misshapen by a lifetime of powerless existence.

A yodel sounded. Far down the tunnel yet but headed their way. Jakie didn't want to hear it but it persisted, filling their silence like a midnight bell. Hastening to pull his thoughts together, he remembered one other thing he had set out to discover.

"Your sweater," he said. "It's very unusual—pretty. Where did ya get it?"

Her delight over the kit dropped as her attention reversed back to the sweater.

"Ezra gave it to me," she said proudly, a little mist clouding her eyes. "Ezra's my brother."

Quickly scooping up this information along with his pack, Jakie nodded. Hesitating, he attempted to absorb every inch of her with his eyes. His feet felt immobile. Cemented to the floor. His reluctance to go was beyond tangible, but the yodeling was driving dangerously close. Sheer seconds separated his freedom from an irrevocably blocked escape.

He felt loath to leave her. Leave her with only the sad memory of the baby skunk being taken away. His heart began to beat far too fast. The yodeling grew louder. He considered his few options. It would be nothing for him to put out the light, spring at the opening door and sprint himself and the girl free, while the hapless courier remained trapped in the terrifying darkness with a plateful of rotting food.

But the plan was still too green. A sprout bursting early through the tarmac, destined to wither and die in the absence of a fertile place to grow. No—he would get the girl—Lily—free. He would promise himself that. But not until he was sure they would not be caught. He'd seen well enough the reward offered to those who failed to succeed. And he was in no way eager to have anything to do with such things.

The falling footsteps were clear now. The yodeling had morphed into a rather frantic song.

"I'll come back for you," he whispered hoarsely. "I'm going to get ya out of here...I promise."

She looked up at him with wide, trusting eyes but she didn't respond. Jakie couldn't tell if she just hadn't heard his heart-garbled words or if she'd actually just heard it all too many times before.

Dear Sir,

I hope this letter finds you well. I am writin
to you of my concerns. I have strugled with
myself aginst doing so but I feel you have
givin me no choice now an I must. You
know i have bin a good patient here in your
asylum for these 2 or 3 years now an not
complined to much. But i find myself boi-
lin in my blood sir an i can not help myself
but speak of the things troublin my mind.
As evin you say so yerself that it is best to
speak of such things that is troublin one.
Is that not so doctor??? I will try to be poli-
ght sir but i find it hard to do so. My estim-
ition of you has falen in my eyes. An that is
a sad thing for me for i feels you is a good
man but what you has done reguires some
explnations for me. Suerly you must know
be now that i long to sees my good Husband
an childrin????? Have i said this enough in
my letters to you assuradly???? How can i
more explain my grief at havin them takin
away from me???? I cry every day sir. Every
day i cry till i feel the life will drain right
out of me. It fears me that i will not be able
to take it any more. An then what good will
i be when i goes home. The time has bin to
much. Am i a criminal doctor???? Please be
a good man an tell me what crime i did comit

for i can remember doin none. You know my conduct here is good. i keep to myself an do my work an somes for the nurses as well. if i were to leave nurse B...wonuld surely get little done. An now i am growing suspisios sir that maybe that is why you choose to keep me here evin tho my brain is right to go home now. is it so doctor???? I ask of you to tell me truthfuly now cause i am in such a confued way not knowin why i am held here when i so despartely wants to go home to my loved ones. An now i see sir that my dear Husband has bin to look in on me an i knew nothin of it. i am furious to lern of this doctor did you not think i would be???? after all this time and all my letters beggin you to ask him to come get me???? How dare you do such a thing sir!!!!! i am beside myself with greif!!!! It becomes you to have let him see me. He is a smart enouf man an could of seen for hissefl i was all good now an could go home with him an cause no further troubel. I must see my childrin sir i beg it of you i am frightful of my mind splitin apart soon if i am held here any longer. Please doctor i beg of you to come see me an see for yerself how wells i'm coming along. I know i acted badly at the dance an for this i am dearly sorry. As I said before i do have a cantankorous side an it is not the best of me. Mostly i can control it now but i was takin by such suprise at that girl wearing my sweater that it plum got away on me. An can yous blame me for it Sir???? What a thing to look up and see!!!!! An evin now my blood is hot as embers as i think of it. How could you do such a thing doctor??? You are a good man that is plain to see. But my Dear Husband would have brought that sweater here for me. It was not right

for you to give it to some one else who had
no claim to it. It were my great aunt Hel-
ens sweater givin down to me when she
passed. As a girl i used to sit with her at
times an she was the one that taoght me
how to embroder the flowers into things.
and i got quiet good at such things an that
made her pleased. So can you imagine for
a moment how it was for me to see you
had givin my own aunties dear sweater to
some other patinet to wear??? I have had
to much of such violition sir to much i tell
you!!!! I demand now that yous let my Husband know it is time he come to get me. it
has been well 2 or 3 years now at least. the
pain of my little ones growin up without
me is to much to bear i would rahter be at
least treated as well as a horse with a broke
leg and take a bulett thu my brains to put
me short of such misery. An sir i knows
you dont have little ones yerself but try
to imagin my heart ache at havin my little
baby growin up without me for these years.
She will be walkin by now an she was only a
babe in arms when i went away. i scarce can
put the words on this page of how it tears
my heart to pieces. An i will admit sir at
first i was furious at my dear Husband for
what he done. An hows he tole me he put
the kittens in the swamp to drown them.
We never did agree on such things sir an
he knew as much an i tore up to the water-
hole as fast as my tired legs could carry me
an...oh doctor i dont mean to say to much
but can you evin begin to unnerstand the
horror of that moment when i saw it werent the kittens drowning at all but 5 of my
own sweet babys???? An it were to much
altogther to see thier little bodys floating
in the swamp up side down just floating

among the reeds. Doctor i think if i were to guess rightly that is were my mind finally gave way an i screamed and screamed and ran out in the swamp to save my childrin an i were beside myself with grief an then i got to the littlest one my new baby girl an turned her face up out of the water an it werent my baby at all but just a bit of wood floatin all wrapped up in my babies nightie. An i didnt hardly know what to belive if my mind was showin me right or if i was in some terrible night terrror. an i tried to check the other bodys cause i couldnt know if they were still my childs an i could hardly move in the deep water to my chest an i fell as i did so many times sobbing and crying out for my Husband to comes help an i was almost drownin myself by the time i got all 5 of thems flipped over an could see they were just blocks of wood dressed up in my childrens clothing. But doctor let me assure you the brains can only take so much of a shock like that or at least this was true of mine an i was still fraught with terror and worry trying to get the blocks of wood to the shore and crying so hard i thought my heart would explode an nothin made no sense no more and i couldnt tell that it were ok and my childrin werent drowned in the swamp. I just couldnt tell no more An doctor i will speak frankly for once altho i know it never seems to get me no good but my dear husband finally came to help me an he laughed at my sobbing and said not to be so silly it were all just a little joke. And Sir i can tell you it were no such thing!!!! Not to me it werent. My dear Husband took me up to the house then he had to carry me cause my legs would not work an i was dizzy an fallin an he showed

me the little ones all asleep in thier beds
safe as new-hatched robins in the nest but i
couldn't get my brains to settle down sir an
he had to take me away from them agin. An
he said he was sorry it were just a little joke
an i cant say sir but maybe he was. Wasnt
long after that he offerd to bring me here
for a small rest an sir it werent no decision
for me to make i was no good there no more
my brains were all over the place—

☰ ☰ ☰

Dropping the scribbled letter on his desktop, Dr. Davidson took the pipe from his mouth and knocked it brutally
against the inside of the trash can. Staring down at the
tiny haystack of unlit tobacco, he reached into his pocket,
pulled out a packet and hypnotically tamped his pipe fresh.
Anna and her incessant nonsense. It perturbed him but
today he had more pressing concerns. Concerns that could
not be so easily filed away on the bottom shelf.

Stuffing the pipe back into the corner of his mouth, he
looked impatiently at his watch. The time was interminable. Quarter of nine. Still fifteen minutes before the ward
lights were put out. He knew the curfew was excessively
early. Especially in the summer months when the long rays
of hot days still persisted through the drawn nightshades.
The lights-out rule was a holdover from the days when the
asylum had been self-sufficient. When hogs and chickens
waited to be fed, the small herd of dairy cows milked. Now,
the early bedtime was just a convenience of scheduling.
Patients routinely complained, their dosage of nightly
sleeping pills helping them to comply.

Striding quickly over to the door of his office, Dr. Davidson locked it. His lips formed a dry, thin smile at the satisfying click. He relished the comfort of that impervious
door. No longer was he at anyone's disposal. Finally alone

in the sanctuary of his private thoughts, cloistered safely inside the oak-paneled womb of his office, he could strip away the awful leaden effigy that bore his name. Allow himself to rest, at least for a brief moment, inside the doubting, desirous, lonely shell of the man he truly was.

Crossing back to his desk, he sat down leisurely. Loosened the tie around his neck. Stretched long and yawned loudly. Again, he checked the time. Scarcely two minutes had crawled by.

The whole focus of his thoughts were being overwhelmingly drawn by two things—an insatiable desire to be near the girl and his little box full of tricks that would enable him to do so. Damning the time, he pushed back abruptly and slid open the desk's heavy bottom drawer. He would only get things ready, he promised. It would not do to attempt to alleviate himself too soon. He'd found that out the hard way once. His slow veins running clear too soon, his dulled euphoria lifting, leaving him to navigate his way back out of the tunnels with nothing to aid his resplendent claustrophobic fear. It was a mistake he dared not repeat.

With great precision, he attempted to concentrate his fumbling hands on emptying out the open drawer. Stacks of reports, files, papers. All taken out and placed systematically on top of the desk, care taken to maintain the progression of order. Noisily, a folder burst free of his hands, fluttering papers across the floor. Cursing, he scooped them together roughly, shoving them back in haphazardly. The calm sense of presence that had enveloped him only moments before was gone. Hands shaking, eyes intense and watery, he felt himself morphing into an animal of rabid need. Pushing and groping his way through the remaining items, he finally seized upon a nondescript, rectangular box. Hastily drawing it onto his lap, he hesitated, listened, then rose to check the locked door once more.

Satisfied that it was indeed secure and that he was still safe from the impertinent Nurse Mildred barging in to flutter her lashes like a battered butterfly and insolently question his directives, he again reposed at his desk and slowly opened the box.

Its contents called out to him like the promise of pirate's gold. A yellowed tourniquet. A long surgical needle. Beside them lay a small vial of sweet rest. Swallowing, licking his cracked lips, he dove into the preparations with a familiarity that should have been frightening to him. Easing the sharp needle into his greedy desire, he laid his head back and sighed, drawing the dulling venom up through him, eager for it to penetrate his anxious mind. His body began to relax, welcoming the hot infiltration that began to float him even now just beyond the reach of his constant companions—worry and doubt.

Withdrawing the needle, he laid it on the desk. Taking his left thumb, he absently twirled the thin gold band that encircled his right ring finger. The ring had belonged to his father. Its presence on his hand had provoked many a hedged question over the years. His answers had always been evasive, if not downright dismissive. He felt the vagueness of the ring's origins bloomed a sense of intrigue around him. Shrouded him with an aura of much-needed mystery.

Catching a look at his watch, he was complacently astounded to see it was half past the hour. Cramming the contents of the drawer somewhat back into place, he attempted to shut it. Taking up the rickety ladder-back chair from the other side of his desk, he maneuvered it in front of his tallest cabinet. Balancing precariously on the seat of the chair, he strained upward, patting impatiently across the dust-covered top of the shelf. His hands returned him nothing. He groped about some more, covering the space corner to corner. Puzzled, he gingerly got down from the chair and tried to think. Had he put it somewhere else? He couldn't remember doing so, but it was quite evident that the doll was no longer where he thought it was. Was it possible that Margaret might have moved it when she was nosing about his office, pretending to be cleaning? Doubtful. She was little inclined to stretch beyond her more immediate capabilities.

Nurse Mildred came to mind, and he stopped to consider this. It was obvious she'd been hurt at being tricked into bringing him the doll. But whether she'd been hurt because he'd caused her to break trust with the girl or whether she was just bitter because he hadn't welcomed her into his plan remained a question. She was a constant paradox of loyalties. One day a plodding, trusted plow horse, the next as fickle as a feline. At any rate, it couldn't be helped. The doll was gone and his time was slipping away also. He'd have to go without it tonight. The girl would have already been given her sleeping pill by now, and he liked to slip into her room just before she nodded off. When she almost seemed to welcome his visits, soft and dreamy and receptive.

Slipping through the tunnels with ease, he observed the grim shadows thrown against the walls by the few ceiling lights. He felt distant from them. Impenetrable from the inside. Tapping lightly on her door, he quickly let himself in. Save for the lump of sweater lying on the floor, the room appeared to be empty. The girl was not sitting on the edge of the bed, waiting for him as she usually was. He glanced at the rude latrine. Empty. Puzzled, his eyes roved the cavernous space, searching into the dark corners as his flashlight exposed them. Finally, he found her, crouched low in the overhanging gloom of the far wall.

"Come now," he cooed as he stepped toward her. "Whatever are you doing, hiding like that?"

Drowsy eyes watched him. She drew back as he approached.

"What's this, my sweet?" he whispered, bruised. "Not back to that silly old game are we?"

Taking her by her slim hands, he pulled her to her feet.

"Let's go sit on the bed and have a little chat, shall we?"

Her head nodded. Likely not with consent but with the effects of the sleeping pill. He chose to believe it otherwise. Slipping an arm around her tiny waist, he helped her wavering feet find their way over to the bed and sat her down. Positioning himself beside her, he wove an arm around her shoulders, pulling her closer as he propped her upright against him.

Something is not right, he fumed inwardly as he stroked her glossy hair. There was something changed about her. He could feel it in the small tremor of resistance still hopelessly trying to gain control of her limp body. The way she had peered out at him from her hiding place. Fearful. In a way she hadn't been since her earliest days in the asylum.

His mind was a mad dance of slow questions. He wished the stupor of the drugs gone. He needed to reason clearly. Could it have been the betrayal of taking away her doll? Impossible. Even Nurse Mildred—with her unnerving skill of divining—had failed to see beyond that. Perhaps, in defense of her violated ego, Mildred had simply chosen to divulge his plan to the girl. *Possible*, he thought. With the constantly shifting loyalties among the staff, he found he seldom knew whom he could actually trust anymore.

The girl's arms were cold, and he rubbed his cupped hands over them firmly. Noticing the discarded sweater lying on the floor beside the bed, he reached over to pick it up. Something tangled beneath it clunked to the floor as he drew it upward. Suddenly fighting through her inertia, the girl pulled free of him, reached down drunkenly and snatched the little doll up into her arms.

Dr. Davidson glared at it, incredulous.

"*Where* did you get that?" he hissed lethally.

Not able to fix her eyes on him any longer, she closed them, curling herself like a cocoon around the doll as she dissolved back into sleep.

His fingers instinctively searched for the wound elastic that bound her hair back from her face into a loose braid and released it. Absently, with a remote anger, he mentally began to draw up an order for Nurse Mildred's immediate dismissal. The impertinence of the woman. How *dare* she go against doctor's orders. He had hurt her. He had seen that. Far more than he had ever intended. But still, that in no way gave her justification for her actions. It was not hers to simply override his decision and return the doll to the girl. Nor snoop about in his office. The idea of it stopped off the blood in his veins. He'd be hard-pressed to explain that little injection kit hidden away in his bottom drawer. He'd already felt her prying eyes on him when he knew his comments had fallen short of the mark. His head nurse had never been stupid; he certainly knew that. She was wily—agile. Dangerous if she were to ever turn the tables on him. He dropped the dismissal note from his mind. Such an easy solution would simply not be an option.

Pressing all his cares about the asylum free of him, he turned his attentions to the girl sleeping against his arm. The thickness in his mind so easily swept it all away. Vanishing it out from under him the way his footprints had disappeared in the sand those few times that his mother—reluctantly—had allowed him to join in on their seaside escapes. Wrapping himself around the girl, he nestled her easily onto his lap. She slept on, unperturbed, the little doll huddled into her, the sweater loose about her shoulders.

He smiled down at her beatific face, a single finger glazing over her long neck, pale and elegant, like the swans that graced the edge of the lake. His eyes moved over her, her body supine but chaste in the hospital nightgown. The buds of her breasts had blossomed. The regular meals had nourished her back toward an acceptable weight and vitality. Improving under the asylum's care but not yet completely well. Only last week, Nurse Bea had noted on the chart that the girl's monthly had ceased again. Such an occurrence was not uncommon with the emaciated ones, but the setback had bothered him all the same.

Moaning lightly, she shifted in his arms, her head tipping her face open to him. Her mouth moved with silent emotion and he thought for a moment she might speak in her sleep. Her tongue, like a tiny pink kitten, searched about softly. To his disappointment, she did not speak but again fell still. Her only movement was the slight lifting and falling of her breast as it followed her rhythmic breathing.

A feeling beyond him pulled him forward, drawing him down magnetically toward her soft mouth. He kissed her—deeply—soulfully—then drew away. She lay as before—unmoved. He felt a pain—ancient and raw—opening up within him. He longed for her eyes to blink open, for a familiar smile to trickle across her lips as she kissed him back. Sighing, he rested his head against the stone wall. He knew it would never be. That this visceral thing was all he would ever have.

"*Ma chérie, ma chérie*," he crooned softly as he began to rock her gently.

It was the pet name by which he had once overheard his father address his mother. It had not gone over well. Her rancid glare and the vicious tinge of mockery that crusted her laugh had ensured his father did not do so again.

Barely skimming the top of the girl's head with his lips, he began to rock her a little more deliberately. He'd be at a loss to know how many midnight hours had waxed and waned finding him doing the same thing. He felt a rare comfort being with her. A safe umbilical happiness, which had evaded him his whole life. He called it love. Sometimes, he supposed he had to allow, he had perhaps rocked her a bit too hard. But he did not like to think about that.

The unblinking eyes of the doll stared up at him. It unnerved him—that thing. He attempted to slide it free from her arms but to no avail. Even in a deep sleep, she was still protective over it. Sliding the sweater from her shoulders, he blotted out its face. He glanced down as something fell free from inside of the sleeve.

A red feather.

Dr. Davidson jolted upright. What on earth was going on? The returned doll may have been Nurse Mildred's doing. But this red feather smacked hard of Jakie Hewitt. How was such a thing possible? Without the benefit of a key, the room was impossible to enter. Was the man a ghost? *Of course not, you fool,* he chastised his railing mind. Jakie Hewitt was just a man. And a simple man at that. If he had given the girl that feather, then either he and Nurse Mildred were in cahoots, or else there was some other way it came through these granite walls.

Carefully repositioning the girl on top of the bed, he picked up the feather and began a slow, methodical search of the room. His mind ran rampant with paranoid accusations, stopping first at one and then the other of his staff, digging back into memories to ascertain what slant they had taken against him. But it was no use. His weary mind was not up to the task. He sighed as he continued to inspect the wall. It felt as if the whole asylum had turned against him. His thoughts fell to Dr. Uldrich, and he felt perhaps he had found the root of the problem. The man had been doggedly undermining him since the first day. Somehow— and Dr. Davidson still did not know how—Uldrich had managed to secure permission to treat several of the asylum's patients, including Norman Headly. And the damning thing of it was, Headly appeared to show progress for his having done so.

Dr. Davidson turned to examine the back wall. He'd almost given up his search as futile when the beam of his flashlight exposed what seemed to be a small indentation. Up high, by the ceiling. Reaching on tiptoe, he inspected it further. Tiny particles of dried greenery caught on the rough edges. Taking his pipe from his pocket, he slid the stem deep into the black void.

So that was it, he thought. Closing his eyes, he tried to recover his bearings. He too remembered the abandoned beginnings of an entrance tunnel that lay just beyond the wall of the cellar room. Like a weasel, it seemed that perhaps Jakie Hewitt had used it to further his own purposes. Well, Dr. Davidson nodded, he just might be able to put the place to good use himself.

CHAPTER 20

J akie honked the horn and imagined the sound. Another one of the ingenious Mr. Brewster's oversights. Sitting jauntily in the driver's seat of the makeshift car that claimed his living room, Jakie gazed out the single-paned window in front of him and into the trees across the dirt road. Smiling, he waved at himself as his reflection waved back. It looked good on him, that car. Added a sense of civility and respect that his pedestrian life in the asylum had slowly stripped away.

Tapping a finger against a nonexistent bowler, he bid the refrigerator hello and wished several passersby a very pleasant day. Stretching leisurely, he checked the weather. Clear blue sky. A perfect day for a drive. Skimming his hands loosely across the top of the steering wheel, he pretended a wide, arcing right turn. Time to flee the congested city streets for the full, fertile fields that lay beyond. A drive in the country would do him well. The rhythmic hum of the tires sang a vacant song. One that encouraged his mind to drift free of itself, floating as placidly and content as a leaf drifting down a stream.

He felt absolutely, deliciously full of the girl—of his Lily. Not just his thoughts but every permeable piece of him. *And the impermeable as well*, he offered happily. He felt himself a lucky man. Never before could he have imagined his days so filled with color. Only now did he realize just how low he had stumbled. Had lost connection with the very essence of himself, failing even to preserve the ghost of faint hope. And perhaps it had been easier that way. A total surrender, relinquishing a lost self he could not remember nor found any promise that it could ever be recovered again.

Signaling right, he eased off of the expressway, first shifting down and then up as he negotiated the ramp, then stepped heavily to escape clear of the confining traffic. Overtaking a rickety truck, he passed by easily, laughing heartily at the aggrieved meat-and-potato-fed faces gawking over in disapproval at his joyride speed.

He relaxed as he traversed broad forests and tidy farms. A dust-colored, sleepy village parted a main street as he approached, and he purred down it slowly, nodding and smiling amicably, returning the shy waves of the locals as they ogled his spiffy roadster. Picking up speed as he again found the open road, he closed his eyes and tipped back his head. The wind was warm and friendly, its supple fingers streaming his hair away from his sun-bronzed face. Following the ribbon of packed-dirt road winding away in front of him, he grew immensely happy at having left the city's turmoil behind. He felt easy here, free. Like he belonged.

A catchy tune began to dance through his mind and, opening his eyes again, he reached forward to a hole slit into the dashboard where a radio was to have gone. Rolling his thumb and finger around the invisible knob, he selected through a plethora of songs. Several familiar melodies floated to him, but their words did not. Turning the radio off again, he set to whistling.

"Cheeeer-a-dote, cheeer-a-dote-dote-dote, purdy, purdy, purdy...whoit, whoit, whoit, whoit, what-cheer, what-cheer... wheet, wheet, wheet, wheet...cheer, cheer, cheer—"

He grinned over boyishly at the empty seat beside him and imagined Lily smiling back. She would love the open road as well. The fresh air. The sun's palm caressing the soft planes of her face. And he would enjoy giving it all to her. Show her a world far more kind and beautiful than the one he suspected she had known.

Closing his eyes again, he visualized their cross-country dash, her head laid trustingly against his strong shoulder as he drove. Following Mr. Brewster's detailed maps, they'd wind their way down through the states and on into the anonymous freedom of Mexico. Probably they would have to stop for a while along the way, but Jakie wasn't worried about that. Fields to work, houses to paint, barns with roofs that begged fixing before the next onslaught of spring rains. Life provided a multitude of tasks for someone with his various skills. And the few things the money could not buy them, the forest and streams would generously supply.

He drove on this way for quite some time, smoothing out the intricacies of their escape. Of course, there was still the unsavory business of attaining the long-buried maps. Folded and sealed away in the Mason jar under Mr. Brewster's decaying hands. He hoped the maps would still be intact. He didn't much care for the idea of taking a completed job and digging it up again, but he could see no other way. Apparently, Mr. Brewster was coming up for another resurrection.

His mind wandered up the stairs of Cottage Five. To the suitcase that bore his borrowed name and the photograph of a woman with hauntingly familiar eyes. He would hoist the trunk out of the attic window and take it with them, strapping it down to the back of the car. His mind had found no answers to the swirl of questions the suitcase had raised, but he knew he felt an undeniable connection to those strange items found beneath its assumed base. If he were ever to have a chance at weaving together the threads of his frayed life, the contents of the suitcase might provide him with the tools he would need. He tried to envision himself as a new man. Happy and vital and free. With welcome surprise, he found in his heart of hearts that he already was. Joyously, Cardinal's song burst once more from his lips.

"*Cheeeer-a-dote, cheeer-a-dote-dote-dote, purdy, purdy, purdy—*"

Then, reaching faintly through his reverie, he heard her answer back. Startled, his eyes flashed open, at once checking the still-vacant seat beside him. For a confused moment, he thought he'd become deceived by his own imagining, but then the song sounded again.

"*Whoit, whoit, whoit, whoit...what-cheer, what-cheer... wheet, wheet, wheet, wheet...cheer, cheer, cheer—*"

This time the direction was not faint but clear to him. He searched outside the window as a fawn flutter drew his attention that way. The distinctive bird, with her coral beak and raised crest, bobbed patiently on a low branch of the spruce tree, alertly awaiting the return call of her potential mate.

Jakie pressed back into the seat of the car and howled with laughter.

"Be off with you now, ya little minx," he called out jovially. "You're far too late, I'll have ya know."

Eyes sharp, she quivered her feathers enticingly.

"I mean it now, darlin'. My heart's already been given away for the rest of the dance."

Unconcerned, the female cardinal—a bird that often mates for life—shook off this news with no apparent hard feelings and, catching a sudden breeze, soared out of sight.

Chuckling to himself, Jakie shifted the car into high speed, Lily back at his side as he prepared to sprint across the unmanned border in front of them and on into a new life in Mexico.

An unexpected rap at the door called him back.

Scrabbling free of the car, he strode quickly to answer the knock, a little embarrassed at the chance his cross-country expedition may have been seen.

Dr. Davidson stood crookedly on the weathered stoop, looking urgent.

"May I come in?"

"Of course," Jakie replied, barely having time to open the door wider as the doctor slipped through.

They stood in an extended silence, Dr. Davidson taking stock of the place as Jakie patiently waited to see what he had come for. Watching the doctor's quick gray eyes scan over his private space, Jakie began to take stock of it himself. The shiplapped walls were rough and dirty, tired sawdust insulation spilling out in several places. The plank floor sported numerous pools of dry rot, which Jakie had learned to step around. Shredded curtains defaced the windows. A small refrigerator, which had retired many years before, gobbled up a corner of the cramped space, the door gasping open, its shelves commandeered and stuffed full of all sorts of useful junk.

"Make some tea?" Jakie offered, hoping to divert the doctor's attention. Jakie had never viewed his home through someone else's eyes. Up until now, he'd had no visitors. *Cozy* was the word he always would have chosen to describe his living quarters. Now he could plainly see it was really less than a tumbledown shack.

"No. No tea, thank you," Dr. Davidson replied, waving a shaky hand through the air.

Keeping an inquisitive eye on him, Jakie set the kettle on to boil anyway. Excusing himself, he stepped outside to secure a few quarter-split chunks of wood, then fed them into the ancient stove's fire chamber. It was obvious to him, despite the doctor's best façade, that the man was a case of nerves, in dire need of something calming. Rummaging through his dusty cupboard, Jakie found a chipped and crackled mug and attempted to swipe it clean. Gesturing for the doctor to sit on his one good chair beside the square wooden table, Jakie stepped over to the hood of the car to gather a few leaves of sweet-fern to flavor their tea.

"Wha...you...Jakie...how the devil did *that* get there?" Dr. Davidson sputtered accusingly.

"Been there ever since ya came in, sir," Jakie said, frowning as he filled the mugs with hot water. "Didn't see it?"

Dr. Davidson's color rose. He mumbled something indistinguishable. Impossible as it seemed, it was evident that he actually had not.

Setting the steaming tea on the rough tabletop, Jakie stepped back out onto the porch and swung a heavy five-gallon pail inside to sit on.

"Honey?"

Dr. Davidson looked across at him blankly.

"For your tea," Jakie explained, already rising off the pail to get the amber-colored jar from the top shelf. He'd never before seen the doctor so distracted and off of his game. An urgent mewling interrupted him, and Jakie stooped down to a cloth-filled basket beside the wood stove and scooped out a squirming black-and-white ball of fur.

"What in God's name—"

"Baby skunk," Jakie replied, bringing it over to the table for Dr. Davidson to see.

"Where's its mother?" the doctor asked warily, easing away from it as he made a quick glance around the room.

"Dead, I s'pose. Found it abandoned," Jakie said as he quickly fashioned together a miniature bottle and set about feeding it. Remembering what he'd first gotten up to do, he reached high for the honey with his one free hand and set it on the table.

"Where on earth do you get these things?"

Blowing cool a sip from his tea, Jakie nodded outside.

Taking the offered honey, Dr. Davidson worked to wipe a spoon sort of clean with his noncooperative hands and stirred some into his mug. The whole of his countenance was awkward and off balance.

"About *that*..." he gestured to the car as he set about clearing his throat. "It would seem a bit against the institution's rules."

Taking up the spoon the doctor had just put down, Jakie calmly added some honey into his own tea, stirring it slowly as he grinned down at the nursing skunk nestled into his lap.

"Been there a long time, doctor."

"Has it?" Dr. Davidson spouted, then fell silent with a look of furious disapproval on his face. It was clear he felt foolish and ill-advised. Diminished in his role as overseer and director of the asylum's activities. Jakie knew the doctor prided himself on having an eye on every facet of the institution's web. But the truth was he'd readily neglected to concern himself with this distasteful corner, preferring to leave Mr. Brewster and—after him—Jakie, to dispose of the asylum's waste.

"Been here for ages. Mr. Brewster liked to tinker at it from time to time. Shame is, he never quite got it done."

Dr. Davidson shifted on the chair. It creaked in complaint. He took a sip of tea. It tasted awful, and he screwed up his face. He took back the spoon that was now in front of Jakie and added more honey.

"Well, still, it's against the rules."

"Can't see where it's caused too many problems as yet," Jakie replied wryly, setting aside the empty bottle and curling the contented skunk back into its basket.

The doctor's eyes fidgeted about the room, and this time Jakie noticed them settle on a few items he'd failed to see on his first go-round. An ax sitting just inside the door. Knives on the counter. And above the living room window, a rusted two-man, crosscut saw. The whole damn place was a violation of the rules.

"No, I suppose not," he conceded. "Does it run?"

Jakie nodded. "Seems to."

Dr. Davidson shook his head almost admiringly. "How the devil you think ole Brewster was planning on getting it out of here?"

Jakie shrugged. "Maybe he wasn't."

"Maybe," Dr. Davidson mumbled, not quite convinced. Jakie knew the doctor held some fond memories of Mr. Brewster, a once well-regarded physicist. In his early years in the ward, Jakie had listened on, amused, as the two intellectuals had shared some interesting debates. They'd jousted over the chessboard as well, right up until the day Mr. Brewster had soundly beaten him and Dr. Davidson had realized it was a game he could no longer afford to play. But that was long before the decay of Mr. Brewster's brain finally ate him into a digger of graves. Eventually, Dr. Davidson had had him moved over to the cemetery shack, where he could at least benefit from being busy for part of the day. And, although the doctor had never cared to admit it, Jakie firmly suspected the move also obliterated the day-to-day reminder of how easily a brilliant mind could be whittled away.

Looking over at the macabre roadster, Dr. Davidson frowned. He eyed the complex machine. Jakie could see a finger of suspicion needling him as the decline of Mr. Brewster's mind began to cast itself in a brighter light. *Checkmate*, Jakie almost said out loud.

"Well, the dementia was setting in pretty bad toward the end," the doctor said, almost to himself. "Perhaps he meant to just drive it out the window—"

"Be a mighty tight squeeze," Jakie replied, draining down the rest of his tea. "Who knows? Maybe he thought he could just make the whole thing disappear with him in it."

Dr. Davidson snorted derisively.

"Anyhow, you should have told me about it, Jakie. It takes up most of the...your home. Surely you want it out of here?"

Jakie smiled obscurely.

"I'll have that done then. As a favor. And maybe you could return one for me."

"*No!*" Jakie said abruptly.

Dr. Davidson's eyes jumped up to meet this bold refusal.

"Not *no* to the favor, sir. But to the car. I'd like it left where it is. It's become plenty useful to me." He directed the doctor's attention back to the car so he could see for himself the reams of fruits, berries, and leaves drying on top of any and every flat surface.

"Suit yourself then." Dr. Davidson shrugged distractedly. Shifting once again atop the vocal chair, he coughed dryly, his demeanor turning icily serious.

"Can I trust you, Jakie?"

Not quite sure how to answer this, Jakie said nothing, waiting for the doctor to further explain himself.

"Everything's changed around here. Around the institution. Since Uldrich came. Staff loyalties shifting on a daily basis. It's become impossible for me to know who I can trust anymore. You always seemed a fair man to me, Jakie. I need your help."

Jakie drew back and studied the doctor's face. The request was odd. Not because Dr. Davidson had requested his help but because he had chosen to say it that way. Times past it had been, *Jakie, this needs doing,* or, *Jakie, I'd like you to—* But never, *I need your help.* There was something pained and desperate about such frank raw wording.

"It involves the girl," Dr. Davidson added, and Jakie's hackles set to straight.

Dr. Davidson shrunk back a degree in the face of Jakie's protective alarm. He shifted about a bit, obviously searching carefully for the right words.

"She's in danger, Jakie. Uldrich is set on getting her into his program, and I don't know how much longer I can protect her from him."

Leaning back against the wall, Jakie said nothing. His head stormed full of his thundering heart, and he worked vainly to calm it. Silently, he called out for Coyote's counsel but no counsel came. Knowing he had to find a way to think clearly, he fought hard to find a point of stillness within himself. For a long while he said nothing, just stared at a blemish of dry rot beneath the table. Dr. Davidson sat in the uncomfortable void, his increasingly physical agitation indicating his displeasure at the lack of response.

Jakie's eyes rose to meet the doctor's questioning glare, briefly catching his own reflection in the oval mirror beside the door. His eyes were lucid and determined. Dr. Davidson sat up a little straighter. The change was so tangible that it actually altered the structure of Jakie's face. The doctor shifted once more on his chair. He was adept at operating in a theater of brokenness, but Jakie could tell he was quickly beginning to understand that this was something different altogether.

"How can I help her?"

Dr. Davidson exhaled a relieved breath.

"Ah. Good. I was hoping I could count on you, Jakie." And then more brusquely, "You've been watching the girl—"

Jakie grew rigid with protest but said nothing.

"Bringing her things? Berries and herbs? *Feathers*—" he added quietly, pulling the stark red cardinal feather from his cardigan pocket and laying it on the table between them.

Jakie watched intensely as Dr. Davidson fumbled his pipe free from his other pocket and placed it in his mouth. It angered Jakie, seeing the feather here. His gift stripped indiscriminately from Lily's compliant hands. He wondered if she had tried to save it. Struggled against the unjustness of it.

Dr. Davidson clacked his pipe absently against his teeth, clearly awaiting an answer. Jakie chose his words carefully. Obviously, his visits had been exposed. To what extent remained the question.

"I gave her some things from the forest," he hedged.

"Through the hole in the wall." It was not a question.

Jakie looked over, a bit surprised. So, the doctor hadn't suspected him of being inside Lily's room after all.

Dr. Davidson misinterpreted Jakie's look.

"Yes, I found your little hole, Jakie. The last time I was down there. And when I went around back to investigate further, I also found the tunnel and that space you've carved out before it. Quite clever, really. But a *complete* violation of the rules. Do you actually stay out there?"

Jakie could see no reason to lie. Clearly, the doctor had found his hideaway. Had seen his bed and tools. His stove vented to the outside, the leathery strips of sun-dried fish and the racks of drying medicinals. And, most damning of all, the long burrowing tunnel that led to the small opening high up in the girl's room.

"Sometimes I stay there," he admitted. He did not like where all of this seemed to be headed. It was blankly obvious he'd broken enough of Dr. Davidson's precious rules to have himself easily transferred away to a different asylum, perhaps even one with tighter security. It was a prospect he'd been threatened with several times before.

"I only wanted—"

An impatient hand waved his explanation away.

"Of course. We both only want what's best for her, don't we?"

Jakie indicated agreement, but he found himself a bit thrown off on suddenly finding himself added to the doctor's roster.

"What I'm about to ask you to do is surely to come as a very strange request, Jakie. It will give you some idea of the complexities of the situation I now find myself in. If word of it gets out, my position here at the hospital will most assuredly be revoked. Do you understand that? You can discuss it with no one. Ever. Do I have your word on that?"

Jakie nodded vaguely. Other than Coyote, who did he have to tell?

"Good," Dr. Davidson murmured, the chair shuffling around beneath him as he strove to find a comfortable stance. His face was tight with exhaustive worry. A mask of extreme fatigue formed the base beneath it. Taking the pipe from his mouth, he cupped the bowl with both hands in an attempt to still them. Their irresponsive trembling troubled Jakie, although the doctor seemed far too preoccupied with other matters to even notice them.

"I need you to take her and disappear for a while, Jakie."

He paused briefly, obviously waiting for Jakie's surprised reception to such a request.

"*Disappear*, doctor?"

"I need her gone, Jakie. As soon as possible. Dr. Uldrich has managed to find his way over my head. God knows how but he has. He's already secured permission to treat several of my patients in spite of my recommendations against it."

He stopped to clear his throat, latent anger curling his hands into taloned fists around the bowl of his pipe.

"He wants the girl, Jakie. He's tried to convince me that his Sleep Therapy will help her. I'm not so sure it will to be honest. There've been improvements in some of the patients, I have to admit. Others have not fared so well. You know what the girl is like, Jakie. She's delicate. I'm afraid he'll change her completely."

Jakie sat quiet within himself and tried to absorb what he had just heard. A thin thread of compassion offered itself to the tortured man sitting across from him. It had sounded strange to hear such a confession tumble from the doctor's mouth but hear it he had. Dr. Davidson—the man whose opinion had held such profound power to alter all of the patients' lives—was afraid. *How easily are the mighty humbled by the beauty of a simple songbird*, Jakie thought ruefully.

He studied the doctor's demeanor, trying to find a path through his own thoughts. Dr. Davidson slumped on his chair, given over at last to the discomfort, a bruised wreckage of his former self. Clearly, things in the asylum had been unraveling around him for quite some time. Despite a feeling of caution tinged with acute jealousy, Jakie felt very sorry for the man. Noticing the doctor had never referred to Lily by her name, Jakie placated himself with one thought. Obviously with the doctor, her hand of trust had only extended so far.

"Do you think she'll go with you?" Dr. Davidson whispered, eyes watery with emotion as he sought out a space of sanctuary on the floor.

Jakie nodded proudly. Prouder than he had any right to be, as such an acceptance of trust still remained to be given.

"I'll go now," Jakie exploded, shoving up off the pail with exaggerated purpose.

"No! No, Jakie. Not yet. There're things you need to know," Dr. Davidson protested, switching seamlessly back into a man used to having things under his control.

"I'll go tonight then," Jakie continued, caught up in the urgency of his mind. "We can easily slip over the wall under the cover of dark."

"That's the thing, Jakie," Dr. Davidson interjected loudly. "You absolutely *cannot* take her off of the hospital's grounds."

"But, you just said I need to take her—"

"*Not* off of the grounds!" Dr. Davidson spat vehemently. "Not yet. If you got caught, things would end up worse than they already are. That kind of exposure would only help deliver her right into Uldrich's hands. And you as well, for that matter."

Jakie felt a raw sick helplessness gnawing at his gut. He frowned over at the doctor, confused as to what was to be his role in the plan.

"You have to hide her *on* the grounds, Jakie." Dr. Davidson explained hastily. "Only for a month. Until I can write her off of the books. After that, she'll no longer be a ward of the institution. She'll be completely outside of Uldrich's grasp. At that point, I can discreetly have her placed in a home in the city. Someplace where they can teach her the necessary skills to live an independent life."

Jakie listened while a slow avalanche heavily crushed his heart. He knew the doctor's plan was right. It was the best way forward for Lily. But he also knew, painfully so, that the best way forward for Lily would also take her away from him forever. He knew the only answer was to agree. But he simply could not find it in himself to utter the words.

"She'll be safe, Jakie. Isn't that what we both want?"

The nod came of its own accord.

Dr. Davidson brightened considerably. "Think of it though, Jakie. Once you've been missing for that month, you'll be written off the books also. You'll be a free man. Able to walk right clear of here yourself."

Jakie frowned over at the doctor, checking to see if he was joking. The serious set of his bedraggled face indicated otherwise. Incredulous, Jakie's eyes settled on the roadster garnishing his living room. After all these years, Dr. Davidson still failed to realize that Jakie had remained confined behind the asylum's protective walls not as a captive but purely out of convenience.

CHAPTER 21

J akie shook his head, smiling as he opened the door of the cellar room. Dr. Davidson had ensured that it had been left unlocked. He had also ordered the shattered light bulb outside in the tunnel to be replaced. Very helpful gestures, neither of which was of any particular benefit to Jakie. He preferred to move through the anonymity of darkness, his senses providing him with a clarity of sight that others found uncanny. But Dr. Davidson's tidy, accurate mind did not work in the same way as Jakie's. It was compelled to fix. To better the world's perceived failings. The compulsion was a slow, secret, insidious stem that wound its way from the buried bulb of his own sense of inadequacy, blooming in seemingly mundane ways. Jakie had long sensed that its constant twirling, twining turmoil was one of the things the doctor most hated about himself.

Jakie had not brought his slingshot along this time. Such minor inconveniences as a broken light were seldom rectified quickly in the laborious ongoing maintenance of the tired buildings. He worked a small meteorite of coal loose from his coat pocket and lobbed it underhand at the offending fixture. The coal arced high and left of its mark, landing farther down the tunnel with a muffled thud. Frowning, Jakie extracted a second lump of coal. He rolled it studiously in the hollow of his palms then blackened his face, an ancient instinct emerging, almost beyond thought. Some lost ghost of his past moved over him and settled deep. He tossed the piece of coal easily, and it shattered him into muted oblivion. He had known it would. Had experienced the satisfying crinkle of glass within every sinew of his body long before the dark rock had even risen through its orbit. Still, the inaccuracy of his first throw bothered him.

Lily sat on the very lip of her bed, doll in arms, wide watchful eyes following every movement of Jakie's silent entry. She wore her sweater, its few remaining buttons done up primly. A small bag of toiletries rested in her lap. She had been expecting him. Dr. Davidson had made sure of this also. The doctor had not been gone from the cellar room for very long before Cardinal's song had softly signaled Jakie's approach.

Springing at once from the bed to the door, Lily looked up at Jakie expectantly. Her energy was light and effervescent. Dr. Davidson had carried out Jakie's one request well. She exuded no sense of fear, only a trusting excitement. Jakie looked down into the enthusiastic wonder sparkling in her blue eyes and felt lost. He simply could not imagine how such hope could have survived the terrific onslaught of her troubled life. She stood before him quietly waiting. The silence, which had apparently insulated her like a thick coat through years of solitude, had become—for her—a comfortable fit.

Jakie could see she had been told no more than she needed to know, which was little. He had made the doctor promise him that. The overwhelming protective force Jakie felt over every aspect of her well-being had reformed him. He would die to protect her. Kill another. He had been surprised to find that certainty residing within him, but he knew if it came to it, that he would. He had no way of knowing what type of atrocities life had dealt her, but he knew it had been far too many. They registered themselves in the sudden flare of her eyes, the almost imperceptible flinching of her small body as a hand moved toward her a fraction too quickly.

He grinned down at her now as he raised the big black-ened paws of his hands slowly up to gently cradle her face. Softly, he painted out the telltale tones of her pale skin so she would merge as one with the dark as they slipped through the night. Her skin became finely polished jade beneath his hands, and he continued stroking the hills and valleys long after the blackness had transferred from him. She stood passively receptive, not questioning this strange rite of passage. Finally, feeling the weight of her safety perched heavily upon his shoulders, Jakie withdrew his hands.

"Do I look like a loony now?" She beamed with a mis-chievous grin.

Jakie shushed her quickly, and she closed up, stricken. He felt bad, but noises had sounded on the stairs at the far end of the tunnel. He took the bud of her hand, forcing a redeeming smile onto his face, loath to frighten her any more than he already had. Pressing a finger to his lips, he conveyed a gentle apology to her with his eyes. This she seemed to understand, and the soft rounds of her shoulders sagged a little as she again found her breath.

They skirted the tunnel quickly, exiting through a propped-open door, skimming along the sides of the build-ings and across the dew-wet lawn like cloud-shadows on a frozen lake. She followed him will-lessly until they were inside the watchful canopy of the forest's fringe. Here she stopped, and Jakie parroted the move automatically, think-ing she'd grown fearful. But she wasn't fearful. She was stopped in stunned silence, her eyes glittering as she tried to consume all the sights and smells, sounds and feelings welcoming her.

Jakie reluctantly released her warm hand as she knelt down on the furry bed of moss beneath them, buried her face, and pulled a sweet draught of life into her parched lungs. Joy lit her as she laid a delicate touch on all the things closest to her. A bald-headed rock outcropping crusted with lichen. The dried dung heap of some small woodland creature. An exquisite wild orchid, its tiny yellow tongue licking the cool night air. She tipped her doll forward so it could share with her in each new discovery.

Embraced by the umbrella of branches and shrubbery, Jakie relaxed a little. He could just make out a half-silhouette of Cottage Four. The tall pines above them parted ways to open a portal up to the heavens. A small swag of moon smiled down on them. He smiled back tentatively. They had entered an uneasy truce. Mesmerized, he turned to watch Lily's face as she turned it upward to receive the bright light. His arms felt empty and uncomfortable inside themselves. He crossed them over his chest and held on tightly. Nourished by the joy of her discovering, he longed to let her know how perfect she was inside a world that no longer fit. That the only sickness existing around them belonged to those who took good people and broke them down into shattered shells, dry shadows that crumbled into a million fractured grains of sand that the ocean of time eventually—mercifully—washed away. It was not the world he wanted her to know.

But of course, the words fled from him, feeling themselves inadequate to explain why such things should ever be. Bereft of answers, he held as quiet as the motionless trees. Lily turned to him as if she had heard him speak. A concerned frown tainted her face. Jakie held her with his eyes, desperately wanting to kiss the pale plump heart of her lips to let her know everything would be okay. Instead, he kissed the end of his own finger and playfully leaned forward to tap the tip of her blackened nose.

"You like it?" he asked, gesturing around grandly at their forest audience.

Lily nodded eagerly. She stroked and soothed the flora as if surrounded by small pets.

"Brother brought me," she whispered proudly.

"To the forest?"

Again, she nodded, eyes sparkling with remembered delight.

"When Pa was asleep. Pa didn't like me going out the house none. Brother took me..." She paused off to think. "Three times." She crossed her thumb over her little finger and held them up.

"*Three times?*" Jakie flared, failing to hide his dismay as he looked at her raised hand. It sounded like an accusation.

"Yes. Three," she said quietly, curling into herself a little, as if she had done something wrong. "But, I was just a little girl then."

"How little?" Jakie asked gently, awkward and desperate for a little salve to soften the echo of his indignant explosion.

Lily shrugged, her face confused. As if the question itself were devoid of significance for her.

Sighing, Jakie sank down beside her on the spongy moss mattress and lightly took her hand. He wanted to apologize for all the things he himself had not done. He cupped her little hand in the cave of his own. The frail, embryonic seed of her that he would protect and nourish until the inevitable bloom of her truest self. They sat looking up at the celestial treasure chest above them, her silken hair tickling against his awareness as they floated in a comfortable canoe of lost thoughts, neither riddled with the compunction to fill the space with verbal speech.

A rectangle of light broke the semidark façade of Cottage Four. She tensed against him, her eyes searching his face for instruction. Jakie yawned leisurely. He would not have her be afraid. Not here in the forest. This was *his* domain. Here, they could be invisible. She rested again beside him as they watched the old building flicker awake. It should have been a beautiful structure, its multi-eyed brick face spilling with golden light. But it was not. Built with the unpaid toil of former inmates' hands, it remained eternally haunted by its own unforgivable debt. The emotional dysentery roiling through the hallways within sickened the light, mutating it with a pustule greenish tint. Viewed from the arms of the forest, Cottage Four looked pockmarked with disease.

The addition of more lights signaled a search was taking place. Pus-colored rectangles splotched on along the bottom level of the building, gradually working their way higher and higher. Jakie slid slowly to his feet, Lily his effortless shadow. Turning toward the deep expanse of trees, they ghosted their way into the covering, her left hand still cradled in his, her baby secreted away inside the nest of her arm.

Jakie's cave home opened to them as suddenly as if it had just then formed itself into being. Lily was oblivious to its existence right up until Jakie motioned her onto all fours and helped worm her through its camouflaged entrance. Scrabbling back to her feet as she gained the cramped, roughed-out inner room, she gaped around incredulously. Her attention vacillated between the little bed molded into the far back wall, the bountiful drying racks, and the coughing companion of the little wood stove, sputtering smoke from its ramshackle road of vented piping. She looked at Jakie with a mute, wondrous awe. As if he were a magician that had miraculously just conjured it all.

Jakie self-consciously skirted her admiring gaze. He felt a distinct jab of embarrassment as she looked around his humble dwelling. Sensing a rising swell of exhaustion forming beneath the shiny glaze of her enthusiasm, he busied himself with uprooting the cave's singular chair. Despite her youthful age, the girl was unnaturally frail, a lifetime of closed captivity robbing her lithe body of the muscle and vitality it should normally have enjoyed. Sinking onto the tattered and torn cane seat, she collapsed under the weight of the unaccustomed exercise, excitement, and rich lungfuls of fresh night air.

Outside a chorus of tree frogs began to reblanket the night with their shrill song. Jakie relaxed at the sound. For him, the frogs acted as a reverse security alarm, their loud chirping ceasing the moment they sensed their private membrane of forest had been breached.

Opening up a battered metal trunk that served to keep the rats and field mice from chewing apart his more perishable items, Jakie withdrew a puffy eiderdown comforter and settled it over the sparse cotton mattress covering the clay-cut wall bed. Two deflated throw pillows stuffed into a single case combined to make a somewhat sufficient headrest.

"You can have the bed," Jakie said, gesturing toward it as he stooped to restoke the embering fire.

She did not argue nor did she ask where he himself planned on sleeping. He struggled to identify her complacent acceptance. It wasn't that she lacked will or curiosity. He could clearly see these burning in her eyes. And several times, as they'd traversed through the forest on their way to the cave, he'd been forced to hurry her along as a myriad of moon-glittered mysteries caught her fascination. No, her disturbing lack of resistance had not formed from a dull spirit. More than likely, he felt, it was the mutated effect of a lifetime observing that—for her—the privilege of rebellion simply transpired into nothing good.

"Something else I need to show you," he mumbled shyly as she obediently rose from the chair.

Again securing her hand, he led her back outside the cave, through a tangled hedge of thick bramble, and down toward the creek. Here, he indicated with suffocating embarrassment, the spot where they would excrete their bodily wastes. This too she accepted without pause or question. As if defecating in the woods was the most natural of things to do.

Eager to distance himself from the uncomfortable intimacy of this most private of functions, Jakie hurried off through the wet ferns and down to the creek's edge. Moonlight rippled over the shallow rapids like mute piano keys. Crouching into a campfire squat, he withdrew his frayed toothbrush from his pocket, dipped it into the icy water and proceeded to brush his teeth. Taking Lily's toothbrush from his other pocket, he handed it to her. Grinning, she mimicked his movements, scrubbing away with an exaggerated flourish.

He was touched by her obvious eagerness to please him, but he could also sense she was careening close to a tipping point. Flying on a thin vapor of unaccustomed exhilaration, fueled by the vast freeness of the night, she was in danger of emotionally imploding, the internal exhaustion almost having consumed her. She was hopelessly, helplessly underprepared for so much sudden stimuli erupting into her world.

Jakie wound a calming arm around her shoulders, and she cocooned easily into the arc of his body with a relieved sigh. Settling back to a more secure position, he continued to hold her close as he coaxed the toothbrush free of her hand. Easing forward, he swiveled the toothbrushes in the fine gravel, then rinsed them in the smoothly running stream.

Life could have ended right there and he would have been a happy man. But the moon continued to shine down, watching as the soft trickling ripple of the tiny rapids soothed Lily toward sleep. Jakie held contentedly, idly watching the skitter-bugs play across the top of a slow eddy farther up the light-dappled creek. Knowing that their circumstances dictated his choices, he drank in the moment a hesitation longer, then he maneuvered the slumbering Lily with him as he stood up. He grew proud of the powerful forces surging through his body as he easily carried her back toward the cave. The weeks of relentlessly digging and scraping his entrance to her cellar room, combined with the newfound sense of purpose he had found in his love for her had all begun to transport him forward into a new vision of himself. He still had no idea who he had been, or where he had come from before being buried behind the asylum's walls. But he knew the man he *thought* he had been was as false as the mistaken name he had come to be called by.

☰ ☰ ☰

As the weeks passed by, the two of them slowly became nocturnal. At night, they emerged to frolic freely in the hushed forest, returning to sleep away the exposing light of day. Lily was enchanted with this new way of life. Her body responded well to the increased exercise and fresh air. She gained weight and a pearly glow lit her cheeks. She learned new words to describe the world she was discovering. She giggled often. For her, time simply did not exist. For Jakie on the other hand, the obese weight of its slow passage suffocated him with anxiety.

He'd scratched several lines into the smooth dirt walls of the cave, Lily watching but never questioning this odd daily ritual. They were getting closer, but the elusive day when they would finally be free of the asylum's grip still remained far in front of them.

Tonight they had stayed out in the forest longer than usual, admiring the full moon, listening to the symphony of the creek. A sudden exhaustion had finally overwhelmed Lily, and Jakie had been upset with himself for keeping her up so late. She'd collapsed onto her bed as soon as they had arrived back home, curled herself tightly around her doll and the baby skunk and fell quickly into a deep sleep. Jakie lay across from her. A thin blanket was all that cushioned the place on the floor that served as his bed. An elbow propped up his head as he watched her sweet face. He was worried about her. About the tiredness, which did not seem to dissolve as quickly as he thought it would once they had the whole forest to nurture her. If anything, it seemed to be growing worse. He considered whether he should ask Dr. Davidson for help. But that course of action was all but closed to him. They had agreed not to have any contact with each other during the entirety of the thirty-day period. Dr. Davidson had made it clear he could not run the risk of having anyone discover that he was aware of their location. Such a strategy seemed wise and fair. Still, having offered Lily the best he knew of the forest's healing ways, her continued fatigue made Jakie's hands feel empty and insufficient.

He held a million questions on his tongue, longing to get to know every moment of her. But he'd learned that too much prodding only served to cause her to retreat back into the shell of her silent self. Feeling a fall chill breathing through the doorway, his eyes searched out the extra blanket squared up in the corner beside the bed. He'd only just barely thought of getting up to cover her with it when her eyes opened to his and she smiled.

"You should be sleeping," he said.

"So should you."

Jakie shook his head.

"How come?"

"'Cause when I close my eyes, I can't see you."

"But I'm still here."

"I know."

"Are you scared I'll leave?"

He shook his head again. The deep orange glow of the fire warmed the room, the heat rising and pulling a cool draft through the door. Shadows flickered over their faces as they lay looking at each other through the darkness. Her hand lightly strummed over the furry ball nestled beside her. The high hum of silence permeated the cave.

"Are *you* going to leave?" she asked, barely audible.

"*No.* Never," Jakie proclaimed earnestly, surprised by the question.

Instead of relief, her face registered a look of pain. Jakie scrambled around inside his head searching for the right words to erase it.

"Ezra left."

"Where to?"

"The war."

Jakie nodded.

"Why do people go to the war, Jakie?"

He thought about this for a long moment.

"To try and help fix things, I s'pose."

She brightened a little.

"Ezra was good at fixing things...he didn't never come back though—"

Jakie noticed a slight tremor run through her. Rising up to his feet, he stepped across the room to pick up the wool blanket. A fast flame flew out from under it the instant his hand lifted the corner. Quick as thought, Lily sprung from her bed and seized the squirming tail of a garter snake.

Jakie coiled back in alarm, instinctively reaching behind him for the shovel. Gently restraining the frantic snake, Lily eyed him sharply. The little skunk flagged its tail. Sheepishly, Jakie set the shovel back against the wall. Cold currents rippled his spine. He watched with utter disgusted amazement as she laughingly tried to coil the unwieldy snake into a green-and-yellow bangle around her forearm.

"You're not scared of it?" he sputtered stupidly.

"Are *you*?" She giggled, offering the wriggling mass up toward him.

Jakie drew away quickly and frowned. She almost seemed to be toying with his obvious displeasure.

"Don't really like snakes all that much," he mumbled.

"I had one. When I was little. In the cellar 'neath the house. Sometimes it would curl up on my tummy. Brother said I kept it warm."

She smiled over at Jakie proudly, and he unsuccessfully attempted to smile back. It looked like a grimace. He was eager to keep her talking; the occasions were rare when she readily opened up about herself. But he was even more eager to rid the cave of the frantically straining reptile she had twined around her hands.

"Maybe we should put it outside—"

Outwardly, she did not answer him, but her nonverbal reaction made it perfectly clear how little she thought of this plan. Jakie grinned at her resistance. This was new. The first glimmer of willingness to fight back for her own self-interest. He wanted to kiss her. But first, he wanted to get rid of that damn snake.

"Why don't you just hold it for a bit, and then we'll let it loose in the forest," he suggested. "It'll be happy out there."

This she could see the sense in, and she readily agreed. When Jakie had initially risen to get the extra blanket, he had planned to sit next to her on the bed. Now, he quickly tossed the blanket to her and instead settled himself back down on the hard floor. He glared caustically at the intrusive reptile.

"Did *you* live in the cellar?"

She laughed gaily, as if it were an absurd question.

"No, silly. I lived in the house then. Just if company came by, I had to go down the cellar and keep quiet. We didn't get much company though."

Jakie chewed internally on his next question for some time. They fell into a comfortable hush. He always found himself straddling some invisible border between drawing Lily out of herself or having her suddenly retreat away from him, back inside her protective walls. She seemed contented now, the skunk curled beside her, the little snake having calmed into her hands.

"Did you ever go to school, Lily?"

"Oh, no. Not me. Ezra taught me to read some. 'Fore Pa put me up the barn."

"Why'd he put you in the barn?" Jakie asked, angrily pulling a screwdriver from a can and roughly working the dirt free of his nails.

Her eyes softened a little at his angered face.

"Like I tole you...Maw said she'd had enough of me fallin' an' such. Said I fell when I was holding one of the little ones. Which weren't true but Pa believed her. It weren't so bad though. I got my own room. And Ol' Brown. Sure did miss that snake though."

Jakie flicked his eyes to hers to see if she was teasing him. She didn't appear to be.

"Did your pa bring you here?" He offered the question gently, not wishing to upset her.

She fell quiet for a long time, and he looked up fearing he'd lost her. Finally, her soft lips quivered, then parted as she answered him.

"No. Not Pa. Neighbors. They were scared of me. There were stories. Pa was long dead by the time they happened along. I tried to tell Ol' Brown, *'Don't lay down, Brown. Don't lay down.'* But he got too tired. His water was all gone. I couldn't get outta of my room. Neighbors kept saying it was the best thing Pa's wife ever done. Should of run off years before."

She fell quiet now under the weight of the memory, a deep sadness taking her. If it weren't for the sight of that repellant reptile lying in her lap, Jakie would have gone over to her and chased her pain away with his aching arms. He was reticent to open any more wounds, but he also sensed the opportunity was ripe for the one last question that burned day and night inside his mind. Their time at the asylum was drawing to a close. If he didn't at least make an attempt to follow through on his hunch, he was not sure he could ever forgive himself. Summoning forth his courage, he pressed on.

"Lily, where did you say you got your sweater?"

"Ezra."

"Do ya know where he got it?"

"Sure. It were my mother's. My real mother's." She glowed quietly. "She gave it to him 'fore she died."

Jakie nodded lightly.

"My other mother, she said my real momma *cracked up* 'fore she died. That she tried to drown all us little kids. That sure made me real sad. But then Ezra tole me that weren't right. Said she'd gone an' got the story all mixed up 'cause she were none too smart. Then he 'tole me what really happened. That our real momma took us kids to the pond to have a swim. And the turtle came over and we rode around on its back, but then it forgot we couldn't swim and it went under the water and we got all wet, but momma was there to dry us all off again, so it were all okay. Oh, Jakie, you should of heard it. Ezra tole the *funniest* stories!"

"Sounds like," Jakie murmured.

His mind was astir with the possibility. Several times he went to speak, then found his voice shut up. What if he was wrong? What if his meddling brought nothing but more painful memories into her already troubled life? And yet, a part of him felt sure of what he wanted to do. It would mean taking a huge risk. A risk that would cost them everything if it proved too big. And yet, something in him was compelled to take it. He had to take Lily and go back one more time inside the bowels of the asylum.

"Lily," he said confidently. "I have someone I want you to meet."

☰ ☰ ☰

He saw the abstract look claim her a millisecond before the first seizure stole her from herself. Stiffening, then collapsing, her shattered body slipped from the bed before he could cross the room to reach her. A ribbon of green and yellow flashed free of her hands. The skunk scurried inside the pillowcase. Her head struck the ground with a hollow wooden thud.

He felt helpless as he frantically pulled the thick eiderdown to him and stuffed it around her. The spasms jerked her violently, loosening it again. A small slash of blood trickled down her forehead, and he attempted to wipe it away with his hand. It blurred larger instead, and he cursed his inability to do anything to help her. Finally, he laid his warm hands lightly on top of her spasmodic body, closing his eyes and humming to her quietly. His hands yielded to the earthquake of movement beneath them, making no attempt to restrain her. Jakie's emotional pain felt physical.

An eternity passed before the electricity had coursed its way through her. It left her spent. Gathering her up inside the quilt, Jakie lifted her back onto the bed. The skunk snuffled around, finally cozying up with its little head resting on her arm. He placed her doll beside it. Unfolding the spare wool blanket, he nestled it over her, tucking tight the edges to ward off drafts. Taking a washcloth from the basin, he blotted away the bloodstained spittle from the corners of her mouth. Lily blinked blearily. Aware but exhausted, she made no effort to move. Leaning forward, Jakie kissed her bloody forehead as an infinite sleep carried her away.

Sitting on the floor, his back resting against the edge of the bed, he rubbed his face awake with his hands. The trauma of helplessly watching her seizure had transported him outside of himself as well. Somehow, the distance seemed necessary. Across from him, the fire glowed hot.

His mind warred within itself about the seizures. Part of him hated them. As if they were a separate entity taking her from him and torturing her needlessly. The other part of him urged that he should not imagine any part of her to be flawed. That this perceived imperfection was no less a part of her total perfection. Jakie railed against the thought. He could hear Coyote's earthen reasoning. That

Jakie must find a way to love all of her. That none of it was separate. He hadn't heard Coyote's voice for a very long time.

Gradually the fire cooled, but the close womb of the cave remained comfortable. The walls had absorbed the heat and would gradually release it, keeping them warm as the fire was allowed to burn out for the day.

Jakie sat listening to the soft purr of her rhythmic breathing. He was growing more anxious to get her away from the asylum. She had almost burned herself on the stove this time when she fell. He refused to think of what might have happened had he not been there. He was exhausted. His body longing for sleep, he once more brushed soft lips across her forehead, then exited the cave.

CHAPTER 22

Jakie was sweating profusely as he ripped away the wide knotty-pine boards framing the living room window. It was not from warmth that he perspired. Fall had bitten the air hard that night. The sweat poured forth from his anxiety. He needed to remove the window out of the wall, but its rusted nails were resisting him noisily.

Finally, his bloodied hands wrestled the last board free. He prayed the barbaric racket he was making would not be overheard. He looked through the glass at the car. He still wasn't sure how he planned on getting it out of the cabin or if he even could. Several times, he had measured the width of the window, somehow hoping the time before he had measured wrong. But its width had remained immovable. Several inches too small. It was not much and yet it was everything. The roadster remained stuck. Jakie had searched around for other, easier options. Something—anything—that perchance Mr. Brewster may have overlooked. But this had remained the only option he could come up with. He would remove the window in its entirety, then chisel away with his ax at the thick logs surrounding the opening. It would be hard work and noisy, but he felt confident to handle that. However, it would also consume an enormous amount of his time, and time was the one thing he no longer had.

Time had become a stranger to him. In a way, he was glad to feel the resistance of it pushing back. It was one of the first things to dissolve in asylum life. The urgency of it. At first, its absence was welcome. However, as purposeless days wore on, one became nostalgic to feel its relentless tug-of-war once again.

Looking through the darkness at the collaboration of chinking and wood shims surrounding the window, Jakie frowned. He wished he could take out his flashlight and make sense of the jumbled, fused mess. Relying on the sight of his hands instead, he palpated the materials, filling the gap between the window frame and the cut-off edges of the hewn logs. There seemed to be an excess of it.

Pulling loose a wedge of chinking, a thick roll of newspaper fell to the porch floor. Jakie probed blindly around the hole it made beside the window frame. More materials fell away. Quickly, Jakie began to pull free the wads of chinking and paper stuffed around the window's perimeter. There was far, far more packing than was reasonably practical. Kicking aside the rat's nest of filler materials growing under his feet, Jakie released a throaty laugh.

Clearly, the clever Mr. Brewster *had* had a fully evolved escape plan after all. Whether the decaying tangle of his mind had hidden it from him in the end, or whether the old man had simply chickened out of following through on his carefully laid plans, no one would ever know. To Jakie, it mattered not. He felt a ghostly jolt of kindred support that chilled along his sweaty spine. Feeling around the inside edge of the window, he found three long spikes reaching out to secure the window into place. He stuck his hand into the gap left by the displaced insulation and stretched out his fingers. He couldn't be sure—but he felt damn willing to bet—that the additional space he'd just uncovered would add up to be just enough to ensure the roadster's final exit. Tipping his head toward the cemetery, Jakie paid silent homage to a brilliant man.

Poking a canvas strap through the opening, Jakie fastened the window to a pulley system hanging from the porch rafters. The three long spikes remained the last barrier. Working furiously, he hooked the first battered head into the claw of his hammer and began to wrench it loose.

Screeee—

The riveting screech stunned the still night. Jakie ceased his pulling. Breathing hard, he listened deeply for any sign that the God-awful wail had jolted someone to come looking his way. He hoped the noise would be mistaken for the trunks of two trees rubbing together. Abandoning his task, he stepped off the porch, crossed the narrow strip of dirt road, and climbed high up into the top limbs of the spruce tree. Systematically, his eyes scanned the hill behind the cabin, the field of buried bodies, and finally over toward the Cottages. All appeared to be in order. If one could call it that.

Descending the tree, he decided he could only afford to pull the nails out with short, intermittent bursts. Again, it would require a premium of time, but there would also be less intensity of sound in the sporadic pulls. Less cause for anyone who might overhear to conclude some sort of progress was attempting to take place.

Exhaustion was seriously marring his thinking by the time he'd finally loosened the window and swung it free. Its removal left a gaping hole in the wall of the cabin. Jakie looked sadly at the dismal display of his former home. Not really a home at all, he realized now. Just a ramshackle hovel filled with broken-down things. Jakie's sadness lightened as he looked back toward the roadster filling the living room. With the window now removed, the car seemed more preposterous to him than it ever had. But it was also now visually obvious that the vehicle would actually be able to fit through the window frame after all.

Adrenaline firing him more fully awake, Jakie ran over to his work shed and knocked apart a half-assembled coffin. Packing a stack of rough-planed pine boards back to the cabin, he fashioned together a workable ramp. This he maneuvered into place over the exposed window ledge, lining up its edges with the car's front tires. The tires were long flat, and he growled for mercy as he wasted more valuable time searching for the hand pump to bring them back into service.

The approaching dawn was bearing down on him like a runaway train. The faster he worked the closer he felt its unswerving approach. There was simply no time to adequately fill the tires, so he just inflated each one a small bit. He would have to top them off just before they made their final escape.

Securing an ancient come-along to the sturdy tree opposite the cabin, Jakie attached its oft-repaired chain to the frame of the vehicle and began it on its ascent up and out of the living room. It was backbreaking, onerous work. Like birthing an elephant out of an ear. But slowly and surely the come-along was successful in uprooting the car onto the pine bridge. It tottered on the precipice for a moment, as if deciding whether it really did want to be extricated from its cozy home. All at once, it tipped forward and began to roll. Too late, Jakie realized that in his preoccupation with trying to figure out a way to get the vehicle removed from the cabin, he had been completely remiss in thinking through his plan in case he was actually successful in doing so.

Success began to roll his way now. He threw up his hands to stop it. His heroic efforts were of course quite useless. He stood motionless beside the come-along on the other side of the road, face frozen, shoulders scrunched, as he watched the car roll down the slope of the ramp, bounce heavily off of the porch, then come to a crunching stop by his feet.

"Oops. Sorry," he whispered to the memory of Mr. Brewster. His mind circulated through a marvelous myriad of things such a harsh bump could have shaken loose. He shook his head at the eruption of noise that had seemed intent on spilling into the night. His only hope now was that anyone hearing his nocturnal thrashings would just assume that anyone being so garishly noisy obviously could have nothing important they wished to hide.

Running a hand over the wood-paneled sides of the car, he circled it with admiration. He had never realized before the depth of craftsmanship that had gone into Mr. Brewster's work. The vehicle had served him well as a drying rack for his herbs; he'd never really had cause to look at it much beyond that. Now that the car was no longer defined within the scale of the tiny cabin, Jakie was surprised to realize it was much smaller than he'd ever thought. Small, but still adequate—he hoped—to carry himself and Lily over the red-and-blue lines drawn like veins all over Mr. Brewster's maps.

☰ ☰ ☰

By the time Jakie had winched the car backward up the hill and in behind the doors of the farrier shed, he was beyond spent. Lingering faces pointed fingers at him from the shifting shadows. Their voices hid inside the soft shivering wind, accusing him of only wanting to keep Lily next to him because of his own beastly desires. They shouted out their nasty taunts and—finally—he shouted back. Collapsing to the floor, he leaned against the creosote-soaked wall of the shed. He had to rest. He was seriously beginning to doubt his ability to actually follow through with his plans.

Wearily, he placed wedges of wood in front of each tire to secure the vehicle in place. He struggled to push the voices away. They were not helpful. Salacious tormentors that he swore were no part of him. And yet, in spite of his denial, they remained. For years they had remained. Accusing, whispering, taunting. He had tried to close his mind to them. Ignore them. Outrun them. It had all been in vain. They persisted daily. *Perhaps,* he thought, *the voices were not outside of him at all. Perhaps, like Lily's seizures, they were just some integral part of his own perfection.*

Clearly these were Coyote's thoughts and standing up, he shook them clear of his head. The exhaustion was really beginning to stumble him now. Making his way once more down to the cabin, he threw a short length of garden hose over one shoulder, then rummaged through a drawer for a battered tin funnel. Grabbing up the heavy five-gallon pail from off the porch, he struggled to make his way back up the hill. Opening the car's gas cap, he stuck the funnel into place and proceeded to fill up the tank. He would have to sneak back tomorrow night, take the now-empty can over to the staff parking lot, and siphon it full again.

He moved once more to the front of the car and looked down dubiously at the bumpy slope. They would get only one chance to roll the car down it, pop the clutch, and hopefully compress a spark of life into the engine. If that moment went according to plan, then they would be set to sail off into the sunset. If not—well, there really wasn't much of a backup plan. If the engine failed to turn over for him and Lily, then the two of them were just going to have to run like holy hell.

Ξ Ξ Ξ

Jakie shadowed his way through the partially illuminated attic. Wiping his hands for the hundredth time on his filthy hanky, he worked to keep his heaving stomach in place. He had been successful in getting Mr. Brewster's maps, but it sure wasn't a job he ever cared to have to repeat.

Squatting once again before the blue steamer trunk, he opened it up wide. Anxiety churled his gut. His mind was astir telling him something was not right. Beyond exhausted, he pushed the thought away. Nights of thin sleep had made him unsure of himself. Living under the constant stress of being Lily's sole protector had left him emotionally drained. The experience of impotently watching the dystopic sight of her suffering the seizure had triggered awake an age-old fear. It haunted him. He had a plan for their escape, but not all of it had become clear to him yet. He knew the gravity of failure would be beyond his ability to bear.

At any rate, he knew he had no intention of waiting around until Dr. Davidson could again take back control of Lily. The doctor's utter infatuation with her was embarrassingly obvious. It reeked of a dangerous instability. And even if the doctor did follow through on his stated intention to place her in a home where she could be taught the basic skills of a self-supporting life, Jakie highly suspected that that life would be lived out as the new housekeeper of Cumberland House.

Jakie pulled his thoughts back to the task at hand. There was no time for daydreaming. Bleary eyes searched once again over the mysterious womanly contents as he pulled open various drawers. Politely folded blouses awaited inspection. He found his hands immobile, reticent to touch them. To touch *her*. Whoever she was—or had been.

Disciplining his hands into the blouses, he felt diligently for anything that might serve him as a future clue. The trunk would not be coming with them when they left as he'd first planned. There was no time. To move it down the stairs would be onerous. And he could imagine clumping it down the stairwell would create enough noise to jolt even the catatonics awake anyhow. No, it would have to stay behind. Whatever he took now was all he would ever have. As far as he knew, it held the only pieces he had about his former life. He felt like a puzzle that had been severely shaken. Parts of him seemed to have held together fairly well. But then there were fragments, and indeed whole sections, that had gone completely missing. Once he fled the asylum, he would never come back. He was mortally sure

about that. Whatever parts of him remained behind in the
trunk would be lost forever.

The cool fabric of the blouses slipped over his hands
like loose skin. Lifeless arms and bosoms rose and fell with
his movements. The spectacle unnerved him. It felt inces-
tuous. He could not stop himself from wondering if the
blouses had once bloomed over the soft curves of his own
mother. He withdrew his hands.

Outside the transom window, he could see the fingers
of dawn beginning to peel back the velvet curtain of night.
The stone gargoyle above the window scowled down at
him. Its tongue stuck out grotesquely. Jakie returned the
gesture. He wondered what sort of depravity of humor had
allowed that thing onto the building in the first place.

Plucking a violet-flowered blouse up by the shoulders, he held it up to the light seeping through the window. Pretty. Unfastening his pack, he stuffed it in. Sorting
through more drawers, he selected then rejected two short
wool skirts, replacing them with longer ones and a pair of
loose trousers. His fingers slid open a drawer of silk stockings. He slammed it shut. Combing back through the other
drawers, he selected a color-splotched silk scarf adding it
to his bag instead.

Yawning, he admonished himself to stay focused. He
had much to do yet. Night was slipping away, and he still
had to make his way undiscovered back to the cave. And yet,
the more he tried to focus, the more elusive focus became.
It swam away. The room grew airy and vapid. He felt drunk.
Voices started. He told them to stop. Above him, the gargoyle smirked down through the broken windowpane.

Jakie glared back at it. Slowly, its lips began to curl into
a snarl. He could hear it snickering. Mucous-laden saliva
drooled from its mouth. Its eyes glowed a color of red that
did not forebode well.

Jakie waved his arms menacingly at the inert beast. It
transformed back into the silly stone caricature of itself.

Jakie laughed dryly. Rising, he began to parade through the rows of shelving. Pressing his flashlight on, he painted its beam up and down and over the stacks of suitcases, trunks, and boxes. He laughed again. A bit louder. Wilder. Taking down an innocuous-looking box filled with yellowed papers, he hurled it across the attic floor. Stabbing randomly at the various pieces of luggage with his flashlight, he exposed each one of them for what they truly were. Grabbing them roughly down, he sent them crashing to the floor. They made a massive racket. Several of them burst open as they fell. Jakie celebrated their disorderly dethronement. Lies. Every last one of them. Filled with nothing but filthy lies. He ran his fingers through his hair. It remained standing furiously.

The gargoyle had helped him. The stupid beast had given it all away. He was not up in the asylum's attic at all. It was so clear to him now that he wondered how he could ever have been so easily deceived. The voices had almost fooled him once again. Cunning bastards. But he could see the truth now, and the truth would set him free. Such was the promise given. The attic—the asylum—did not even exist. He was simply caught up inside the recesses of his own mind. The bags and boxes scattered around him were nothing more than the mute symbols of his own compartmentalized thinking.

Footsteps sounded heavily in the stairwell. He laughed at them. Loudly. Derisively. They kept coming. Standing taller, he pointed his flashlight toward the door and commanded them to stop. Voices joined them. Incensed, Jakie screamed at them to cease. Bats flew from the rafters. The voices and footsteps turned urgent at the sound of his shout.

Abruptly—the illusion of his mind gave way to a heart-sickening reality. Not only *was* he up in the asylum's attic—someone was rapidly approaching up its only exit. Jakie Hewitt was trapped.

"Think, Roper. Think," he ordered himself, then stopped. *Roper*. What an odd way to have referred to himself.

The creaking commotion on the attic stairs did not encourage further introspection. Suddenly, he remembered the anonymous battered suitcase with the baling-wire handle. The one filled with reams of discordant ropes and a half-deck of playing cards. Stumbling over himself, Jakie raced back through the rows of scattered luggage, beaming his light, hoping, pleading, cursing, and praying to find that one nondescript case. With his captors set to barge through the attic door at any moment, it remained his only viable hope.

His foot found the suitcase first, Jakie half-hurtling over the top of it, both arms swimming as he struggled to regain his balance. Grabbing open the lid, he clumped the coils and curls of rope onto the floor. He didn't know if they could lower him all the way to the ground, but they sure as hell were going to help shorten the fall. His hands flew into a fit of combining the ropes together. Intricate figure-eight knots emerged that felt as comfortable to tie as lacing his shoes. The clusters of knots looked a mess, but they tested strong.

A burly shoulder was applying itself furiously to the attic door. Smash—relent. Smash—relent. Jakie could hear the brittle boards beginning to give way.

Clambering back over to the still-exposed contents of the steamer trunk, his hands flew wild through the heaps of clothing. He grabbed the picture of Ms. Jacqueline K. Hewitt and tossed it in his pack. Straining to control his panic, he began to whistle, trying hard to void the relentless smashing of the door from his head. He had to think clearly now. No movement could be wasted. No opportunity sacrificed.

Raking the bottom drawer empty, he concentrated hard as he placed his shaking hands onto the panel of the false bottom. Pushing and pulling, he maneuvered it frantically as he attempted to work it free. It held fast. So immovable that for a moment he wondered if he had only imagined the whole false pretense of it. But his hands disagreed. They quivered with an energy that knew no doubt. Jakie realized that he—this Jakie he'd become—had to get out of the way. That the knowledge and skill needed to slide past the intricate maze of the panel was held deep inside him. Inside the world of the man he once was.

Closing his eyes against the pounding pressing in around him, Jakie emptied his mind into a singular place. It was the space he'd entered all those long years ago when he fixed his eye on the heart of his prey. Here he held his focus. With a foreign sense of confidence, his hands moved easily through a sequence of tiny cryptic movements. Angry shouts outside the door distracted him, pulling him forward before he could finish. Cursing loudly, he tried to force the panel. It held firm. Desperate to regain those few pieces of himself, he searched around him frantically for something to wrench open the false bottom. Nothing presented itself. The shouts and smashing grew louder and louder, until they began to feel like they were erupting from within him. He shook his head violently to dislodge them. Eyes casting back up toward the gargoyle. An idea exploded in his mind. Shoving everything back inside the steamer trunk, he grabbed the mass of ropes and wove a quick mesh around the trunk's sturdy sides. He clambered catlike up the shelves, pushing and heaving luggage out of his way as he went. Flying a loop up over the gargoyle's neck, he jerked it tight. Pulling the sleeve of his jacket down over his left hand, he smashed the remaining window from its pane. Pulling with every ounce of desperation within him, he began to pulley the trunk up toward the window. Everything creaked and complained at the unexpected load but, teeth gritted menacingly, he continued to pull. Finally wrestling the luggage through the windowpane, he lowered it hastily to the ground below, gasping with the exertion it required to keep it from tumbling into a free fall.

Behind him, the door received its final death blow. It splintered and split, then crashed heavily to the floor. A short stunned pause, then a heated squabble ensued. Having finally obliterated the barrier between themselves and their quarry, his pursuers now found themselves quite unwilling to be the first one to step on through.

Seizing their brief moment of indecision, Jakie slipped himself through the window. Tying the end of the rope around the gargoyle's neck, he grinned at the indignant stone beast, then rappelled down under the rising dawn of light. Hitting the ground hard, he scrambled along the edge of the building toward a wheelbarrow leaning up against it. Struggling the blue trunk free of the tightened ropes, he wished he had time to pull out his knife. Listening intensely, his mind wound into a maelstrom of anxiety as the voices above him spread out in a search of the attic. It was only a matter of time before they realized it was empty and the coming morning revealed the long rope dangling freely outside the window. Summoning up every last bit of his strength, he hoisted the trunk onto the wheelbarrow, labored it into the shadows, and disappeared from sight.

CHAPTER 23

Nurse Mildred pulled the rough blanket up around Anna's shoulders and tucked it in. The musty tunnel was cheerless and cold. There was no suitable spot to rest one's eyes. The whole place was an objection against itself. Remaining motionless on the gurney, Anna kept her eyes closed. Nurse Mildred stared absently at the sign addressing the door across from them. *Study of Human Ecology.*

"You doing okay there?" Mildred asked as she puttered about the stretcher, fussing futilely with the blanket.

"It's not too late you know. We could still go back upstairs."

She peered down at the pinched eyes. If it weren't for the steady stream of rhythmic breathing, she might have sworn there was no one at home.

"Can you hear me, Mrs. Mason?" she pleaded. "There's no one who's making you do this. You do understand that, don't you?"

Silence.

"Then why—"

A sigh. Weary. Impatient.

Nurse Mildred looked back across the hall. She began to chew on the edge of a raw knuckle as the blurred congestion of noises grew louder beyond the door. Reaching down, she took the old woman's bony shoulders in her hands and shook the eyes awake.

"*Anna,*" she said urgently. "Maybe you should just think about—"

"It's all I do, nurse—is think—"

"Well, maybe we could try—"

"Doctor said he'd make it go away. Every bit of it." She turned her head and again closed her eyes.

Make you go away, Nurse Mildred thought but didn't say. She'd already tromped on more than enough feet around the asylum lately with her seldom-silent disapproval of the various carrying-ons. More than once, the precarious nature of her job security had been hinted at. Her senses clearly told her that something was astir about the place. And it would come as little surprise to her if the unctuous young Uldrich were suddenly introduced as her new boss.

The prospect did not please her. For the most part, she found him far too happy with himself. And his ingratiating manner among the patients reeked of a disingenuous forgery. But still, she had her livelihood to think of. Troublemakers were seldom tolerated. She had certainly found that out the hard way. This would hardly be the first time she would have to forgo acting on her own sensibilities. Restraints, electric shock, induced convulsions, lobotomy. Even the occasional slap had been administered against her better judgment.

Her inability to hang her professional self up in the cloakroom at the end of the day had created a chasm between her and the other nurses. They felt her moody and unsocial. Which she was. Purposefully, she lagged behind as they chatted themselves free of the asylum each shift change. She listened from her envious prison as they easily discussed shopping trips, exchanged recipes, and made dates for afternoon tea.

Abruptly, the door to Uldrich's room flew open, and the man himself appeared. Snapping his head first one way and then the other, he scouted out the empty corridor.

"Where's Bea?"

"*Nurse* Bea is tardy this morning," Mildred clipped as tartly as she dared. She did not care for the fact that Uldrich had arranged for Nurse Bea to bring Mrs. Mason down to his treatment rooms. Such transfers were normally undertaken by the attendants.

"Ah, well, never mind then. I'll catch up with her later." He turned his attention toward the stretcher.

"So, what do we have here?"

"*This* is Mrs. Anna Mason. You signed for her. Remember?"

Dr. Uldrich eyed Mildred sharply. "Of course I remember. Volunteer. Correct?"

Nurse Mildred shrugged.

"Is she asleep?"

"No."

"Well, we'll just let her sleep then. She'll be okay out here until the girls can get the room ready. Hang on a sec'. I'll get the other one for you to take back up—"

"What other—" Mildred said to his back as he disappeared out the door.

She stood hostilely waiting in the gloom, as the noises beyond the door grew steadily louder—coughing, talking, laughter. It sounded like a party. Leaning against the gurney, she tapped her finger into the blanketed shoulder. There was no response.

Finally, the door opened again, leisurely, and a pert nurse stepped through. She walked half-facing backward as she led someone by the hand. Moving somewhat unsteadily, Mary Lawson followed her into the tunnel.

"Mary!" Mildred cried out, so surprised she was barely able to coil back an urge to wrap the girl into a robust hug.

Mary looked at her with a startled uncertainty. Smiling thinly, she looked away.

"Doesn't she look great?" Dr. Uldrich boomed, as he joined them in the tunnel.

"A bit gaunt—"

"Nonsense. She looks wonderful," Dr. Uldrich said with a flick of his hand. "Here, let me demonstrate how effective her therapy was. Mary—

"Mary," he said again, stepping closer to her as he snapped his fingers. "Mary, look at me. The nurse here wants to know where your husband is."

Mary's eyes scurried across the faces watching her, scavenging for a clue.

"Come on, girl. I haven't all day. Where's your husband?" he pressed a bit more urgently.

Overwhelmed with confusion, she sought refuge looking down at her feet.

"Surely you didn't *lose* your husband, did you?"

Curling up her shoulders, Mary's face crumpled as a single strangled sob escaped her.

"Doctor—" Mildred warned.

"Let it be nurse! It's an integral part of the therapy."

"Mary," he said brusquely. "Look at me."

She did so.

He softened his voice.

"Do you know where your husband is, Mary?"

She shook her head.

"Do you know *what* a husband is, Mary?"

She shook her head again.

Dr. Uldrich looked over at Mildred with a self-congratulatory grin. It was not returned.

"Well, never mind, maybe your nurse there can help explain it to you. So, what do you think?" he asked Mildred.

Nurse Mildred was a volcano on the verge. She chose each word with extreme caution.

"What have you done to her—"

"Blotted out some of the more undesirable traits and had them replaced. Quite simple really—"

"Aye-aye-aye, doctor. Don't you see what you've done?"

Dr. Uldrich screwed up his face.

"You've only gone and addled the poor girl's egg, that's all—"

"Addled her egg? What's that supposed to mean?"

"Oh...well, maybe Nurse Bea can help explain it to you, sir."

And without a backward glance, she took Mary by her compliant hand and began to slowly make their way down the tunnel, Dr. Uldrich's stream of outraged protest bouncing resoundingly off the crumbling brick walls.

☰ ☰ ☰

They literally bumped into Nurse Bea as soon as they started up the stairs leading to Cottage Four.

"Ooo...you scared me!"

"You're late," Nurse Mildred flared. She was in no humor for theatrics.

"Just a little." Bea shrugged with a shrill giggle. She tried to worm her way past them.

Mildred, immovable, blocked her path.

"And just where do you think you're off to?"

"Dr. Uldrich's rooms," she flipped back. She was in a hurry, and she was obviously finding their body blockade most irksome.

"I've already seen to the patient you failed to transport this morning."

"Oh...thanks. But I have something I want to tell him."

"What?"

Bea was reluctant to say. But Nurse Mildred's stance was making it pretty clear she wasn't letting anyone by without a good reason.

"Dr. Davidson's been tipped on the whereabouts of Jakie Hewitt and that spastic girl," Nurse Bea babbled out excitedly. "They're going off to get them right now."

Mildred's face opened up with undisguised surprise. Nurse Bea tried for an opening.

"No! Here...you see Mary back up to the ward. There's a bed open in *A*."

"By myself?"

"Of course by yourself."

"But what if she acts up on me?" Nurse Bea pouted.

Mildred gently patted the top of Mary's hand, then gave it to the other nurse.

"Mary will cause you no such problems, Nurse Bea. I can shamefully assure you of that."

☰ ☰ ☰

Mildred intercepted Dr. Davidson and his group of attendants halfway across the cricket oval. Uncomfortably obese, she was in no condition to be chasing off over wide-open spaces. Fortunately for her, the sedentary lifestyle of the bookish doctor found him similarly taxed. Loudly cursing his inability to carry forward, he slowed to a stop, wheezing for breath as he watched her labored approach.

"Go back." He waved angrily. "Go back. I've no need of you out here."

Ignoring the order as if she had simply not heard it, she bumped through the crush of attendants and crowded herself up close to the irate doctor. Stabilizing herself with his arm, she bent over in a noisy attempt to catch her breath.

"So," she gasped. "You found him?"

Shadowing a grimace, Dr. Davidson eased himself free of her weight.

"Yes."

"And the girl?"

"She's with him...so I'm told."

"Someone tipped you to their whereabouts then?"

"Yes."

"Who?"

"For God's sake, Mildred! It's not any of your damn business *who!*"

She drew herself up and slightly away from his explosive hostility. She had never before seen the doctor so animated. A hissing, red frenzy of nerves, his voice squeaked up into an unnatural register. Her curiosity was piqued.

"Just asking, that's all. Why the big secret?"

"There is no *secret*, Nurse Mildred," he exploded again, eyes bulging with intensity as he tried to suppress the volume of his words. "It's confidential. Now, please, go back to the ward so we can carry on before the brute runs off with her again."

"Well, with all that girl's been put through, you can't very well be barging in on her with this bunch. She'll need to see someone she's come to trust. That's probably me, doctor. Wouldn't you agree?"

She smiled innocently. Dr. Davidson's face began to twitch. He shot a barbed look her way, but with all the attendants' eyes upon him—he didn't dare to disagree.

"Fine. Follow along then. But we'll not be slowing down to wait for you. And I'll need absolute silence when we surround his den so the cagey dog doesn't steal off with her again."

"Well, heave-ho then, Sally Ann," Nurse Mildred said cheerily, having now regained both her breath and her pluck.

Cork-screwing his face, Dr. Davidson struggled to hold his tongue.

Impeded by her years of domestic inactivity, Nurse Mildred groveled along behind the group. She clawed her way up steep embankments and slid down mossy slopes. Thorns caught at her uniform, roots at her feet. She was *not* quiet. Whatever she lacked in physical conditioning, however, she more than made up for with her remarkable resilience. More than once the doctor's face registered bitter dismay as he searched behind him only to find her steadily trudging on.

Taking advantage of yet another stop, the winded Mildred again sidled her way up beside the doctor and flopped herself down by his feet.

"So, you've been this way before."

Alarm registered across his face.

"Years ago. Why do you ask?"

"Just seem awfully shore of the way, that's all. Had never thought you to be such an outdoorsman."

She smiled her simple smile up at him. The one she knew he hated. The one that belied her true intentions.

"I was given excellent directions, Nurse Mildred. Exceedingly excellent directions."

"Yup." She nodded slowly. "Seems like."

Scowling, Dr. Davidson hissed around at the group.

"Listen. All of you. From this point on there is to be no talking. None. Not from anyone. Hewitt might be half-deaf, but he's also as canny as a cat. He gets an inkling of our approach and he'll be off again with that girl. And there's no telling what he'll do to her."

Mildred looked around her at all the dull, nodding faces. She shook her head. Most of them had known Jakie for years. A passive, friendly, helpful man with a penchant for healing. Now, despite any evidence to the contrary, they felt him an ogre. Dangerous. She sighed dejectedly.

They moved on as a semisilent shadow through the woods. Mildred continued to observe Dr. Davidson's familiarity with the path. He never paused to consult a map, and yet his movements were decisive. Her suspicion grew almost to the place of once again querying his newfound ability. The group suddenly fell to a halt. Dr. Davidson had raised a hand into the air. Instantly, the attendants began to form a tight semicircle against the hillside. It was obvious they were responding to some sort of prearranged signal that she had not been party to. They looked suddenly bigger, more fierce and alive. Like alley dogs—threatened.

A caustic grin cut open the doctor's face. His eyes danced with nervous anticipation. A whole cathedral of alarm bells went off in Mildred's head. No man in his position should be enjoying the hunt quite this much. Looking over at Oswald, the doctor nodded as he indicated a small opening in the shrubbery. Drawing two canisters from his pockets, the burly attendant stroked alive a match and lit them. Putrid black smoke billowed into the air. Stepping forward quickly, he parted the underbrush further and hurled the smoking cans deep inside.

An almost instantaneous eruption of strangled coughing rewarded him, and the men sent up a spontaneous cheer, then scrambled about for dense sticks and hand-sized boulders.

☲ ☲ ☲

Jakie crawled out first. He made no attempt to escape. At a glance it was clear how tightly woven was the knot that surrounded him. Even if he were able to overcome his captors, he would have to escape without the girl. He would not do that. Their capture was his fault—his failure. Crushed by fatigue, he'd slept carelessly, his good ear to the ground, rendering him virtually deaf. Reaching back through the bramble, he helped Lily forward. Upon the first explosion of gaseous fumes, he'd leapt up, wrapping her and her doll tightly inside the wool blanket. The acrid, burning smoke having reached through to her now, she emerged gagging and sputtering, blurred eyes running with tears.

What she saw obviously frightened her immensely. She coiled back, blinking with confused terror at the hostile nightmare surrounding their home. The distressed skunk slipped free of her, and she crawled after it as it tried to re-enter the smoke-filled cave. Grabbing it up, she curled herself around it tightly as Oswald attempted to shake it from her grasp.

"Leave it!" Dr. Davidson bellowed. "Let her keep it for now. I'll deal with it later."

Scrambling to his feet, Jakie moved toward Lily. A fury of needless, brutal blows leveled him. Four of the attendants held him flat to the ground while a fifth one searched him for weapons. Finding the hand-forged blade strapped to Jakie's leg, the attendant undid it and waved it around for all to see.

"Bet *he* was the gaw-damned ringleader of that bunch that jumped me—" Oswald growled and several heads agreed.

Lily became a kicking, screaming, frenzy of panic as Oswald returned his attention back to her, his big hands clamping down around her thin hips, as he dragged her roughly toward him. Smirking churlishly, he laughed at her useless attempts to displace him.

"See here!" yelled Dr. Davidson. "Do be careful of the baby."

"Just a doll," Oswald spat, ripping it free of Lily's protesting arms and flipping it at the doctor's feet.

"Not that you imbecile. Can't you see the poor girl's with child?"

Everything ceased. All struggle. All breath. All thoughts of mutual intolerance. The only focus for one and all became the soft round of the girl's stomach. Grabbing the edge of her blanket, Oswald ripped it loose, exposing the telltale evidence.

"Wha...no!" Jakie wailed. "I never...I never touched her. Nurse Mildred...please—" he pleaded.

"Ah, ya dirty pig!" Oswald snarled, letting go of the girl with one hand and delivering Jakie a cracking blow to the head.

Collapsing onto his knees, Jakie begged up at the doctor. Blood ran red from a gash by his ear.

"Please. Dr. Davidson...please. You know I'd never—"

"Immaculate conception I suppose, Mr. Hewitt? Very well then. We have ways of fixing even that—"

The man's face had changed. He looked down at Jakie with an almost calm serenity. But the light had gone out in him. Clearly, something sinister had wormed its way in and rotted out the very core of his decency. Suddenly, Jakie realized with horror just how deep this game of double cross could potentially go.

☲ ☲ ☲

Word that Dr. Davidson had been tipped as to Jakie and the girl's whereabouts flew quickly throughout the wards. Speculation ensued about who would have been privy to such knowledge. Bets were placed. Arguments ensued. All semblance of order dissipated as patients and staff alike milled about the grounds, awaiting the recovery party's return. A game-day excitement percolated the air.

Jakie was finding little occasion to use his feet as he found himself forcibly hauled along between two attendants. Devastated by his failure to protect her, his only thoughts were on how Lily was coping with such an unexpected, hostile intrusion. Unable to see her, he struggled for a moment to look back her way, Oswald's eager fist encouraging him forward once again.

The stark pain of the blow startled Jakie back into the reality of the nightmare surrounding him. A commotion of noise called his attention, and he looked up to see a smattering of the Cottages' patients strewn about the lawns, awaiting the group's approach as if it were some sort of gruesome medieval parade. Peripherally, he could see Mr. Seymour standing in the shadow-cloud of an old oak. His wide wagging face was worked up with an opposition of words Jakie could not hear. Shaking his tattered ledger at various staff members, Mr. Seymour freely stroked names from the halls of life with a devout abandon.

Beyond him stood Phillip, soggy kitchen mop still in
hand. He fluttered Jakie a tremulous wave, his searching
blue eyes storm-blackened with worry. Up ahead on the
path, Jakie could see the stone lady, erect on her bench.
Her dark-dyed head held motionless, her gaze fixed on
the horizon as the catastrophic group approached. Sitting
below her on the ground was Mary Lawson, legs splayed
as she slumped bonelessly over herself. Oblivious of the
drama unfolding around her, she was slowly pawing the old
lady's stolen treasures out of the ground and attempting to
secure the filthy bobbles into her own limp scraggly hair.
Her attention was not diverted by the hustle of attendants
dragging Jakie down the path but the old lady's was. Snapping whip-crack-quick up off the bench, the older woman
stumbled forward into Jakie, causing an avalanche of tumbling cursing bodies. Acutely aware of how easily so much
brute pressure could powder her ancient bones, Jakie
fought powerfully to reclaim his balance. Misconstruing
this for a renewed effort of resistance, an entourage of
highly wired attendants swarmed back over him.

"What the gaw—" Oswald hollered incredulously.
"Look out! Bugger's got hisself another knife!"

Jakie looked down at his hands to discover the accusation was indeed correct. He *did* have a knife—sort
of—stuffed between his rope-bound hands. An old knife.
Rusted. With a slight bend to one side. He looked over to
catch a sly wink from the stone lady, just before Oswald's
hulk hurtled into him. Throwing his arms up in an effort
to protect himself, Jakie felt too late the blade of the knife
impact Oswald's barrel chest.

"Ah! Crazy gaw-damn bastard stabbed me," Oswald
bleated as he stumbled backward.

Jakie shook his head in innocent protest as he looked
at the knife still protruding from his hands. The bent blade
stood briefly at an odd angle, looped through a slow arc,

then broke away completely, falling to the sidewalk with a clarifying clatter.

"Run Jakie! Run!" a voice shrieked, and Jakie looked over to see Phillip jumping up and down, punching the rag-topped mop into the air like a cheerleader's pom-pom.

For some reason this shrill suggestion struck Jakie as a profitable option and, leaping free of the hands reaching his way, he began an all out dash for the green comfort of the distant trees. Careening his head around for a quick look, he glimpsed the old woman clapping a quiet fury with her tiny gloved hands. Still slumped into a heap below her, Mary Lawson joined in with erratic, slow-motion applause, her head searching around as she looked for the source of excitement. Having lost his composure completely, Dr. Davidson spun in tight circles, screaming expletives as his attendants gave chase.

"Bully for you," shouted Mr. Seymour, wildly spanking his Bible up against the trunk of the oak tree. "Right bully for you!"

Jakie fled for his very life, the rag-tag crew of patients noisily cheering him on. He held his bound hands up in front of him as he ran, the unnatural position even further impeding his gait. Twice he stumbled and almost fell, scrambling madly as he regained his footing. He could feel those bastard dogs clawing at his back, the whole damn pack of them rabid with hate.

Above it all, he could hear Phillip's distinctive high-pitched voice wailing itself into a frenzy.

"Run! Run! Run! Run like a devil, Jakie! Run like a Black Devil!"

☰ ☰ ☰

Jakie came to just as the last restraint was being ratcheted tight. Completely immobilized, his body was a consummation of pain. A swampy fog thickened his thinking.

Quite some time passed before the commotion around him divided itself into voices and movement. Slowly creeping open his eyes, he scanned the room. White. Sterile. Silver trays full of silver instruments. A vicious bright light glared down at him. Panic exploded. Grappling for control, he forced his eyes back half-closed, listening intensely to discern who else was occupying the small space with him.

To the left of him, a heavy body lumbered about, breathing loudly. Drawers rattled open, then banged shut with an aggravated expression.

"This one? Or this one here?"

Jakie could hear the hard cold clinking of metal.

"Oh, for God's sake, Mildred. It doesn't matter. Either one will do. No. Not that. I've no need of it. Hurry it up a bit will you, so we can get to it."

The terminally slow opening and closing of several more drawers answered him.

"I'm *waiting*, nurse."

Jakie felt hollow. Removed from himself. He followed the sound of Nurse Mildred's laborious shuffle as she made her way back toward the table he was strapped to and positioned herself across from the doctor.

"What's your hurry? It's shore not like he's going anywhere."

"My *hurry*, Nurse Mildred, is that I have rounds to get to yet. I certainly hadn't expected to find myself in here this morning—"

"Could easy enough wait—"

"It can't *wait*, Mildred. You saw yourself what he did to her."

"Did I?"

"Of course you did. We all did."

She took a deep, measured breath, then released it slowly.

"I saw what *someone* did to her, doctor. Shore enough. But how can we be sure it was—"

"Of course it was him—"

"What about the attendants? Wouldn't be the first—"

"Don't be ridiculous. Wasn't an attendant. Hewitt was the only one with her—"

"Last bit, shore. But we've not examined her. Who knows how far along—"

"I don't need to *examine* her to see what's in front of my very eyes, Mildred! Hewitt *violated* her. And it's my job, as the head of this institution, to ensure it *never happens again*. Now—if you would *kindly* remember your position here—I would quite like to *proceed!*"

Dr. Davidson's words bounced loudly around the room, their sporadic emphasis like the erratic movements of a novice as the high wire begins to wobble.

"All right! Steady yourself down a bit, doctor. You'll be no good for surgery all worked up like that."

She sighed heavily as she moved up and stood beside Jakie's head.

"It's not *that* kind of surgery, Nurse Mildred," Dr. Davidson muttered, lips scarcely moving, teeth clamped in a tight grimace. "I'll need you down this end."

"Down there?" she spat. Her distaste was palpable. "What for? I thought we'd just give him a little zap to the head."

Dr. Davidson smirked.

"A little zap to the head won't be anywhere near as effective as what I plan to do down here, nurse. Come now—I need you to hold it."

"*It?*"

"His penis, Mildred. I need you to hold it steady while I cut."

"You gonna cut off his winkie!" she gasped.

Jakie gasped too, but the massive dose of barbiturates they'd plugged into him had suffocated his brain. He was essentially useless to himself. A primal terror pounded his

heart as he felt his trousers being unzipped and his man-
parts being handled roughly.

"No, Mildred. I'm not going to emasculate him."

Jakie and Nurse Mildred shared a collective sigh of
relief.

"Have you ever seen a two-headed snake, Mildred?" the
doctor asked distractedly.

"Can't say I have," she replied, shaking her head as she
studied the doctor's absent face. "Has anyone?"

He continued sorting through a tray of gleaming instruments, picking up scalpels of various sizes and inspecting
them carefully, not answering her question.

"They're rare—" he finally rambled on. "An oddity.
But they do exist. That's what it will look like. I'll slice it
straight down the middle—"

Nurse Mildred swooned as she gripped at the edge of
the table with white-knuckled hands.

"Doctor—I don't believe you ever did tell me how you
knew where they were hiding—"

"I never told you, Mildred, because you have no need
to know!"

"Well...I'd *like* to know—"

The accusing tone of her voice distracted him away
from his selection of tools.

"It's not your business, Nurse Mildred!" he railed. "It's
just not any of your goddamn business! You understand?
Suffice it to say a little bird told me. A little bird that pre-
fers to remain anonymous, all right? Now—just leave it
alone and let's get on with it here."

Crossing her arms over her bosom, Mildred glared at
him. "Doesn't seem right."

"What doesn't seem right?"

"None of it. Maybe we should wait 'til we can talk—"

"There is nothing that needs talking about, nurse.
Now—are you going to help me here or should I see if
there's someone else who would like your job?"

"But—"

"No, Nurse Mildred. Decide—"

She looked up at Jakie's battered face.

"But, doctor. I just can't help but feel that we are about to mutilate an innocent man."

Dr. Davidson glared back at her.

"Decide, Nurse Mildred."

Jakie drifted below them in a mental fog. Bits of whispered gossip overheard from the nursing staff floated back to him. How Mildred had been terminated years before from other hospitals for her outspoken insolence. Without any other means of support she had apparently suffered greatly, the poverty almost claiming her. The memory of the stark helplessness seemed to nod her head for her.

"Good," Dr. Davidson clucked dismissively. "Here. Use this—"

"Wait. I think he's coming to—"

The doctor cast a disinterested look Jakie's way.

"He's fine. I'll be quick."

Nurse Mildred watched Jakie's face. He once again opened his eyes fully, and their mutual fear communicated between them.

"He's waking up, doctor. Just let me get him a bit more. It'll be more humane," she pleaded.

"Oh...well hurry it up then—"

Jakie felt a painful pinching, then the hard bite of the restraint loosening as Nurse Mildred turned to amble away.

He watched through a thick haze as she walked back toward him with a full syringe. Bumping her way around to the doctor's side of the table, she scissored open Jakie's sleeve and pressed the needle against his arm. But the sharp penetration never came, and she held his eye meaningfully as she went through the motions of the injection. Slowly, he became aware of a subtle loosening of the right hand restraint as well.

Wait—she mouthed down at him, and Jakie prayed that he would be able to do so.

He watched her anxiously for a signal as she repositioned herself farther down the table next to the doctor. The doctor handed her a pincher-like tool, and a searing pain burned through Jakie as the sharp instrument bit into his penis and pulled it taut.

"Tighter!" Dr. Davidson fumed eagerly. "I want a straight cut."

Jakie's fists tightened into weapons. He allowed only one word into his mind. *Wait. Wait. Wait.* Dr. Davidson impatiently adjusted the overhead lamp, then leaned in closer toward Jakie, a fine scalpel vibrating in his tremulous hand. The single-toothed blade just barely nicked Jakie's flesh before it was sent flying to the floor by Mildred's hand.

Instantly, Jakie flew up and wrapped the ballistic doctor in a furious arm lock. Still with no idea where the plan went next, Jakie was just insurmountably relieved to have everyone away from his private bits. He stared frantically at Nurse Mildred as the doctor squirmed loudly, facedown in his arms. She stared frantically back at him—and then efficient as ever—she stabbed the doctor with the needle and unloaded half of the syringe. Slowly the man's struggling ebbed and finally ceased, and Jakie let him slide to the floor.

Rapidly unbuckling the remainder of the restraints, Jakie pushed himself free of the table. His trousers fell to his knees. He yarded them back up again, eyes avoiding Nurse Mildred's face.

She had busied herself trying to hoist the doctor up onto the surgery table. Jakie joined in the effort. His head felt estranged from him, and he had to focus hard to keep himself upright. Silently, they refastened the restraints around the comatose doctor, then looked up at each other. Mildred's face showed she was just as stunned as Jakie to suddenly find herself swirling halfway through such a reck-less non-plan.

"Thank you, nurse—"

"Don't be thanking me none—" she said, holding onto the side of the table as—with great effort—she lowered herself onto the floor. "I must be as crazy in the head as the rest of you for doing this. But soon's they come in and find this mess—I'm telling them you done it *all*."

Taking the syringe from her pocket, she pumped herself full of the remainder of the drugs, then laid herself out flat. Jakie stood for a half-second, trying to comprehend all this before he bolted for the door.

"Jakie!" she called up after him. "Take the doctor's sweater with you. They put the girl back in the tunnel room. The keys are in his pocket."

Ξ Ξ Ξ

Jakie burst into the cellar room. It was empty. Standing stu-pefied, Dr. Davidson's sweater still dangling from his hand, he surveyed the space for a long moment before he realized where Lily was hiding. She'd once again cocooned herself tight inside a blanket and curled into the remotest corner beneath the iron cot. She did not answer his calling. But he could see her stark blue eyes watching as he slowly lowered onto his knees and began to gently pull her toward him. Wide eyes fixed on him, she did not resist. Slowly, she sat up and softly touched the red welts that covered his face. The blanket slipping loose, a furry bundle scampered free. Scooping the skunk up, Jakie helped Lily onto her feet.

"We gotta go. Ain't safe for us no more."

Clutching her doll tighter to her chest, she said noth-ing. It was obvious the traumatic events of the morning had chased her back inside herself. He only hoped her faith in him had not been irreparably torn. That she would still trust him enough to let him lead her free of the asylum.

Moving toward the door, he grinned when she shadowed him so closely that she actually stepped on his heels as he paused to open it wider.

Nothing was fitting the way he had planned. Not once had he worked through the logistics of a daytime escape. He'd always imagined their vanishing to occur under the helpful cover of night. Stepping into the vaguely lit tunnel, he slipped Dr. Davidson's cardigan on in a thin attempt at disguise. It was not much, but it was all that he had. Lily looked over at him and frowned treacherously. An explanation would have to wait. He knew it was only a short window of time before the wolves were at their backs. Pulling Lily's blanket up around her shoulders, he tried to make it look like a shawl. Taking the little skunk from his hands, she cozied it down inside the blanket with her doll.

Creeping through the tunnel, they slipped down one corridor and turned a corner into the next. Jakie stopped. Up ahead of them a steel gurney was parked against the wall. A pathetic wad of blanket was held down by canvas restraint straps. Jakie could just barely discern a frail body lying beneath them. He hoped against hope that the patient's face would be turned away from them.

He motioned Lily for silence, then remembered how uncalled for the gesture was. Barely breathing, they continued to make their way forward. The person on the gurney was motionless. Drugged or asleep. Perhaps even dead. The narrow width of the tunnel was cramped by the stretcher. They would have to ease close to get by it. Neither of them relished the thought. Jakie could feel Lily tensing up behind him. He reached back and took her hand. Quietly, they inched their way up even with the small still body. Mentally, Jakie cautioned Lily to not look down.

Suddenly, she froze. The patient's eyes had popped open. Jakie tried to pull Lily forward. She resisted, held immobile by the sharp glare gleaming into her. He pulled forward a little more urgently and Lily eased toward him.

An old claw reached out, catching at the hem of Lily's sweater. She drew back quickly, the movement unseating the blanket from her shoulders and half-exposing her doll.

"Lily!" the old woman croaked, and now Jakie looked down as well. Mrs. Anna Mason lay like a lost scrap on the gurney, securely buckled down. Her haunted eyes were on fire as they stared at the doll Lily hugged to her chest. "My baby—" she choked. "Give me my little Lily—"

"She's *my* baby," Lily said possessively. "Ezra gave her to me—"

"Ezra'd do no such thing!" Anna hissed. "He's a good boy—"

Confusion twisted Lily's face.

"You know Ezra?"

Anna's voice grew stronger on a glimmer of pride.

"Ezra's my son."

Lily and Anna glared at each other through a cloud of disbelief. Jakie's mind circled around itself, seeking clarity. Time was not theirs to spare. But still, he could not ignore the pieces of disrupted lives falling into place all around him.

"Anna," he ventured. "Mrs. Mason—don't you see? This girl is your daughter. That's why she's got your sweater. Ezra gave it to her. Don't you see? It's been a long, long while since you been gone in here."

Anna said nothing. Her face held impassive as she continued to stare up at the girl. Lily shot a look of great displeasure Jakie's way.

"My mother weren't a loony," she said with a rising dignity.

Anna's weary eyes flickered as she reached up to touch Lily's amber hair.

Lily moved beyond Anna's reach.

"My mother weren't no loony, Jakie," she insisted loudly. "Brother told me she died when I were just little. But she were a *real* smart lady—"

Signs of activity could be heard in Dr. Uldrich's rooms. Jakie knew there was no time to explain to Lily the connection he could see formulating in Anna's eyes.

"Mrs. Mason," he said urgently. "We've got to go now. Before it's too late. We're running free of the asylum. Come with us—"

Anna continued to study Lily. The determined set of her fine jaw. The glow of righteous indignation that brightened her pretty face.

"No. You go," she said quietly, the vagueness returning to her eyes. "It's best left this way...go."

Closing her eyes, she turned her face toward the wall, gnarled fingers tangling around frazzled clumps of hair.

Jakie reached out and gently touched the old woman's shoulder. A silent sob convulsed her. He opened his mouth to protest. The raspy scrape of the inside bolt opening on Dr. Uldrich's door changed his mind. Squeezing Lily's hand tightly, he sprinted down the corridor as quickly as Lily was able to go.

Using Dr. Davidson's pocketful of keys, they slipped effortlessly free of the tunnel and up onto the first floor of Cottage Four. Senses scanning around him, Jakie hurried toward the back door. Passing by a small room, he almost knocked Lily over as he doubled back to enter it. Shopping about the orderly cloakroom, he selected a long, ample-sized navy coat and helped Lily into it. Straining to encompass her blanket-shawl, skunk and baby doll, the coat made Lily look like someone twice her size. Reaching up on a top shelf, Jakie took down a small white hat and set it at a slight angle on top of her head.

Catching a glimpse of herself in the reflection of the window, Lily giggled. Jakie smiled as he softly whispered her quiet, then led her back out into the hall. The squeaky approach of two young nurses cut off their escape through the back door. Someone—hoping to brighten the front entrance hall—had placed a lovely bouquet of bright chrysanthemums on the oak sideboard. Jakie helped him-self to these as well, plucking them up vase and all. The two chattering nurses glanced over at the displaced couple standing by the wall.

"I'm sorry, sir," one said cursorily. "Visiting day is Sun-day. You'll have to come back."

"Looking for the cemetery," Jakie mumbled, indicating the flowers.

"Oh. Yes. Of course. It's over that way." She waved a hand vaguely in the air. "It's quicker if you go out the back door. Would you like me to show you?"

"No, no. We'll be just fine, miss. Thank you," Jakie declined as he looped his arm through Lily's and began to make his way purposefully down the thickly waxed hallway.

They exited down the back steps of Cottage Four with great care, the sudden sunlight challenging their sight. They walked with an exaggerated slowness. From any amount of distance, they would have easily passed for an elderly, mourning couple, making their measured way over to grieve a lost friend or family member. As it was, Dr. Davidson's and Nurse Mildred's compromised positions had evidently still not been discovered, and no one paid them any attention at all.

Rounding up over the crest of the hill and out of sight of the asylum, Jakie offered the vase of chrysanthemums up to a random grave and broke into a slow lope. Lily trotted along at his side, struggling to maintain her bal-ance wrapped up in the oversized coat with her squirming entourage of skunk and baby doll.

Stopping outside the farrier shed, Jakie wrestled open the squeaky door. Again taking Lily's hand, he attempted to lead her inside the gloomy enclosure. Hesitating, her trou-bled eyes searched into him warily. Knowing their moment of opportunity was preciously short, he tried to urge her forward. Her resistance answered back strongly. Almost beside himself now with frustrated apprehension, Jakie finally made the connection; the forlorn shed was probably not too dissimilar from where she had lived out a great deal of her lonely life. Of course she'd be loath to enter such a place once again. Letting her hand go, he pushed the doors open farther, then went in by himself.

His hands trembled as he snatched away the tattered blankets and burlap sacks that hid the little roadster from sight. Twice he stopped, cocking his head to listen into the distance, fearing he could hear them coming. All that came back to him was the low echo of Coyote's laugh.

Lily stepped cautiously inside the shed, watching brightly as the vehicle emerged from beneath the coverings. She placed a hand against the blue steamer trunk and pushed on it encouragingly as Jakie wrested it from the wheelbarrow and hoisted it onto the car's rear deck.

Perspiring heavily from the gravity of their situation, he laced the trunk down as best he could, then once again took Lily's hand. Leading her to the passenger's side of the car, he helped her into the seat. Other than the windshield, the vehicle had no windows or doors. Lily sat in still, upright anticipation, her blue eyes wide with fearful excitement.

"I didn't never get to go in the truck before—"

"It's a...really? Never?"

"No. Not me. Pa didn't never take me to town with the other kids."

Jakie nodded tightly as he kicked the blocks out from under the tires. He grimaced down at the long, steep slope of hill in front of them that he was hoping would catapult the engine to life. Putting the shift in neutral, he heaved himself against the vehicle. The car rolled forward easily, as if it had been waiting all its life for such a moment. Jakie jumped in beside Lily and grabbed the wheel.

"Best hang onto your hat, Lily! This is gonna be one helluva first ride."

The car gobbled away the hill, bouncing and lurching drunkenly as it raced toward the bottom. Lily's scream deafened Jakie's good ear. Grabbing a gear, he popped the clutch, the back power of momentum almost sending him and Lily head first into the windshield. The motor gasped as if it had been suddenly choked, then sputtered awake. Jakie was sure Lily's terrified scream would have been heard 10,000 miles away, but he grinned widely just the same. Although he'd envisioned it countless times, it was hard to believe the scheme had really worked, and now Mr. Brewster's legacy was sailing them off toward the asylum's gate.

Jakie desperately wanted to put his arm around Lily and pull her close to him. The way he always had in his daydreams. Effortlessly. Confident of her approval. Now, in the reality of the moment, he didn't dare. The car rattled and shook as it bumped along the dirt road. He wasn't even sure if he knew *how* to drive, although he seemed to be doing a pretty good job of it. But he knew if he allowed the engine to stall, they were done for. The manic jumpstart on the hill had succeeded in jolting the motor awake, but it was going to take a good deal of steady driving to generate the battery full of sustainable life.

His hands busy with the steering wheel and gearshift, he looked over at Lily and smiled. Her face was white. Her eyes sparkled full of exhilarated tears.

"Oh Jakie!" she gasped breathlessly, reaching over and grabbing his arm fiercely. "That was *so* much fun! Can we do it again?"

Taken up by her innocent spontaneity, he laughed out loud and she joined him. She seemed to be entirely unaware that they were halfway through a daring asylum escape. Hating to have to quell her enthusiasm, he shushed her silent as he nodded toward the main gate looming up ahead of them. His heart bled a little as she readily accepted his command and curled back into herself.

The over-attentive gatekeeper had already strolled out to greet them, bulbous brown eyes ogling the car as they rolled to a stop. A squat man packing a big belly, his thinning hairline warned of future baldness. Yellow teeth indicated an enjoyment of black coffee, while the florid flush of his nose hinted at a dependence on something far stronger.

"Morning," he said, nodding his head at Jakie. "Ma'am."

Keeping his head low, Jakie played the engine with his feet. He was terrified it would stall. Looking up at the gate, he nodded back toward the man hoping that would be the end of the matter. The gatekeeper did not seem at all concerned or agitated, which struck Jakie as a very good sign. Clearly their attempted escape had still not been found out. He eyed the gate in front of him expectantly as the gatekeeper made a great show of inspecting all the unusual details of the car. The massive gate was closed but not locked. Jakie considered whether the sleek roadster had sufficient distance to pick up enough speed to just blow right through it.

"Well-dy, well-dy, well-dy," the gatekeeper sang tonelessly as he again wandered around to the driver's side and leaned himself up against the flared fender. "Can't say I ever seen ones these before."

"Import," Jakie mumbled.

"Ohhh...yup. From the States?"

Jakie nodded.

"Looks like yuh been a lotta places," he said, eyes snooping over the labels covering the trunk.

"Looks like...yup," Jakie agreed.

"You friends of the doctor then?"

Jakie's nod was stilled by a flash of steely-blue eyes. Reaching into the pocket of Dr. Davidson's sweater, he plucked out the pipe and clacked it against his teeth instead.

"He's up from the States too, ain't he? Dr. Uldrich?" the gatekeeper asked, stooping over as he lit the pipe.

Jakie smiled thinly, choking a little on the smoke as his eyes again suggested the gate.

"We-ell, I guess you should be getting on your way. Looks like rain and you've no top," he observed without making the least bit of effort to move clear of the car.

"What kind of car you say this is again?"

"I...uh..." Jakie faltered.

The bulbous eyes queried a little deeper over Jakie's roughed-up face.

"It's a...Brewster," Jakie sputtered quickly.

"A Brewster! Well-dy, well, well. Not every day you get to see one of those—"

A plaintiff mewling escaped from Lily's borrowed coat. The gatekeeper's fleshy eyes narrowed with suspicion.

"What you got in there?"

Jakie turned to Lily, holding her gaze intently as he tentatively unfastened a button, slipped his fingers inside the coat and briefly drew out the doll's tiny hand.

"Oh...yup...a baby," the gatekeeper said, his suspicion deflating.

"Getting hungry," Jakie warned with a serious set to his face.

"Oh, yup-yup-yup," the other man yelped as his flustered face flushed red. "Well I—oh-oh. What's this? Looks like we got us a runner."

Taking the pipe out of his mouth and tossing it onto the dash, Jakie swung his head around to see what had called away the man's attention. Off in the distance, he could just make out a mad dash of bodies racing toward the gate, the obvious hefty bulk of Oswald forming the lead. Frantically looking back up at the gatekeeper, Jakie worked hard to keep the explosion of anxiety in his heart from invading his face.

"Don't mean to hurry you none, sir. But you'd best be getting yourself outta here," the gatekeeper said apologetically. He moved quickly now toward the gate, unlatched it and drew it open. "Once we get ourselves a runner 'round here, the whole damn place gets locked down. No telling how long it might take to get you and the missus outta here then—"

Jakie gunned the car through the gate and out onto the main road, the burst of speed snatching the hat off of Lily's head and flying it down the highway behind them. Covering her mouth with both hands, she failed to suppress a delighted squeal. Jakie laughed out loud, euphorically, at her wide-eyed wonder, and she accompanied him with an effervescent giggle. Her laughter bubbled up through him like champagne—a very fine vintage.

He drove on in petrified silence for quite some time, making constant checks over his shoulder. Remembering Mr. Brewster's detailed instructions, he eased off the main road and felt himself relaxing as the comforting country-side began to slip by. True to his daydreams, the exhausted Lily sidled up close beside him and laid her head against his shoulder. Easing his arm up, he put it around her and pulled her closer. Poking its little head out, the skunk nosed around then retreated back inside its warm wool den. The sprinkle of rain had almost ceased, and the whole world glistened around them.

"Look!" Lily exclaimed, pointing ahead of them, up in the sky.

"Rainbow," Jakie said grinning down at her. "You never seen one before?"

"Sometimes I did. What is it?"

"A promise."

She looked up at him and frowned.

"Some folks say if you can get to the end of it you'll find a pot of gold. It's like a promise from God that everything is gonna get better. That things ain't never gonna be so bad again—"

"Oh Jakie!" Lily laughingly interrupted. "That is *such* a funny story—"

The End